Flirting
IN ITALIAN

Flirting
IN ITALIAN

lauren henderson

DELACORTE PRESS

Copyright © 2012 by Lauren Henderson
Jacket art copyright © 2012 by Britt Erlanson/Getty Images

Visit us on the Web! randomhouse.com/teens

Educators and librarians, for a variety of teaching tools,
visit us at randomhouse.com/teachers

Library of Congress Cataloging-in-Publication Data

Henderson, Lauren.
Flirting in Italian / Lauren Henderson.—1st ed.
p. cm.
Summary: Spending the summer in the Tuscany region of Italy on
a secret mission to solve a family mystery, a teenaged English girl is
distracted by her exciting American roommates and some sexy Italian
boys on Vespa scooters. ISBN 978-0-385-74135-4 (hardcover) —
ISBN 978-0-375-98999-5 (lib. binding) — ISBN 978-0-375-98452-5 (ebook)
[1. Identity—Fiction. 2. Dating (Social customs)—Fiction. 3. Tuscany
(Italy)—Fiction. 4. Italy—Fiction.] I. Title.
PZ7.H3807F1 2012
[Fic]—dc23
2011036332

The text of this book is set in 12-point Goudy.
Book design by Kenny Holcomb

Printed in the United States of America
10 9 8 7 6 5 4 3 2 1
First Edition

Random House Children's Books supports the
First Amendment and celebrates the right to read.

For all the Lucas, Giacomos, Giovannis, Riccardos, Francescos, and Sebastianos I danced with during my party years in Tuscany; for Sabina Broadhead, who was always beside me when I was dancing on tables, and whose house the girls visit for the party; and in fond memory of Golia the donkey, who lived there and was exactly as described in this book.

Ci sono trenta modi per salvare il mondo,
ma uno solo perché il mondo salvi me—
che io voglia star con te, e tu voglia star con me.

There are thirty ways to save the world, but only one
way for the world to save me—if I want to be with you,
and you want to be with me.
—Jovanotti

Prologue: London

The picture in front of me is like a magnet, drawing me closer and closer, till my shoulder is nearly brushing against its antique gold carved frame. It's like looking in a mirror, and it's holding me spellbound. I can't look away from what's almost my own reflection.

Eyes, dark, with a slant up at the outer corners that my mother calls almond-shaped. Hair as dark as my eyes, wavy today, frizzy and wild when it's damp. Skin that's sallow in winter, needing sunshine to warm it up, turn it pale gold. A short, curvy figure and a small waist, made even smaller in mirror image by a corset much lower-cut than I would ever wear; I'm spilling out over the top.

In this enchanted mirror, I look truly lovely. My hair

is piled on the crown of my head, which makes me look taller, and it's decorated with small white pearls, which gleam subtly against the dark mass of carefully tonged and arranged curls. There's a matching pearl necklace around my neck, cool and delicate, and the square-cut neckline of my sea-green taffeta dress is trimmed with lace that feels as soft as chiffon. It looks as if I have a beauty spot on my cheek, and I lean in, trying to see if it's really there or just a speck on the glass. . . .

"Miss? Miss! You can't touch the paintings!" barks the guard.

I jump, startled out of my wits. I've forgotten that I'm in an art gallery with other people around. The security guard is a young woman, and she is tapping me on the shoulder, indicating that I need to step back from the portrait, which I'm so close to by now that my nose is butting up against the glass.

"Oh!" she exclaims as I pull away and mumble an apology. The guard is looking from me to the portrait now, and her jaw has dropped, something you read about but don't often see; her mouth actually gapes wide for a moment.

"My goodness me," she says, shaking her head. "Look at that resemblance! No wonder you were looking at it so closely! You might be twins, dear. Are you related?" She laughs. "Funny way to put it—she's been dead for hundreds of years! I should have said, are you from the same family?"

"I don't know," I say slowly, stepping back from the portrait.

"Well, you must be! It's positively uncanny."

She peers from me to the girl in the portrait. For the

first time, I focus on the background behind the girl in the beautiful taffeta dress; she's standing, quite composed, with one hand on a table stacked high with books, in what looks like the turret of a castle; the stone walls are curved around her, the windows small. Behind her is a picture on an easel, a landscape in the process of being painted. A wooden palette lies on the shelf below, brushes fanned out decoratively. To her right, through the narrow turret window, is a panoramic view of green hills, cypresses marching down them in a winding curve that leads to the valley below. On the windowsill a large tabby cat basks happily in the sunshine. It's serene in her little private room. Books to read, a picture to paint, a cat to play with, a beautiful view.

I look at the square brass plaque next to the painting. It doesn't offer much in the way of information.

Portrait of a Young Lady: Unknown painter, school of Carducci, c. 1750.

"Excuse me—do you know if they have any postcards of this in the shop?" I ask.

The guard shakes her head regretfully.

"I doubt it, dear," she says. "We only stock ones of the really famous paintings. The Canalettos and the Hogarth. And the Watteau, of course."

I came to see the three Canalettos, which are masterpieces: views of Venice. I'm doing coursework on them for my art history A-level. My teacher said not only would it be a wonderful experience for me to see the real thing, but it would sound excellent in an essay to slip in a comment about having visited Sir John Soane's Museum. Examiners love that kind of thing.

But now my face falls in disappointment. I've read about Sir John Soane, after whom the museum is named. He traveled to the Continent in the late seventeen hundreds, for two years, when he was twenty-five. That was quite common then, doing what was called the Grand Tour—young men visited France and Italy to have adventures and collect sculptures and paintings. Sir John Soane did that on a huge scale: he ended up as the professor of architecture at the Royal Academy, and his house became a world-famous museum.

That doesn't mean that everything he bought on his travels was a masterpiece. Some things he just picked up because he liked them. Like this *Portrait of a Young Lady*. Clearly, he bought this without knowing who the painter was—or the name of the young lady.

I bite my lip. I don't know anything about the portrait. I can't even buy a postcard of it. So how am I ever going to find out who the girl in the painting is? I have to discover why on earth a girl who lived in the late eighteenth century—in Italy!—looks so like me she could be my twin sister.

Seeing my woeful expression, the security guard takes pity on me and walks over to the other side of the room and looks away. Quickly, I take a photo or two on my mobile, then fiddle with the flash settings and take several more. "Photos not allowed," the guard now says as she turns around and sees me. I put my mobile phone away.

I want, very much, to go on staring at the painting, to see if there are any clues I can find in it, any secrets that it might yield on close examination, but this discovery feels intensely private. I don't want to share it with some random woman: I want to keep it for myself, hugged close to my chest.

"Thanks," I mumble, turning away.

Mercifully, the man downstairs at the information desk isn't familiar enough with *Portrait of a Young Lady: Unknown painter* to recognize me as its living incarnation. He looks up its details on his computer and tells me that Sir John Soane's biographer has "tentatively identified" the location of the painting as the Castello di Vesperi, in Tuscany.

"Nothing concrete on the subject of the painting," he continues, scrolling down the screen. "But obviously the assumption is that it's a family member. An unmarried young lady. No wedding ring. Probably a daughter."

He glances at me. "I'll print you out the information we have on it, if you'd like." I nod and smile my thanks. "Fascinating chap," he adds. "Doing a school project, are you? You know Sir John's tomb was the model for the red telephone box?" He grins. "That's usually the favorite fact on the school tours."

He's handing me the piece of paper that he's just printed. I reach out to take it.

"Thanks," I say, but he doesn't release it; he's looking, now, from me to the portrait, which has come up on his computer screen.

"How very interesting," he says. "She looks exactly like—"

"Yes, I know," I say quickly, tugging on the paper. He's not grasping it that tightly, and it comes loose from his fingers. I fold it in half, shove it into my coat pocket, and turn away, crossing the hall toward the entrance door.

My head's spinning. I don't know how to feel or what to think. The museum faces Lincoln's Inn Fields, which is a wide green expanse as big as a cricket pitch, bordered with huge old oak trees. I cross the street, so distracted I almost get run down by a very grumpy cyclist who yells abuse at me as he swerves around me dramatically to make his point. It's March, still too cold for sitting on the grass. I walk over to a wrought-iron bench near the bandstand and sink down on its chilly surface, tucking my coat under me for an extra layer of warmth.

Between the thick gnarled roots of the oak trees, I can make out small patches of snowdrops, fading back now because spring's on its way, and crocuses, white and mauve. The occasional bright yellow daffodil, slight and fragile, is opening up, looking for the sunshine. I shove my hand into my pocket and pull out the piece of paper from Sir John Soane's Museum, unfolding it and laying it on my lap.

The portrait of the girl who looks so like me is reproduced in a small black-and-white rectangle on the top left of the page. The lines of text beside it are barely a paragraph: there's pitifully little information on the girl from the seventeen hundreds who happens to be the spitting image of me.

It may seem that I'm making much too big a deal of finding my double. After all, it could just be coincidence. With all the historical portraits in the world, there must be hundreds—thousands—of accidental resemblances. People must look at oil paintings from centuries ago and see their own faces staring back at them more frequently than anyone realizes.

But most of those people don't have the same nagging feeling that has torn at me, made me wonder about my looks, my coloring ever since I was old enough to be aware that I don't resemble any of my family—my mother, my father, my aunt, my grandparents. None of them. At all.

My mother and her sister are both tall, fair, with high sculpted cheekbones and deep-set blue eyes. Classic Scandinavian blondes, like their Norwegian mother. My dad is Scottish, sandy-haired and stockily built, with pale skin that freckles easily and hates the sun; his eyes are pale blue-gray, his lashes as sandy as his hair.

And I'm their short, brown-haired daughter. Sallow skin, big dark slanty eyes, a small curvy figure with boobs and a bum, quite unlike my ex-model mother, who's slim as a wand—exactly like *her* mother and sister . . .

Family photos are like a game of Odd One Out. I've gone through old photo albums, looking for a picture of anyone who looks like me, and never found one, despite my mother's vague comments, made from time to time, that I must take after the "dark Scottish" side of my father's family. I've lost count of the times that people have asked me if those tall blond people are really my mummy and daddy. I've had strangers assume I'm Italian, Greek, Cypriot, or Spanish; I've been into Lebanese and Turkish delis and had the guys behind the counter speak to me in their language; on holiday with my mum last year in Sri Lanka, the locals thought I was half Singhalese. I've basically got the coloring and bone structure (ugh, my round cheeks) of someone from a Mediterranean country, evolved for glorious golden sunshine, hot baked earth, bright blue sea.

Not at all the cold-climate looks of my parents.

And no, I've never dared to ask my mother if I was adopted. The possibility has been in my mind for years, of course, ever since, when I was quite young, I read a book where the heroine turned out to have been stolen from another family years before. I don't for a moment think that my loving, sweet mum could have done anything like that. But it's not as if I have brothers or sisters who look like me, or like our parents: I'm an only child. Which could make it a real possibility that I was adopted because they couldn't have a baby of their own.

But that's where I've always stalled in the past when this idea has popped into my mind. Because my mum is really open and honest with me. She doesn't lie, she doesn't keep secrets, she's always answered any questions I've asked her. Besides, there are plenty of families where kids are adopted; it's not a big deal, not something people need to keep secret. I know at least three girls in my school who are adopted, and no one thinks twice about it.

If I weren't my parents' biological daughter, I simply don't believe that my mum wouldn't have told me the truth long ago, when strangers started to comment on my looks, to say that I didn't resemble my parents. Surely Mum and Dad would have said something then, sat me down and explained that the reason I look so different was that they couldn't have kids and had adopted a little girl who needed a home? It wouldn't have been difficult. I love my parents to pieces. I would have understood; I wouldn't have been that upset. I know how much they love me, and they've always made me feel really secure. I'd have asked questions, of course, but Mum would have answered them honestly. I know she would. Because she always does.

No, that's the part that doesn't make sense. I just can't believe that my parents would keep something this big from me. It's completely the opposite of the whole way they've brought me up.

I turn the paper over in my hands and realize how cold they are: I forgot my gloves, because it's sunny out. But March in London is still cold, the spring sunshine is pale and weak, and my hands feel frozen to the bone. I fold the paper, put it back in my pocket, and stand up, rubbing my hands together.

I'm getting the Tube straight home so I can look up Castello di Vesperi, the "tentatively identified" location of the turret room depicted in the portrait, on the Internet. And I know what I'm going to do then. It'll be the first big secret I've ever kept from my mother: I'm going to find some way to visit the castello. It's the only way I might conceivably find out anything more about the girl in the picture, her history, her family.

The girl who's the mirror image of me.

My Daughter's Leaving Me

"*Signore e signori*, please fasten your seat belts and return your seatbacks and tray tables to the upright position," says the airline steward over the PA. "We will be landing in Pisa in fifteen minutes. *Signore e signori, siete pregati di allacciare le cinture di sicurezza* . . ."

I peer through the window beside me. Bright blue-green sea below, such a vivid aquamarine that unless you saw it with your own eyes you wouldn't believe it could actually exist in nature. Little white flecks dance across the azure blue, waves tossed up by the wake of the occasional boat. And then the deep aquamarine fades to a lighter blue as the water becomes more shallow; the coast comes into view. It's my first glimpse of Italy, and it takes my breath away. It's the start of July, full summer, and the sea and land are bathed in dazzling golden sunshine. I can see a marina along the coastline, tiny dots that must be fishing boats and yachts moored in an inlet. The seashore is the color of pale terra-cotta, but beyond it, beyond the miniature red roofs of the buildings that cluster around it, there's rich green marshland. I know (from the in-flight magazine, not a more impressive source) that the Leaning Tower of Pisa stands in the Field of Miracles, and I squint, trying as hard as I can to make out a white pillar on a bed of green grass, but no luck.

Italy! My anticipation is intensifying so powerfully that I'm breathless. My mum says that when I was a little girl, I would get so excited at the prospect of a treat that I would barely be able to breathe; I'd rock back and forth, hyperventilating, making little gasping noises, eyes like saucers, mouth open. I twist away from the window, focusing on the gray marled fabric of the seatback in front of me, trying to calm the frantic pounding of my heart.

Italy. It's really happening. My adventure—maybe my real life—is about to begin.

And at that thought, my heart sinks. I'm feeling suddenly, horribly, guilty.

Because I left my mum behind. For two whole months. We've never been apart for that long, and I don't know how she's going to manage.

Even worse, I'm secretly, shamefully, glad. *Glad* to be leaving my mum, to be free for maybe the first time ever in my life. To be alone, without her always there, able to work out who I am in the space her absence will give me. Though

I'm sitting in a cramped airline seat, arms tucked into my sides so I don't accidentally whack my neighbor, I feel as if I have more space to breathe than ever before.

Maybe that's how it always works; maybe you never realize how squashed in you've been until the restrictions vanish, and you can finally stretch out your arms. I feel as if I could whirl around again and again.

I should be in pieces about leaving Mum. I must be a really bad daughter.

I fumble for my phone, then remember I can't turn it on midair. So I slip my laptop out of my bag for a brief moment and open it up; I've saved the photo of the portrait on it as well, just in case I lose my phone.

I click to open the picture, and get the same shock I always do as it comes up onscreen. I stare at myself, at hair decorated with pearls, at a green taffeta dress, my eyes looking back at me, and I know that I've done the right thing in leaving my mother behind to come on this quest to find out where I come from. And why on earth this girl from eighteenth-century Italy is my mirror image.

Because as I snap my laptop shut, I know that anyone who saw a resemblance like this would move heaven and earth to find out the reason behind it.

Ever since I saw the portrait in Sir John Soane's Museum, I plotted and schemed and strategized so successfully that I surprised myself with the sheer extent of my capacity for covert action. The first thing I did was drop the name of the Castello di Vesperi into conversation with my mum.

Faux-casually, of course. I've just done my final A-level exams—English, French, and art history—and the plan is for me to study art history at Cambridge University, if they let me in. In the autumn, I'll sit the Cambridge entrance exam and go for interviews at the college I've applied for, which means my studying isn't over, even though the A-levels are. I'm still supposed to be reading art books, going to galleries and exhibitions, building up my knowledge as much as possible. So it's very easy to tell my mother, over dinner, that I'm going to an exhibition at the Wallace Collection tomorrow with my friend Lily-Rose—paintings from the Castello di Vesperi in Chianti. Her eyes don't even flicker; she forks up another piece of grilled chicken, smiles at me, and says that sounds lovely. No recognition of the name at all.

I test it out again, at the end of dinner, as I'm stacking the dishwasher; I mention the name of the fictitious exhibition again, and how much I'm looking forward to it.

"Goodness, you *are* keen!" Mum says. "You've been out at museums all this week!" She yawns. "Time to collapse on the sofa, don't you think? What film shall we watch tonight?"

So that's totally conclusive. No recognition of the name di Vesperi at all. Mum is the worst liar in the world, which is probably why her brief attempt at an acting career failed completely: she's incapable of pretending to feel anything she doesn't. It's probably why she was such a good model, though. She's as transparent as a pool of water; every new emotion is instantly registered on her face. We have some of her most famous photos hung in the flat, and I love them all, because they capture Mum's expressions so perfectly—wistful, happy, thoughtful, loving. She told me once that photographers she worked with learned how to trigger her emotions: they'd yell "Think of cute puppies, Daisy!" if they wanted her to smile, or "Your boyfriend said he needs to take a break!" if they were after romantic melancholy.

And the most famous photo of all, the *Vogue* cover where she's holding an orchid in her hand, staring at it with a misty, tender gaze in her big blue eyes, her blond hair falling down her back: in that one, she said, the photographer told her to look at the flower and think of what she loved most in the world.

"And of course," she'd said, hugging me, "I thought of you, my lovely little baby girl. Because you're everything in the world to me."

I love my mother more than anything. I really do. But she isn't everything in the world to me. And sometimes, wonderful though it is that she loves me so much, it can be a bit—I feel so guilty even thinking the word—it can be just a little bit . . . *suffocating*.

Mum wants to be my best friend, my confidante, my older sister, almost. Thank goodness, she's not one of those weird mothers, like my friend Milly's, who acts like she thinks she's our age: Milly's mum likes to come along on our shopping trips to Topshop and H&M, buy miniskirts even shorter and tighter than ours, listen to the same music we do, flirt with boys we know, insist that we call her by her first name. She made a huge scene when Milly wouldn't accept her friend request on Facebook. Mum's not like that, even though she could get away with tight minis much better than Milly's mother. Mum looks really good for her age; she works out, takes tons of vitamins, eats very lightly. The night I got home from Sir John Soane's Museum, she made boiled new potatoes to go with the poached sole, but she only ate one, and I finished the rest. I think Mum diets too much, but she says it's from being a model, and that's why she'd never want me to do it as a career.

Fat chance. Literally. I'd need to grow six inches and lose twenty pounds, for a start. Mum loves me so much that she doesn't see anything ridiculous about mentioning me and modeling in the same sentence. And if there's a secret she's hiding about why I'm not tall and willowy and blond like her, she's unaware of any connection that might exist between my looks and the di Vesperi family. That's very clear.

I simply don't have the nerve to ask her directly about the resemblance. Because it would be suggesting that she might not actually be my mother—or that my father might not actually be my father. It would upset her more than anything—even more, I honestly think, than her divorce from Dad. I simply couldn't deal with the fallout. I'm not brave enough to broach that sort of question to a mother who's done nothing but love me to pieces since the day I was born.

So I proceed inexorably to Step Two. I've already Googled the castello and the di Vesperi family. There isn't much information on them at all; I was really disappointed at first. Almost all of the entries are about the estate and the different kinds of wine and oil they produce; the closest I got to a mention of the family was a comment that the Principe di Vesperi, the prince whose family's owned the castle and estate for centuries, isn't in residence most of the time, and the di Vesperis have hired someone called an oenologist, which means a person who supervises growing the grapes and the actual making of the wine. There's nothing on the family history. Nothing that would help me find out the name of a girl who might have been seventeen or eighteen around 1750, who hung out in a turret room in the castello in the company of a big ginger cat.

But then, far down the third page of entries, I strike gold.

"Mum?" I say in a would-be casual tone a few days later, when I've had enough time to work out my strategy, have answers planned for every question she might ask or objection she might raise. "You know my art history teacher said I should really use my summer to broaden my range of knowledge for the Cambridge entrance exam?"

Oops. I cringe. I rehearsed that much too much. I sound about as casual as a high-speed train doing 140 miles per hour.

Mum is arranging flowers in the huge, three-foot-high glass vase that sits next to the living room fireplace. I've picked this moment because arranging flowers makes her happier than any other activity I can think of; she hums to herself as she does it, a soft pretty little thread of sound.

She turns around, a spray of cherry blossom in her hand, an abstract, dreamy expression on her face.

"What was that, darling?" she asks.

I get a second chance.

I repeat what I said before, but add a lot more "ums" and pauses, so I sound a lot more relaxed. She nods, half her

17

attention still on the vase and the cherry blossom branches that are already inside it, framed by tall fronds of green leaves.

"That's why you've been going to so many galleries," she says vaguely.

I sigh.

"The thing is, I don't think it's enough," I say, frowning in concern. Unlike Mum, I'm very capable of dissembling when I need to. "I think I should be doing more."

Mum's beautiful big blue eyes fill with concern.

"Darling!" she exclaims, putting down the blossom and turning fully to me. "What kind of thing? I know how important this is to you!"

I do love my mother very, very much.

I take a deep breath.

"Well, I'm getting a bit worried about not having a classics background," I say, propping my bottom on the arm of the sofa closest to me. "I've been doing some research on what the art history faculty wants, and a lot of the previous students have done Latin or Greek or both."

"They did have Latin at St. Tabby's, didn't they?" my mother says, biting her lip. "But you did German O-level instead."

"*That* was a mistake," I say gloomily. "I was terrible at German. I was lucky to get a C. All their sentences are backward. I mean, who *talks* like that?"

"Oh, never mind," Mum says consolingly. "You know I told you that all the German people I've met spoke perfect English anyway. Like the Norwegians," she adds, smiling.

Mum's been living in London for twenty-five years; by

now she has only the faintest trace of her Norwegian accent. And her English really is perfect.

"Your French is very good," she continues.

"Hopefully," I say, crossing my fingers. "I won't get the A-level results till August. But that's sort of what was on my mind." I tilt my head to one side. "I was thinking maybe I should try to learn another language."

"Latin or Greek?" Mum says incredulously. "What, in a couple of months?"

"No!" I grin at the mere idea. "I was thinking Italian—"

"Oh!" She brightens, her eyes sparkling, "That sounds like a really good—"

"In Italy," I say, and watch her expression like a hawk. She looks, to my surprise, genuinely excited.

"Oh, that's lovely!" she exclaims. "I've been wondering what to do for a proper summer holiday! I know we're going to stay with Mormor in September—she's rented the cottage on Sognefjord again for us and your aunt Lissie—but you and I should get away too, shouldn't we?"

Mormor is my grandmother—it's a funny word that actually means "mother of your mother." Mum's dad was my farmor, and my dad's mum would be Morfar, etc. I love going to the cottage in Norway; it's painted red with bright white trim and a slanting roof, like something from a fairy tale, and it has a deck from which you can dive into the lake, with its clean clear water and views to the mountains beyond. It's always just me and Mum, Mormor and Aunt Lissie—Farmor died three years ago, and though Aunt Lissie has lots and lots of boyfriends, Mormor wants the fortnight in Sognefjord to be just us. The women in the family. (Mum, unlike her sister, never has boyfriends. I used to like that it was just the two of us, after Dad left, but now I'm beginning to feel it's about time for things to change.)

"We could travel all around Italy!" Mum's saying, waving her arms in great excitement. "Venice—Florence—Rome—Naples! Do a big trip!"

"The Grand Tour," I mumble, thinking of Sir John Soane.

"What?"

"Mum . . ." I have to burst this bubble now. It's not completely unexpected. I thought my mother might jump at the opportunity to spend the summer with me, abroad. There's a phrase she uses constantly—

"Mother-and-daughter time!" she exclaims, clapping in sheer pleasure, her blond hair tumbling around her shoulders.

I start again, as gently as I can. "Mum, I don't think I'll manage to learn Italian if it's you and me together, staying in nice hotels. Who are we going to talk to, waiters? I was thinking I should go and do a residential course in Italy for a couple of months. Immerse myself in the language, see lots of art, study a bit of history. . . ."

Her face falls, and my overbright voice trails off at the sight of the disappointment and sadness written so clearly on her beautiful face.

"Oh," she says slowly. She looks around her, as if she's forgotten the layout of our living room. She takes a couple of steps sideways, almost shuffling toward the armchair that matches the sofa, and she reaches out to its back, resting her hand on it for support.

I don't know what to say. So I stay silent as she lowers herself into the armchair, sinking into it heavily, like an old lady.

"Oh," she says again, even more quietly, looking down at her hands.

I feel absolutely terrible. Words rise to my lips: assurances that I love her more than anything, that I don't want to hurt her, that I won't go to Italy by myself if she doesn't want me to, that I'll spend the whole summer with her instead.

But the trouble is, I don't want to say them. I really *do* want to go to Italy. By myself. Mum's expectations for me are like a weight on my shoulders, and I find myself itching to shake it off.

I've been staring at the carpet, the weave and the pattern, so I don't realize for a while that Mum has raised her head and is looking at me. It takes all the courage I have to meet her gaze, and when I do, my heart melts.

Because in her eyes I see nothing but love.

"Oh, *Mum* . . ." I throw myself across the space between us, falling to my knees in front of her, wrapping my arms around her legs, burying my head in her lap. "I'm so sorry—I didn't want to hurt you—I won't go, I won't do the course—"

"Don't be silly," she says, stroking my hair, her voice so gentle that it triggers the tears that have been building up. I start to cry into her jeans as she goes on:

"Of course you have to go off by yourself. What was I thinking? You're nearly eighteen! If you weren't taking a gap year, you'd be off to university in the autumn! I'm so lucky I get an extra year with you. I should be counting my blessings, not trying to hang around your neck all summer when you want to be off with girls your own age." She bends down to kiss my head. "Tell me about this course. I bet you've picked one out and know everything about it already, don't you? You're always so organized."

I raise my head, my face smudged with tears, which Mum wipes away with the hem of her sweater.

"It's in Chianti," I say eagerly, "in the middle of Tuscany. Really close to Florence and Siena, in this lovely fourteenth-century villa with a swimming pool. This Italian lady runs it every year—she takes about four to six girls, so it's nice and small, and you learn Italian, do art tours, go riding, learn watercolor painting and ballroom dancing, study Italian history—there's even a flower arranging class and a course on the wine and food," I add, thinking that this will appeal to Mum.

She doesn't react the way I expect, however. Instead of looking pleased that I'm taking an interest in one of her hobbies, her eyes widen in surprise; she seems completely taken aback.

"Darling," she says, "flower arranging—*ballroom dancing?* You know what this sounds like to me? Finishing school!" She frowns in confusion. "That's the kind of thing my model girlfriends used to do, so they could learn to be rich men's wives. They used to teach you how to climb in and out of Porsches with your knees politely together so no one could see up your skirt. It was for girls who weren't that bright. Like me." She grimaces. "But you're so clever! Why do you want to go to some sort of *finishing school?*"

Because Villa Barbiano, where the course is based, is in the valley below the Castello di Vesperi. And the lady who runs it takes her students on a private guided tour around the castello, which is otherwise strictly closed to the public. It says so on the website.

"It looks really pretty," I say rather feebly. "And the art history part of the course seems very thorough. They have lots of guided tours to private art collections that you'd normally never get to see."

"Well, you'd know all about that kind of thing," Mum says dubiously. "But wouldn't there be something a bit less—I don't know—posh thick rich girl? Darling—*ballroom dancing.*"

"I really want to do this one!" I plead. "I can skip all the bits I don't like. And it's only for a couple of months. I can still come to Norway afterward. And by then, I'll be rattling away in Italian!"

"*Ciao, bella!*" Mum says, giggling. "That's what all the boys say in Italy. You'll see. I remember that from modeling in Milan. *Ciao, bella!*" she repeats, waving her hands around and smiling reminiscently. "They ride Vespas and offer you lifts on the back. Oh, darling." She pulls me up to sit next to her on the arm of her chair. "You're going to have a wonderful time."

"I hope so," I say, hugging her.

Words are trembling on my tongue. I want, very badly, to ask if there's anything she wants to tell me. Anything that she might not have felt comfortable telling me before. Anything remotely to do with Italy. Or the fact that I look so different from my Norwegian relatives.

23

But she's being so lovely, so supportive, that I simply can't ask. I can't pry into a possible secret that my mother may have chosen not to tell me.

"I'll tell your father," she says. "But I'm sure he'll be fine. One thing I will say for him, he's never stingy with his money."

Dad left Mum over ten years ago, for an awful Danish woman with a name—Sif—that sounds like a brand of toilet cleaner. (Dad really does like Scandinavian women.) I hate her. It's not that I blame her for stealing Dad away—I mean, I do blame her, but it was Dad's fault much more than hers. She's just a horrible cow who wants to pretend Dad didn't have a life, or a wife and daughter, before she met him, and she does everything she can to stop me seeing him; she even got him to move halfway around the world, to head up an investment fund in Hong Kong.

But at least Mum and Dad didn't have a messy divorce, like the parents of a lot of my friends. No custody battles over me, or making me tell the judge who I want to live with, or sending me to mandatory therapy, ugh, like poor Lily-Rose, who had to go to a counselor for two whole years. Mum said Dad was great in the whole settlement thing. She had savings of her own, from her modeling days, but he's taken total care of us both, giving us enough money to buy this lovely flat in Kensington, ensuring we don't want for anything. Mum isn't remotely extravagant—we don't live some sort of jet-set life. But if I want to do a two-month course in Italy, which costs, I must admit, what looks to me like an awful lot of money, I don't need to worry for a moment that we can't afford it.

24

And yes, I know how lucky I am. I really do.

"Maybe I could come to visit for a weekend?" Mum says in a small voice. "I could stay in Florence, rent a car, come and see where you're staying . . . you could be my guide and take me round the galleries you've been to. . . ."

"Oh, Mum! Of course!" I hug her even tighter. "And I'll email you the whole time—I'll have my phone, you can ring me whenever you want to—"

"I won't ring you every day," she promises in an even smaller voice. "I promise. I won't be one of those awful smother mothers. Honestly, I won't."

And though a little warning bell is ringing inside my head, she's being so wonderful that I ignore it and tell myself that I believe her.

"Violet! My baby! Violet, darling . . ."

Mum is sobbing, full-out weeping, a river of tears pouring down her face, taking a lot of her mascara with it. That's the real downside of her inability to pretend to emotions she doesn't feel; it also means that she has no control over them. This has led to the occasional embarrassing incident when I've had tiny parts in school plays (tears of pride, overapplauding at my split-second curtain call as Peaseblossom or Second Lady). But nothing has ever been as remotely bad as this.

The worst part is that I'm frozen to the spot. I know I should be hugging her, reassuring her, but I'm so scared by the idea of getting sucked into the scene she's making that I just stand there by the departure gates, one hand on the pull handle of my carry-on bag, the other holding my passport and boarding pass. It's the most awkward place for a scene that I can imagine. Anything more public would be hard to picture.

"Violet, darling . . . I tried to be brave, I really did!" Mum's sobbing, her arms outstretched to me. "But it's two months! *Two months!* I'm going to be so worried about you all the time—I don't think I can bear it!"

"Madam, could I ask you to move a little to the side?" one of the security guards says, visibly uncomfortable. "We do have quite a press of travelers today—"

"My daughter's going away!" Mum wails. "She's leaving me! My daughter's leaving me!" And to my horror, she grabs on to the arm of the poor woman, who looks as appalled as I feel.

"Madam—" she starts, looking around frantically for help.

For a few awful, shameful seconds, I seriously contemplate dashing through the gate and joining the line at Passport Control. It's moving fairly quickly; in the minutes it will take Mum to recover any shreds of composure, I'll be into Security, where if she tries to follow me, she'll be detained by the guards.

I'm a bad daughter even to think that. A terrible daughter. Not only am I leaving my mother on her own for two whole months, I'm fantasizing about running away from her and possibly getting her arrested.

Galvanized by guilt, I dash over to Mum's side, peeling her hands off the security guard, apologizing profusely.

26

"I've never really gone away before," I mumble. "She's very upset . . . sorry. . . ."

Mum collapses on my shoulder, folding over me like a rag doll because she's so much taller than I am. She looked so lovely today, I was so proud of her; in her slim gray trousers and white linen sweater, her blond hair pinned back from her face, a big silver necklace wrapped around her neck and cascading down the front of her sweater, she looks so young and smart. I could see men glancing sideways at her admiringly as we walked through Heathrow, and my heart swelled with happiness at how fantastic she looked, how great she was being, holding my hand, swinging it back and forth, talking about what a wonderful time I was going to have in Italy.

She's been so brilliant, too, during my exams. For the last few months I've been revising nonstop, drilling myself in French conjugations, learning Shakespeare quotes, staring at Rembrandt self-portraits till I dream about his face every night, and Mum has been a star, making sure I have my favorite meals, dragging me out to get some fresh air now and then, reassuring me when I break down and panic that I'm going to have mental blocks in the exams and forget everything I've learned.

She looked after me, and now I have to look after her, I tell myself as I pat her back and do my best to tell her I'll be okay, that two months will go by really fast, that there's nothing to get upset about.

But a nasty little voice inside my head points out that I threw my messy sobbing fits in private. Not at the departure gate at Heathrow airport.

27

I dart a glance around me to see if anyone's staring. And I promptly see two girls standing by the currency exchange, whispering together, all-too-obviously staring in our direction. I notice them at once because they're both carrying big white bed pillows wedged under their arms, something I've never seen before. They look older than me, with smooth hair pulled back elegantly from their faces, which are equally smooth and so well made up that if they were in uniform, rather than jeans and hoodies, I'd think they might be air hostesses. One's white, curvy, with lots of blond hair, and one's black and very slim; they make a striking pair, and from the way they carry themselves, it's clear they know it.

The black girl meets my eyes for a moment, and smirks; she turns to say something to her blond friend, who laughs in response.

Cow, I think angrily. Maybe it's the fact that Mum and I are being openly sneered at that makes me take Mum's shoulders, lift her off me, and say:

"Mum—I really have to go now. There might be lines at Security, it takes ages to go through."

"Violet, darling, my precious little girl . . . why did I *ever* think this was a good idea?" Mum grabs a tissue from her bag. One thing mothers always seem to have, I notice, are tissues. She wipes her eyes, wincing at the amount of mascara that comes off in the process. "You can always come back, darling. Just one phone call—one text—and I'll be on the next plane to come and get you. I promise. I know it's a long way away—"

Not even a two-hour flight, I think.

"—but I'll be there straightaway!" She grabs my hand

and stares intently into my eyes, her own blurry and red. "And I'll email you every day, darling! Every day! Honestly! Just in case you're homesick! Oh, God—why did I ever let you talk me into this? It's not too late to change your mind, you know!"

Oh, Mum.

"I love you, Mum. I'll text as soon as the plane lands, okay? Try to keep busy! Get Aunt Lissie to come over for a visit—you could have some sister time together!" I suggest in a flash of inspiration. "I'll be back before you know it!"

I give her a last quick hug, grab the handle of my bag, and shoot between the security guards before she can follow me, or break down again; mercifully, there aren't that many people at Passport Control, and I'm at the desk in a minute or so. Handing my passport and boarding pass to the man behind it, I glance quickly back at Mum. It's worse than I thought. She's sobbing again, holding on to the top bar of the security rail that separates departing travelers from the rest of the people in the airport, her blue eyes as mournful and tear-filled as if I were moving to Australia, not just going to another part of Europe for eight weeks.

If I didn't know her, I would definitely think that she was doing it for effect, enjoying being a drama queen. And I can tell that's what the two girls I spotted before think: that Mum's relishing the drama of our parting. They're in the queue behind me, staring openly at Mum and commenting to each other, flashing perfect, even white teeth.

How mean. I don't see how two girls carrying ginormous bed pillows have the nerve to laugh at me! I think furiously, grabbing back my documents from the passport official and dashing through the sliding doors without even looking back at Mum, my shoulders slumping in guilt that I'm abandoning her in such a state.

If things keep going this way, my trip to Italy's going to be a total disaster.

Like Waking Up in THE PRINCESS DIARIES

As soon as I step out of the plane, onto the wheeled staircase down to the tarmac, Italy hits me in the face. Bright
sun blinds me: it's like stepping onstage, a bank of white
light forcing you to blink, raise a hand to shield your eyes.
I fumble in my bag for my sunglasses, holding up the people behind me. Warm, humid air wraps itself around me
insistently, demanding that I unzip my jacket, pull off my
cotton sweater, bare my arms and neck to the blazing mid-
afternoon sunshine. By the time I'm down the wobbly metal
stairs, by the time my feet first touch Italian soil, I've wres-
tled off the outer layers I was wearing in the air-conditioned
plane. Everyone else is doing the same dance, wriggling and
writhing as they cross the tarmac, shrugging off jackets,

stuffing them into carry-on cases, the older English men and women putting on the straw Panama hats and ribboned raffia boaters they've brought to protect their white skin from the scorching Mediterranean sun.

Sod that! I can't get enough of it. By the end of these two months, I want to be suntanned and golden from head to toe. I tilt my face up to the sky—it's as bright a blue as the water that borders the Tuscan coastline—and revel in how glorious the warmth is. I was definitely meant to live in this climate. My body's sucking up the heat, flourishing in it; I feel like a sunflower, turning my face to the sun, blooming and blossoming, petals opening wide.

I'm smiling as I enter the long, low white terminal building and navigate through corridors hung with huge framed photographs of olive groves and bright green oil in bottles, of sleek white yachts, of luxury hotels with striped loungers around bright blue swimming pools. The line at Passport Control is very brief for EU citizens, and the airport's so small that by the time I emerge into the baggage hall, luggage is creaking around on the conveyor belts, unloaded from our plane. I see my suitcase and dive for it, pulling it off the belt. Already, my denim shorts, which I'm wearing over opaque black tights, are feeling heavy in the humid air, saturated with moisture, itchy and uncomfortable; I long to pull the tights off, at the very least, but then my shorts would be too—well, short. I bought them specifically to wear over tights—they'd be a bit too much like hot pants if my legs were bare, and I'd feel really self-conscious. I like my legs, but I'm not tanned or slim or tall enough to carry off hot pants anywhere but on a beach. God. Clothes are *hard*.

A girl passes me, looking visibly uncomfortable, her pale skin coated with sweat and her light red hair sticking to her forehead. She's dragging a matching pair of cases, a carry-on and a larger suitcase, in a cheap beigey tartan print that's a bad rip-off of a recent Burberry design. To be honest, it looks as if she bought them at a cheap market, or a pound shop; I can see the binding on the carry-on's already fraying, and clearly a wheel on the main suitcase is broken, because it's squeaking and bumping unevenly, and she's having to haul it along like a sack of potatoes. The Alsatian dog that's supposed to be drug-sniffing the passengers but is lying on the cool tiled floor by the exit door instead opens one eye at the noise as she lumbers past, cocks his ear, and slumps back to sleep again. His handler, chatting with a customs official, is completely uninterested in any of us travelers.

"*Uffa!*" mutters an Italian businessman in front of me as the smoked-glass double doors fly open onto the arrivals section, and his attempt to stride through the crowd of waiting friends and relatives is thwarted by the redheaded girl. Her suitcase seems to have completely broken down; a beige wheel is rolling across the tiles, disappearing under people's feet, and she's come to a halt, trying desperately to lift her suitcase by its handle, blocking the stream of people now flooding out behind her. No one helps; they push around her, cursing, until finally she manages to haul both her cases through the crowd, shoulders slumped. I feel really sorry for her, but I'm busy looking for the person I'm supposed to meet; the paperwork said that we would be met at Pisa by Catia Cerboni, the lady who owns Villa Barbiano and runs the course, and that she would be holding up a card with our names on it.

Of course she'll be here; why wouldn't she? The flight was on time—there's no reason she wouldn't meet it. But it's impossible, when you're alone in a strange country where you don't speak the language not to be even a little bit nervous that you'll be abandoned. Everyone else seems to know where they're going: businesspeople are walking off quickly with their briefcases, and Italians are falling into each other's arms with theatrical exclamations of happiness. I'm pressed forward by the people behind me, and I scan the crowd almost frantically, until with huge relief I see a woman right at the back, by the far doors that keep pulling open onto a bright glorious vista of sunlight, holding up a small white laminated sign reading VILLA BARBIANO.

As I approach her, I bite my lip. She's really intimidating: thin as a rake, her pale linen dress hanging off her deeply tanned limbs, big sunglasses holding back her dyed blond hair. She's wearing no makeup except dark red lipstick, which somehow makes the dark circles under her eyes more noticeable, and she's dripping in gold—heavy bracelets clanking on her narrow wrists, big gold hoops swinging from her ears. Her fingernails are painted the same dark red as her lipstick. And her expression is deeply, profoundly bored in a way I've only seen on Frenchwomen before. Which is *not* a good sign.

"I'm Violet Routledge," I say hesitantly. "Am I the first?"

She nods.

"Catia Cerboni," she announces, leaning forward to peck me on either cheek. "*Ciao*. Welcome to Italia."

She has no Italian accent whatsoever, I notice, impressed.

"There are three more of you to come," she says, looking at her gold bracelet-watch. "I hope they will be here soon. Or I will have to pay for an extra hour in the parking lot."

Blimey, I think. *You're a friendly one.*

Crashing and thudding signals the arrival of the second person in our group: it's the redheaded girl with the broken suitcase. She's close to tears, one shoulder hunched from lifting her big case while pulling the carry-on with her other hand. I dash forward to help her prop the broken one against the wall; Catia Cerboni looks on with plucked eyebrows raised, not lifting a finger to assist.

"You must be Kelly," she drawls at the girl.

"That's right." The girl looks surprised. "How'd you know?"

Catia smirks.

"The other girls are American," she informs us, flicking her gaze up and down first Kelly, then me. "You two are clearly not American."

She says this like it's a bad thing. Kelly and I exchange glances, checking each other out, but also sharing a moment of *She's a charmer, right?*

Kelly's fanning herself, pushing her hair back from her forehead.

"Blimming hot, innit?" she says in a strong Essex accent. "I was freezing on the plane, but it's all right now, eh?"

She's wearing a tight T-shirt, an equally tight denim

mini, and flip-flops, revealing a lot of lightly freckled white skin. The T-shirt, a fluorescent green, is much too bright for her coloring, and makes her look bigger than she is; she's built on a solid scale, with a squarish body that the miniskirt doesn't flatter. I like her eye makeup, though: long strokes of bright green pencil that matches the T-shirt, layered over equally bright blue shadow. It's really fun. Her nails, I notice, are stubby short and painted glittery turquoise. I glance down at my own, whose burgundy polish is chipping badly. I should tidy them up at some point. *Mum would nag and nag me about the chipped nail polish,* I think, and I have a quick rush of homesickness before I determinedly push it back into its box and slam down the lid.

"Oh my *God!*" comes an exclamation, high and nasal enough to cut through even the constant Italian chatter all around us. "This trolley's, like, *drunk!*"

Mad giggling follows this, equally loud, as two girls pushing luggage trolleys come cannoning through the crowd of friends and relatives. People jump aside for them, complaining, but I notice Italian men, young and old, turning to stare after the girls appreciatively. I also notice that all the Italian men—young and old—are wearing their jeans *much* tighter than I'm used to in England. I must say, I definitely like it. I gawk at one boy, about my age, in a really skinny pair of jeans and a short-sleeved shirt tucked into them; you can see his whole body, tall and lean, with a nice round bum, which happens to be pretty much my ideal boy's figure. Unfortunately, when he swivels, checking out the giggling girls, I see his face, and that ruins it. Not only is he not very handsome, but he's shaved his facial hair into a weird line that runs like a chinstrap around his jaw.

I quickly avert my gaze and realize that not only are the two girls heading straight for us, they're the same two I saw at the airport. The ones with the pillows. Super-smart, super-confident. Who were laughing at me and Mum at Heathrow.

They're the two other girls on the course. Oh, *brilliant.*

"It's, like, *wobbling* like *Jell-O!*" trills the blonde, laughing as if this is the funniest joke in the world.

"Use your core strength," the black girl says dryly. "Like Natalie says in Pilates."

"Oh, jeez, I *so* hope they don't have Pilates in Italy!" the blonde says. "I always think I'm going to fall off the ball. It's so *unstable.*"

"That's kinda the *point*, Paige," the other girl says even more dryly.

"Oh! Yay! Villa Barbiano!" Paige exclaims, pointing at the sign that Catia is holding up. "That's us!"

They come to a halt in front of our little group. I see that their trolleys are heaped high with luggage; they must have brought two suitcases each, plus their carry-ons. Their pillows are stuffed into the wire baskets at the front, bulging out like big white airbags.

"Did you think they didn't have pillows in Italy?" Kelly asks bluntly, which makes me snort.

Paige tosses back her blond locks.

"American pillows are the best," she says. "My mom says so."

Catia Cerboni claps her hands.

"*Allora*," she says, "you are all here! Good! Welcome to Italy and your course. I am Catia Cerboni." She sweeps her hand in a big circle in the air, as if she's blessing us. "You will all introduce yourselves as we go to the car," she says, turning on her heel and shooting out the automatic glass doors, clearly in a hurry to make it out of the car park before she has to pay for that extra hour.

"I'm Violet," I say as we follow Catia out into the blinding sunshine, flicking my sunglasses down from the crown of my head. "And that's Kelly."

I nod at poor Kelly, who's busy struggling with her cases once more.

"I'm Kendra," says the black girl. "And that's Paige." She nods at her taller, whiter, bouncier companion.

"Oh, we saw you at Heathrow!" Paige exclaims to me. "Was that your mom? She was, like, freaking out! You must have been like, *Mom, stop embarrassing me!* I'd be, like, *mortified* if my mom made a scene like that! It was like a movie or something—I thought she was going to yell '*Don't take my baby!*'" She wrinkles her forehead. "I don't remember where I saw that."

"Probably a Lifetime movie," Kendra says in what sounds like a sarcastic tone.

"Probably! I *love* Lifetime movies," Paige says happily.

I fall back to keep pace with Kelly, so cross with Paige that I'm literally biting my tongue to avoid snapping at her; I don't want a feud to start before we're even in the car. Kelly's got a good hold on her case now, and is bumping it along, though it's making an awful scraping sound and I doubt she'll be able to use it again.

"Right old natural blonde, that one," Kelly says, nodding at Paige. "Not much between the ears."

I know she means that to console me, and I warm to her. We're walking along a path between banks of green grass on which rounded, odd-looking bronze statues are set at intervals. Wide banners flap in the breeze, proclaiming the dates for the Puccini Festival at Torre del Lago, bright colors against the blue sky. There's even an outdoor café with smiling people sprawled at tables, smoking, drinking beer, eating pizza; Pisa airport is nicer than most town centers I've seen in the UK.

"Come along!" Catia's shouting, and Kelly and I hurry up our steps obediently, crossing through bollards to the parking lot, and a large, rather bashed-about jeep with its baggage door open. The American girls' enormous luggage is taking up almost all the space; Kelly and I, by dint of much pushing and shoving, manage to wedge our suitcases in. I reach up and slam down the hatchback just in time, before one of the cases comes sliding out again.

"Okay!" Catia says, pulling away almost before Kelly and I have managed to jump into the jeep. Kendra is in the front, which I suppose is fair, as she's the tallest, but it would have been nice to have been asked. I'm in the middle, and I glance sideways at Paige, who's already plugged in earbuds and is listening to her iPod, humming tunelessly.

I'm embarrassed to admit how intimidating I find the American girls. They're so confident, as if they own the world. They're as beautifully groomed as if they were models; I assume they've traveled over from the United States, while Kelly and I just had a short flight from the UK, but the American girls, despite having had a much longer journey, look fresh as daisies. Paige's skin is smooth and glowing, her cheekbones accentuated with blush, her lips glossed with clear shine, her lashes thick with mascara. Though she's probably wearing a lot more makeup than me and Kelly, she looks more natural; the English style is to wear theatrical, showy makeup. Kelly and I have lots of eyeliner and bright nail polish on, and it's really obvious, while these two girls are much more subtle.

I glance sideways at Paige's fingernails, perfect beige ovals tipped with white; they put my scabby scraped ones to shame. I curl my fingers into my palms to avoid the comparison. And she smells lovely—like bubble gum and apples. Her hair, caught back in a silk scarf tied at the nape of her neck, is thick and smooth. She has a huge pink pashmina wrapped around her throat, which she adjusts tighter because of the air-conditioning, stretching out her jean-clad legs, humming away.

Everything she's wearing is new and shiny, or looks it. And Kendra's even smarter; diamonds gleam in the lobes of her ears as she turns to look out the window, and her hair, clubbed into a short ponytail, is perfectly smooth, pulled tight to show the elegant shape of her head.

I realize what's taken me aback: the American girls must be the same age as us, but with their poise, their grooming, they seem so much older. They make me feel like a snotty-nosed, scruffy, immature fourteen-year-old, looking up to the sixth-formers at school in awe because they seem so grown up, so trendy. It's *not* a sensation I enjoy. I wonder if Kelly feels the same. . . .

The jeep makes a right-hand turn, rolling me into Paige's side; she yelps in shock, an annoying little yipping noise, like a startled Chihuahua. We've been on the motorway for quite a while, but now we're coming off, onto a slip road, through a series of villages with beautiful names: San Vincenzo a Torri, Cerbiano, Macario a Monti. Almost immediately, the road starts to wind back and forth in tight curves, and we have to hold on tight in the back not to bump into each other constantly. And the jeep starts climbing, the road gets steeper, as we travel up into the Chianti hills; Catia is changing down gears, the old jeep clanking as it adjusts to a sharp incline.

I'm mesmerized by the views. It's like the color of the Adriatic Sea; you don't believe that anything could be that amazing aquamarine in real life, not till you see it with your own eyes. The Chianti landscape is just as extraordinary. It's like a whole series of postcards brought to life. Perfect stone farmhouses built on steep hillsides, with olive groves and vineyards laid out in equally perfect rows, cascading down green slopes in a patchwork of delicate colors: rich green grass, the darker emerald of the vine leaves, fluffy gray-green puffball-topped olive trees, gray stone buildings. Tiny cars, bright flashes of color, wind their way up narrow little roads lined with cypress trees, clouds of white dust trailing in their wake like jet streams behind airplanes. Occasionally, there's a vivid chemical flash of blue, a perfect rectangle of tiled swimming pool.

My fingers are itching to pick up a pencil, crayons, a stick of charcoal, and start sketching. My friend Milly is really into photography, but that's never been my thing; I've always liked to see the picture I'm making grow slowly on the sketch pad or canvas even though I don't have much experience in art.

But now, my eyes wide as I take in one spectacular panorama after another, I wish, with all my heart, that I'd been to a school that maybe did proper art O- and A-levels, not just a few art classes. Because the small drawing ability that I have is not going to be able to do justice to the amazing views that I'm dying to get on paper.

"I feel sick!" Paige whines beside me, snapping me out of my reverie. "I'm getting totally carsick! These roads are *way* too bendy!"

"Open the window and put your head out," Catia snaps, driving, if anything, even faster.

"Ugh! My hair'll get all messed up!" Grumpily, Paige buzzes down the window and pokes her nose out, holding her hair flat with both hands clamped to the sides of her head. She gulps in deep breaths of air as the vehicle lurches along.

"She looks like a dog," Kelly mutters to me. "You know, when they stick their heads out of car windows?"

"A golden Labrador," I mumble back. "Big and shiny, but no brains at all."

Paige is definitely built on a large scale; she's not at all fat, just big-boned, sturdy, like a lacrosse player, which she probably is; she glows with health, and her golden tan is

42

enviable. The more I think about the Labrador comparison, the better it is.

"Any better?" Kendra twists around in her seat to look at Paige. "Do you want to swap places?"

Now, Kendra, I think, *is a greyhound. Lean and elegant, not a hair out of place.*

"We're nearly there," Catia snaps as the jeep turns sharply onto a side road, jouncing and bumping on the dirt surface. Paige sensibly ducks back in before her head gets severed by a particularly enthusiastic bounce. We're traveling up a steep avenue lined with cypresses, as so many of the roads seem to be; the pale dust from the road surface has already coated the bases of the trees and the tangle of undergrowth on either side. The road drops away, to oohs and aahs from all of us as we see the valley below, a village in a bowl of green to our left, rows of vines flowing in straight lines down the hillside on our right. I notice bunches of tiny dark purple grapes growing on the vines, half hidden by the clustering leaves; and bright red roses planted along the edges, climbing up the stakes, twining around them lovingly.

It's so beautiful. I've seen wonderful landscapes before; my mum likes to travel, and of course we go to Norway every year. I've seen Scottish mountains, French chateaux, even the Sydney Harbor Bridge when we went to Australia two years ago. But there's something about Tuscany that stirs up my heart like nowhere else. I want to paint every inch of it. I can't wait to start the art lessons.

It feels like coming home.

All the girls are squealing now as the jeep crunches

over ruts and potholes, throwing us against our seat belts. We're turning through high gateposts, down an even narrower road, almost a track; and then white gleams through the trees and Catia is swinging the jeep to a halt, wheels crunching on gravel, in front of a wide cream-stuccoed villa, pale mauve wisteria climbing up its sides and softening its square lines.

"Welcome to Villa Barbiano, your home for the next eight weeks," Catia says shortly as she unclips her seat belt and swings herself deftly to the ground. "It is eighteenth century, built as a country home for my husband's family, the Cerbonis. Their main palazzo was in Florence, but that has now been sold. We make our own wine and olive oil, and also some goat cheese, which is very popular."

"Goats! Eww! Smelly!" Paige mutters, not quietly enough; Catia shoots her an evil stare.

"I will show you to your rooms," she says coldly, "and then you may unpack and maybe have a swim in the pool before dinner."

We all perk up at the mention of the pool, dragging our cases out of the jeep and following Catia through the big double doors of the villa. Inside it's immediately cool, the terra-cotta tiles of the floor and the white-plastered walls cutting the outside temperature. The house is half in shade, shutters at most of the windows, stripes of bright sunlight stippling the rust-colored floor and the stone staircase we climb. The walls are hung with elegant little watercolors of fruit and flowers, and each hallway we pass has an inlaid occasional table placed against the wall, one of those half-moon shapes with a perfect flower arrangement in a vase on top, like you get in five-star hotels.

I'm amused to see that we have to climb right to the top of the house, under the sloping roof. Catia has put us in the old servants' quarters.

"*Ecco!* Here are your rooms," Catia says as we arrive, panting because of the weight of our cases, at the top of the stairs. She's standing in a wide, stone-floored anteroom with a roof sloping away on either side to long low windows, her arms wide, like an air hostess indicating emergency exits. "There are two beds in each one, and each room has its own bathroom," she informs us. "The beds are made up, and you will find your own towels on them. Every week you will be responsible for taking your sheets and towels downstairs to the laundry. Please do not use fake tan, as it stains the towels and we have to bleach them, which is not good for the environment. There are beach towels by the swimming pool. Do not take your house towels out to the pool. And please do not put sanitary napkins down the toilet, as you will make a blockage."

She drops her arms, turns on her heel, and heads for the top of the stairs, picking her way past Kendra's gigantic suitcase.

"The pool is at the back of the villa," she adds. "Dinner is served at eight-thirty in the dining room. We dress for dinner. No shorts, please. And no skirts so short we can see what you are wearing underneath. This is a course for young ladies, not ragamuffins."

We're all so freaked out by this speech, delivered with

the weariness of a woman who's trotted it out hundreds of times before, that we're frozen in utter silence as Catia's heels click down the stone stair treads, one flight, two flights, and eventually recede into the depths of Villa Barbiano. It's our first bonding moment as a foursome, and it's over in a flash: a swift, panicky glance exchanged by all of us, the realization that we're stuck, for the next eight weeks, in a house with a woman who seems to actively dislike teenage girls.

"You and me?" Kelly says to me as Kendra jerks her chin at Paige and heads across the antechamber to the door closest to her. *It's Brits versus Americans,* I think, rolling my case in the opposite direction. *Scruffs versus glamour girls. Blue nail varnish versus French manicures . . .*

But all comparisons trail off as I enter the bedroom and goggle in shock. It's like a suite, with the bathroom leading off one side, and it's huge. There's a single bed on either side of the room, a hooked cotton rug and white-painted nightstand beside each one. A big white cupboard and chest of drawers match the rest of the furniture, and a few black-and-white prints hang on the walls. It's a blank canvas, simple and elegant, the roof sloping sharply to the right, exposed wooden beams with terra-cotta tiles lining the spaces between them.

But the real star, for me, is the window between the beds. Long and low, beneath the eaves, it frames a view of blue skies, olive groves, and oak trees in the valley below, as beautiful as a painting. Sunlight gleams through it in a long refracted ray, bounced off the eaves, hanging in the air, tiny dust mites suspended in its golden glow, glittering like dots of mica. I run over to the window seat and sink onto the stone embrasure, staring out at the panorama, for the first time really understanding what the expression "feast your eyes" means.

"Oh *wow!*" Kelly echoes my feelings as she thuds into the room. Her case tips to the floor with a crash. "Piece of rubbish," she mutters, kicking it. "Didn't even last one blooming trip." She clears her throat. "Um, d'you care which bed you have?" she asks politely, as screams of:

"Mine!"

"No, I saw it first!"

"I put my bag on it!" shrill from across the anteroom.

"My money's on Kendra," I say, grinning at Kelly. "And no, I don't care which bed I have. Do you?"

Kelly looks as if she doesn't know whether to laugh or cry. Slowly, she walks across the room and sinks onto the far bed.

"At home," she says eventually, "I share with my two little sisters. They've got a bunk bed and I've got one of those sofa-cube things that I unfold every night. We've only got a little council house, and there's six of us. This room"— she gestures around her—"is the size of our entire ground floor. Kitchen, lounge, everything." She swallows hard. "So, no, I don't care which bed I have either."

"You know something funny?" I ask. "I'll bet these are the old servants' quarters. Right at the top of the house, under the roof."

She's thunderstruck.

"You're having me on," she breathes, looking around the huge bedroom in wonder.

I shake my head. "Of course, there'd have been a lot

47

more people in here, all piled in, lots of beds in rows. And there wouldn't have been a—"

More screams resound from the other side of the top floor.

"Omi*god!*" Paige howls. "The bathroom's like *huge*, and it's all *marble!*"

Kelly and I race across the room to look at our own en suite bathroom; luckily the doorway's wide enough to let us both through. We gasp at the sight of the room, which is just as big as our bedroom: at the marble bath, the marble-walled open shower—there isn't even a curtain, it's so big it doesn't need one—and the twin sinks set in a long white marble slab in front of a huge mirror.

"Those aren't real gold taps, are they?" Kelly says in a hushed voice, as if she's in church.

I'm trying not to smile.

"No," I say.

"I might tell my sisters they are," she says, shaking her head in disbelief as she looks around the room. "They'll believe it." Kelly sinks slowly to a squat, her head in her hands. "Flipping, bleeding hell," she mutters slowly. "Buggering, bloody, sodding hell. Sorry. But if you *knew* where I started out this morning . . . what my home looks like . . . This is like—" She draws in a long breath. "Like waking up in *The Princess Diaries* or something."

I have no idea what to say to Kelly. I'm feeling very spoiled and privileged and undeserving when Paige bursts into the bathroom. She's changed into a whirl of white lace cover-up over pink bikini over full-body tan, flip-flops slapping on the tiles.

"Hey! Isn't it cool!" she sings out. "Though I can't *believe* we've only got single beds! I'm gonna keep falling right off it when I turn over! Anyway, we're going down to the pool. You coming? Come on down! Jeez, I sound like a game show!"

She swirls out again, leaving the dust mites whirling in her wake.

We charge back into our enormous bedroom to tear open our suitcases. I realize that looming up before us is one of the major holiday hurdles that any group of girls has to face: the first time they all decide to go swimming together.

I *hate* this bit. It's the Swimsuit Beauty Parade.

Swimsuit Beauty Parade

The parade is brutal, but it's over relatively quickly. There's a flurry of movement as we spread out our towels, settle on the loungers, dart quick looks around us to see if anyone else is watching, and peel off our outer layers. Paige has effortlessly won the Best Pool Outfit competition; her white lace cover-up is gorgeous, and I totally covet it. These American girls are much chicer than me and Kelly: like all my friends, I just wear a strappy top and a little pareo-thingy over my swimming things when I go to the beach or the pool, while Kelly doesn't even have that—she's just pulled the T-shirt and mini she was wearing before over her swimsuit.

But these girls have actual pool-lounging outfits. Paige's pink bikini is coordinated to her pink diamante-studded flip-flops, and her cowboy hat looks really cool with the white lace of the cover-up. You could laugh at her, call her too matchy-matchy, or say she's trying too hard, but to be honest, I think both Kelly and I envy how smart she looks. Kendra has tossed off her own yellow wrap and dived in to swim lengths, her slim, dark shape cutting through the water like a pair of designer scissors, arms and legs long and lean. Kelly and I join Paige in a chorus of oohs and aahs about how beautiful the pool is.

"I mean, I saw it in the photos online," Paige is saying, picking up one in a long series of suncreams, double-checking it's the right factor, and then applying it to her shoulders. "And it looked stunning. But in real life, it's, like, *amazing.* I'm gonna take a ton of photos and make everyone back home jealous."

The pool's at the side of Villa Barbiano, set in a wide green lawn bordered with fragrant lavender and rosemary bushes: the swimming pool comes right up to the border of the lawn, and that side drops away with the slope of the hill with what I think is called an infinity edge. It means that when you're actually in the water, you can float and look at the landscape with nothing to obstruct the view. I find myself wondering what a painting would look like if you did it as if you were in the pool: glittering water below, distant hills in the center, blue skies above, the concrete surround of the pool just visible at the far edges of the frame.

And then I shake my head in confusion. *Tuscany definitely does something weird to me. I've never had this impulse to paint everything I see before. . . .*

I fold my top and pareo and put them on the little dark

green table next to my lounger. Then I start applying sunscreen. Kelly's doing the same thing, and we're glancing over at each other, checking out what I really don't want to think of as competition, but it's so hard not to. With the film posters and ads showing pictures of perfect bikini bodies, the magazines that pick apart celebrities, rating their good and bad bits, it's almost impossible not to do the same. I wish I didn't, but I do. I feel really mean to be relieved that Paige, though not at all fat, is bigger than me, taller and wider, with solid thighs and arms, while Kelly is pale, plump, and clearly miserable in a green one-piece that makes her white skin look almost putrid. I'm very grateful that I've been fake tanning for a couple of months; my naturally sallow skin looks nicely pale brown, and my black polka-dot bikini, with little frills around the legs and bosom, is structured enough that it makes the most of my shape.

Or rather, it does when I look at myself in the mirror, tummy sucked in. Sitting up, walking around—those are very different activities, and I know I'd loathe seeing a photo of myself snapped at those moments.

Whereas Kendra, rising from the swimming pool, pulling herself up to stand on the side with one athletic push from her toned arms, has nothing to fear from anyone's camera phone. We all stare openly at her in her tiny white bikini, the kind that's just a few triangles of material that fasten with a few ties at hips and neck and back. The kind that only models with small, perky, high bosoms and tiny bums can wear. Hello, Swimsuit Beauty Parade? We have a winner.

I think for a moment of my mum in a bikini, long and slim and elegant as Kendra, though she does wear a slightly more mum-suitable two-piece, thank goodness. I certainly didn't get my figure from her side of the family: she, Aunt Lissie, and Mormor are all tall and lean, with long waists that give them totally flat tummies. I look gloomily down at my squidgy one, as I've often done in their company, but this time with the added force of wondering whether I have such a different figure because I'm not actually related to them at all.

I swallow, hard. I texted Mum to say I'd arrived safe and sound and of course got a second flood of relieved texts back: the first, naturally, had already arrived as soon as I switched my phone back on, apologies for breaking down at the airport, best wishes for the trip, pleas to let her know as soon as the plane touched down in Italy. She thinks texts are like letters: she always starts "Darling Violet," writes lengthy paragraphs, and finishes "Love, Mum." The phone has to break them down into multiple messages. It's a bit exhausting, frankly, but I know it means she loves me, so I try not to get too irritated.

You'd better not, I think. *You're going to get lots and lots of text-letters from her in the next eight weeks.*

"That pool's really small," Kendra says dismissively, walking over to her lounger, where she picks up a towel and wipes her face dry. She wraps the towel around her head like a turban and stretches out on the chair, looking like a carved mahogany sculpture of a Somalian supermodel. "I'm going to have to do a hundred lengths a day, instead of fifty," she complains. "It's like I'm bouncing off a wall every five strokes."

Fifty lengths a day? No wonder she has that figure! I think, wincing at my own laziness. I glance at Kelly, who's putting

53

up the umbrella to get some shade; she grimaces back at me, clearly having exactly the same thought.

"You work out really hard!" Paige exclaims, looking down at her own stomach and prodding it gloomily. "You make me feel like a lazy slob!"

I have to give Paige credit: she may spill out everything that pops into her head without thinking first, but she's pretty honest. She laughed at my mum's drama-queen meltdown at Heathrow, but at least she's pointing out her own defects too.

"I do a hundred sit-ups every morning," Kendra says, reaching for her white-framed sunglasses. "You can join in if you want."

"Oh my *God!*" Paige wails. "A *hundred?* I can barely do *three!*"

She grabs a handful of stomach and wobbles it. I am increasingly, reluctantly, impressed with Paige: it takes real courage to wobble your tummy in public.

She looks over at me and Kelly with a friendly smile.

"This place is awesome," she says cheerfully. "I mean, it's smaller than it looks on the website, but everything's smaller in Europe, right? London was really cool. We stayed there last night, with friends of Kendra's mom. My mom and dad thought we should have a rest before we came over to the mainland."

Kelly has lain down on her tummy on the lounger, face on her arms, but now she lifts her head, squinting in the sun, and stares incredulously at Paige.

"When you came over to the *mainland?*" she asks. "You

do know that the United Kingdom is a completely different country from Italy, right?"

Paige's blond eyebrows knit in confusion.

"But it's all part of Europe?" she says, looking at Kendra for help. "I mean, England's like an island, off the mainland of Europe."

"We're a *separate country*," Kelly says coldly. "It would be like saying that Greenland's an island off the mainland of the United States."

"Isn't it?" Paige says, giggling helplessly. "I was never very good at geography."

"Kelly's right," Kendra drawls. "Some of us Americans do have half an idea where other countries in the world are located."

"Are you two friends?" I ask, because I can see that Kelly's still seething.

"Our parents know each other from the country club," Paige says, not a whit upset by being effectively called an idiot by Kendra. "Our moms play tennis together on Saturdays."

"And our dads golf together," Kendra says, self-mockingly now. "It's all *super-cozy*. I wanted to come to Italy for the summer, and I found this course online—"

"But *her* mom didn't want her to go on her own, and she told *my* mom, and *my* mom thought it would be a great learning experience for me—" Paige bursts in enthusiastically.

"And teach you where some other flipping countries are besides your own," Kelly mutters sotto voce.

"—so they thought we'd make a great team," Kendra

concludes, with enough sarcasm in her voice to indicate that she has decidedly mixed feelings about having Paige as her sidekick.

"You hadn't met before?" I ask. I'm always curious about people: Mum says I shouldn't ask so many questions, but I can't help it.

"Oh, we knew each other from the club," Kendra says. "But we don't have the same friends. Or," she adds rather pointedly, "go to the same school."

"Oh no! Kendra goes to the really brainy high school in Jacksonburg," Paige says with devastating candor. "Her friends are all, like, super-smart." She giggles. "Mine just like to party. Hey!" She sits up, leans forward, and shoves her own sunglasses up to the crown of her head. "Talking about partying, I didn't come to Italy for the summer just to hang out with a bunch of girls! No offense, but there had better be some cute boys around here! If not, we'll just have to go out and find them, right? Hunt them down like dogs!"

I can see that Paige has a real gift for saying what everyone else is thinking but is too proud to admit. Of course I've been speculating about Italian boys, lots and lots, but I wasn't going to say it out loud. . . .

"Do you two have boyfriends?" she asks us.

Kelly shakes her head and I shake mine, a little embarrassed at being put on the spot.

"Cool!" she continues, to my surprise. "Kendra doesn't either. And I just broke up with someone. Or he sort of broke up with me. I think. We had a fight and it was all kinda messed up. Anyway, who cares?" She throws her arms wide, smiling so happily I can see almost every one of her big white perfect teeth. "It's summer! You should never have a boyfriend in the summer. You get a boyfriend in the autumn, so you have someone over Christmas! And then you break up with *him* in the spring so you can party in the summer again!"

Kelly and I stare at her, eyes wide. There's a mad kind of logic to this, I suppose.

"That isn't how we *all* roll in the States," Kendra informs us with an ironic twist of her mouth. "Paige just thinks the way she does stuff is—well, how everyone does it."

I'm getting really warm now; even though it's late afternoon, the sun low in the sky above the far hills, the heat of the day has soaked into the concrete surround of the pool and baked the earth dry, and that heat is still shimmering all around us, the air heavy with it. Sucking in my tummy, hoping my thighs don't wobble too much, I sit up, quickly swing my legs to the ground, and walk over to the pool, diving in before anyone has too much of a chance to see me in motion. The water's deliciously cool against my overheated skin, and I swim a whole length underwater because it feels so good. I wish I had the willpower to make myself swim a hundred lengths a day, like Kendra's planning to do; it would definitely slim me down a bit.

And yet, being totally honest with myself, I know I won't. I sigh as my head breaks water at the far end. How is it that some people have amazing self-discipline, and others just don't?

I'm at the infinity edge, and I hold on to the side, the smooth rounded concrete lapped over with water, which trickles gently over it and down into a little trough a foot below, there to catch the overflow. From here I have a great view of the ornamental gardens below, planted with hedges in a complicated geometrical pattern, small flower beds shaped like shields set between them at intervals. The grass of the lawns, seen from above, is drying out, the earth below baked hard and brown by the sun; the grass is wither-ing in the scorching heat. Back in England the lawns would still be lush and richly green; but the Mediterranean climate is harsher, with much longer summers, and—here, at any rate—rockier, stonier soil. Plants that grow here have to be tough to survive. Like the vines, and the olives, and the rosemary . . .

From my elevated perspective, I'm the first to see a bright blue convertible winding its way up the hill with two people in it. *Girls,* I realize as the car nears the house, and I feel my heart sinking: *We have enough girls in this house already. We need some testosterone!* The car passes below me and pulls in to a parking area behind a stand of pine trees; moments later, the engine turns off, the doors slam, and Italian voices, high and piercing, ring out in the still, heavy afternoon air, light footsteps running up a concealed flight of stone steps until the girls emerge on the far side of the swimming pool.

We all turn to look at them. I swing around, my arms wide to either side of the pool surround, and as soon as I catch sight of them I'm really grateful that most of my body is concealed by the water.

Because they're really thin, and really stunning. And they're looking down their prominent Italian noses at us as if we're nasty stains on the upholstery of the pool loungers.

I can't tell if they're the same age as us; maybe they're

a bit older. They're both wearing armfuls of narrow gold bracelets and dangling earrings. Their thick dark hair is cut short, pushed back from their faces, and they're wearing as much makeup as Kendra and Paige, but in a considerably more obvious style. They make Kendra—slim athletic Kendra—look plus-size. Their legs, in their skinny jeans, are like toothpicks. Their heels are three-inch-high studded wooden sandals, and their tight white tops fit their narrow torsos like gloves, lifting over their low-rise jeans to reveal glimpses of near-concave stomachs. They're carrying shopping bags and studded handbags that match their sandals, and they're tanned to the color of caramel toffee.

An absolute silence has fallen as we all watch them go past, swinging their bags and tossing their earrings as if they were on a catwalk. They're chatting to each other, laughing, perfectly aware of our presence by the pool but not deigning to even nod at us in acknowledgment. One of them glances over at us briefly and says loudly to the other, "*Hai visto? Madonna, che maiali!*" as they trip through the back door of the villa.

We all look at each other. I'm biting my lip; Kelly's pulled her towel over herself to hide her body; even the confident Paige and Kendra are visibly taken aback. The four of us have bonded as a group. And though I'm glad that we have, I'd really rather that it hadn't been caused by some frighteningly intimidating Italian girls spitting out a comment about us that, by its tone, was definitely dismissive.

"Oh, *jeez*," sighs Paige, who's rapidly becoming the Girl Who Says What Everyone Else Is Thinking. "How did *this* happen? I wanted some Italian *boys*, not skinny girls who're

59

gonna make the rest of us feel like crap!" She narrows her eyes and waves one fist at the sky. "This proves it," she adds gloomily. "God is *definitely* a guy."

❧

The appearance of the Italian girls, brief though it was, has killed our mood. The sun is sinking in the sky, and I think we all want time to unpack, bathe, and primp ourselves to the nines before dinner, now that we're aware of the level of competition there will be around the dining table. We've discussed the girls and decided that they must be Catia's daughters: the website for Villa Barbiano's summer course mentioned the whole Cerboni family, and Paige, bless her, blurted out that she'd been hoping that this meant a ton of hot sons.

"*Not* skinny daughters," she'd said gloomily as we parted in the antechamber to go into our separate rooms. "Which totally *sucks*."

Kelly showers first, and I unpack; when it's my turn for the bathroom, I luxuriate in the shower for the longest time. I've never had a bathroom like this before, one where the marble-lined shower stall is so huge it doesn't even need a door or a curtain; the water pours down in a wide arc, hitting the stone below, running down into the brass drain, saturating the stone. It's such a novelty that I stand there for ages, stretching my arms, feeling the cool grain of the marble under my fingers, turned at an angle so I can look at the view out of the window, the rising hill behind the house planted with lines of fluffy-topped olive trees, their leaves steely green.

I'm practically in a trance. So when Kelly bursts into the bathroom, jumping across my eyeline, gesticulating frantically, I scream my head off with shock.

"Come and see! You've got to come *now!*" she yells, turning pink at the sight of my naked body and averting her eyes immediately. Despite sharing a room with her sisters, Kelly is turning out to be very modest.

"But what—"

"Just *come!*" She gallops out of the room, flip-flops flapping as she goes. I grab a towel, throw it around me, and dash in her wake into our bedroom, over to the windowsill, where Kelly's kneeling, her body so far into the window frame that it looks as if she's about to jump.

"Look!" she hisses without turning her head. "*Boys!*"

It's War

"*Wow*," I breathe as I hang out the window next to Kelly, seeing exactly why she's summoned me so urgently. I hear a suppressed giggle and turn my head a little to see Paige and Kendra doing exactly what we're doing—huddling in their own window seat, staring at the same riveting sight below. I dart a quick glance up and am reassured to see that the low, slanting roof projects above us far enough that it would be really hard for someone in the grounds below to look up and spot four excited girls clustering at the top-floor windows, half hidden under the eaves, gawking shamelessly at the exciting view.

Whatever prayers Paige has been chanting in the last hour or so have paid off massively. Because in the gravel parking area behind the stand of pine trees, swinging their jeans-clad legs off Vespa scooters, taking off their helmets and tossing back their hair, are two answers to any girl's prayer. Two gorgeous, sexy, strutting Italian boys. Just like my mother said.

A tiny sigh escapes my lips.

"I *know*, right?" Kelly says eagerly beside me, a little too loudly, because Kendra hisses a "Shh!" to shut us up.

The boys are stowing their helmets under the Vespa seats, unzipping leather jackets, adjusting their sunglasses, raking their fingers through their thick hair, taking the steps up to the lawn in a couple of long-limbed jumps.

"They're like an aftershave ad!" Kelly whispers, ecstatic, into my ear. "Oh my God, the one on the left . . . he's *soooo* handsome. . . ."

I honestly can't see much variation between them; they're both slim, designer-stubbled, in fitted white shirts tucked into their jeans, which no cool English boy would do but which actually looks really sharp. Kelly's fave has lighter hair—golden maple to the other one's chestnut—and is slightly shorter, but that's the only difference I can see.

The boys are almost below us now, striding toward the house. Kelly leans out so far to get a last glimpse of them I put my hand on her arm, worried that she actually will fall: when she eventually hauls herself back into the room, she's lit up, beaming from ear to ear.

"*Oh,*" she breathes in enchantment. "They're so *beautiful!*"

And then her face falls, so completely that it would be comic if it weren't poignant.

"*Ugh,*" she moans in misery. "What am I going to *wear?*"

By the time we gather in the antechamber to go down for dinner together, just before eight-thirty, it's clear that Kelly wasn't the only one of us who was spurred on by the snotty Italian girls and the handsome Italian boys to make a huge effort with her outfit. We have a lot less to work with than the American girls and their two suitcases each, which, judging by the deafening noise that came from across the anteroom an hour ago, were stuffed full of every electrical beauty product in existence. Their hair looks as if they brought a hairstylist along in one of their gigantic suitcases; Paige's is caught back with a silk scarf and tonged into curls that fall past her shoulders, and Kendra's is slicked to her scalp and wound into a chignon. They're in bright little linen-print dresses that show off their smooth limbs, accessorized with pearl earrings for Paige and diamonds for Kendra.

"Hey," I mutter to Kelly, "we're the trendy ones. Remember that."

We may not have the invisibly natural makeup skills of the Americans, but I think we look a lot cooler, with the sooty black eyeliner and artfully messy hair that's the fashion in London. I'm in a little dress with a square neck and puff sleeves, sort of deliberately old-fashioned, with a huge multistrand fake-pearl necklace a million miles from Paige's ladylike studs. I've painted a beauty spot on my cheekbone, cherry-glossed my lips, and added some fake lashes; I love to dress up, and I'm determined not to be overshadowed. Lily-Rose and Milly and I experimented for years till we found looks that suited us, and we're proud of our individuality, our personal style.

But Kelly, I'm realizing, is not that confident about her looks. She hates her legs, and insisted on wearing jeans. At least her black top slims her torso, and she's done that blue and green eyeliner again, which I think really suits her. Plus, we've both redone our nails—and our toenails. All considered, I'm proud of the English contingent.

Until we enter the dining room, where the Italians are already gathered, and Kelly goes bright red at the sight of the boys lounging against the polished drinks table, and can't say a word for a good twenty minutes.

"It's nice that you dressed up for dinner," Catia Cerboni says approvingly, coming forward to greet us, razor-thin in a slubbed silk sheath dress and matching short-sleeved jacket. She looks at the two boys, and sighs. "I wish they would put on jackets, but they say it is too hot. *Moh.*"

"*Dai. Mamma, non rompere,*" the taller boy says, straightening up at the sight of us. "*Ciao!* Hello!" He smiles charmingly. "I am Leonardo, and this"—he nods at the lighter-haired boy—"is my friend Andrea. It is lovely to meet you."

Beside me, Kelly makes a choking sound. I don't dare look at her. Not only do the boys push off the table and come toward us, they take our hands, one by one, and duck their heads, kissing us on each cheek, saying "*Piacere,*" which, from my *Easy Italian for Beginners* book, I know means "It's a pleasure." They smell much cleaner than the average English boy, of soap and shampoo and conditioner and aftershave, a waft of pine and citrus and green ferns, delicious and fresh. Leonardo is sexier, in my opinion, darker, with

65

more stubble and deep brown eyes; Andrea is fairer, with pale blue eyes and longer, silky light brown hair.

But if this were my choice of boys for the whole holiday, I think as they hand us flutes of what looks like champagne, pale straw–colored, dense with tiny bubbles, *I could scarcely complain. They're both really hot.*

Oh God. I hope I'm not blushing like Kelly! At least I managed to say "piacere" back at them, which is more than anyone else did . . .

"A toast to welcome our summer guests!" Catia says. "Elisa, Ilaria!" she snaps at the two girls who walked by the pool earlier; they're smoking by the big french doors, their backs turned to the room. Tossing their heads and shrugging, they stub out their cigarettes in the big planter next to them, not seeming to care about the lemon tree it contains. Catia sighs audibly and mutters a reproach that Elisa completely ignores as she and Ilaria wriggle back into the dining room. That's the best way I can describe how they move; though they're rake-thin, it's as if they're somehow managing to rub their inner thighs together as they walk, writhing sinuously. *Gah,* I think gloomily. *Whereas I spend my time trying to get my inner thighs not to rub together. It's very unfair.*

"This is *Prosecco di Veneto,*" Catia informs us, in the tone of one imparting a lesson. "It is sparkling wine made from the Prosecco grape. We drink it in Italy before meals, as an *aperitivo.* It is light and pleasant, not strong like champagne. And we say *Salute* when we toast. Okay! So!"

She raises her glass.

"*Salute!*" she says, and we all echo obediently. Leonardo

and Andrea smile charmingly at us as we take our first sip; the Italian girls do not.

"Introduce yourselves," Catia says crossly to them as the bubbles burst on my tongue. I love the taste; I love any drink with bubbles in it, but this is really delicious.

"I am Elisa," says the leader of the two, her Italian accent much stronger than Leonardo's, her dark curly hair cropped short in a terrifyingly fashionable style that only someone very confident could carry off. She waves a hand at her friend, the gold bracelets on her thin tanned arm jingling as she does so. "Elisa Cerboni. That"—she points at Leonardo—"ees my leetle brother, Leonardo. That"—she points at Catia, with more jingling—"ees my mamma. And thees ees my friend Ilaria. Okay?" She says "okay" with such a strong Italian inflection it takes me a moment to recognize the word. I mouth the pronunciation to myself, trying to copy it. "So now we can sit down for the dinner, yes? I am very angry."

Without waiting for an answer, Elisa stalks over to the long table laid with a white lace–inset tablecloth, and set with gleaming silver cutlery, gold-edged china plates, and arrangements of white roses in small silver bowls artfully placed along the center. She pulls out a chair and slumps into it as I stare at her incredulously, unable to believe she's actually announced that she's in a foul mood; what are we supposed to say to that?

Catia heaves another sigh.

"Hungry!" she says, taking her seat at the head of the table. "Hungry!" She emphasizes the *h* for effect. "'Angry'

67

vuol dire incazzato. 'Hungry' *è affammato*." She rubs her stomach, clearly illustrating what "hungry" means.

"*Ma sono anche incazzata*," Elisa says sourly. "*Perche—*"

"*Zitta!*" Catia snaps.

Leonardo grins at me and Kelly.

"My mother is telling my sister to shut up," he says cheerfully. "That is what '*zitta*' means."

God, I think nervously, is this normal? Do they always squabble like this?

Apparently so. I look around; Ilaria is sitting down next to Elisa, gesturing for Andrea to take the seat beside her, and neither of them look at all fazed by the spat. And Leonardo is still smiling, not remotely bothered either.

"Your English is really good," I say, a bit at random, as Paige, who clearly isn't backward at coming forward, plunks herself down next to Andrea, twirling a fat blond ringlet around her fingers and saying brightly:

"Well, hello! My name's Paige, and it's very nice to meet you!"

"*Grazie!* Thank you!" Leonardo says to me as I take a seat as far away from Elisa as I can manage. "I like my English to be very good. I practice a lot. I like it to be better." He sits down next to me. "My English is much better than my sister Elisa's," he adds affably.

"Your English ees better," Elisa snaps, "because you love to talk to foreign girls. *All* foreign girls," she adds, sweeping her cold, dark, mascaraed gaze around at us to emphasize her message: that her brother is a big slut and we shouldn't be flattered by his attentions.

Ilaria giggles dutifully at this.

"Cool," Kendra drawls, slipping her long, sculpted thighs onto the chair next to Leonardo. "You like foreign girls, and I like Italian boys. Sounds perfect to me. I'm Kendra."

Leonardo takes Kendra's hand and raises it to his lips.

"*Sei bellissima,*" he breathes.

"Ooh!" Paige heaves a gusty sigh. "That's so romantic!"

"Our first course," Catia announces loudly as a small, dark-skinned woman enters the room buckling under a large silver tureen, "will be *fusilli con zucchine.* Fusilli pasta with zucchini and lemon."

We serve ourselves with big, silver-handled spoons as the tiny woman staggers around the table, presenting the tureen to each of us one by one. Then a plate is passed around with a grater and a big hunk of Parmesan cheese, so we can grate our own.

"It is always best to serve the cheese fresh," Catia tells us. "Not already grated." It's clear that she runs this course at least in part because she relishes telling people how to do things correctly, and why; you can barely put your fork in your mouth without Catia telling you how to hold it.

The pasta is delicious; short and curly, with lemon zest flecking the bright green of the grated zucchini. I definitely like it. Elisa and Ilaria, I notice, have taken very little, and are only sipping at their glasses of Prosecco; the rest of us have already finished ours by the time Catia tells Leonardo to open and pass around a couple of bottles of red wine. Kelly, beside me, hasn't said a word since we came into the dining room. Her flush has abated, but when I glance at her, it looks as if she's on the verge of tears: her eyes are suspiciously red-rimmed.

"It's really nice, isn't it?" I say, finishing my fusilli and laying my fork down on the plate.

The table's been laid with a big underplate at each place, decorated with swirls of gold; the pasta dish, on top, is a shallow bowl, and I put my fork on that, as my mother's taught me. Kelly nods quickly, a swift duck of her head, picks up her own fork from where she's put it down on the tablecloth, and places it on her plate as I just did. It looks as if the fork tines left a mark on the white cloth, and she tuts nervously when she sees the green stain, trying to scrape it off with her nail.

"It's fine," I mutter, but she keeps on scratching in a vain effort to remove the stain, a bright red color coming back to her cheeks.

"This is a light Chianti that we make ourselves, here at Villa Barbiano," Catia says as Leonardo fills my glass. "It is a table wine, *vino da tavola* in Italian. Only twelve percent, pleasant but not too strong." She directs a hard glance down the expanse of white cloth at the foreign girls. "In Italy," she says pointedly, "we drink only with meals. *Not* like other countries. When we do not eat, we do not drink."

So don't act like drunken foreign sluts with my son and his friend, I translate. I'd whisper this to Kelly, but she looks frozen, and I'm afraid I might upset her. The little servant is coming around again, to clear our plates, and before I can stop her, Kelly tries to help by lifting not only the pasta bowl, but the underplate too; the woman has to stop her with a quick tap on Kelly's wrist, instructing her to put down the whole thing, then lifting up just the pasta bowl and fork.

Oof. There's nothing worse, socially, than getting your

manners wrong and being corrected by the staff in front of the host. Kelly's seat is next to Catia, and Catia's beady eyes have taken in this entire faux pas.

Poor Kelly. Table manners are so confusing. I mean, how would you know about underplates if someone hadn't shown you? Kelly collapses back into her chair, blood rising in her face right up to the roots of her hair. Thinking quickly, I grab her glass of wine and hand it to her.

"Try some wine," I say, hoping it will make her feel better. She mutters thanks, takes the glass, and dutifully has a sip; then she sits up straight, shakes her hair back from her face, and takes another, longer sip.

"This is really good!" she exclaims, looking surprised. She turns to Catia, her embarrassment swept away in the excitement of her new discovery. "It's, like, *dry*. And light, like you said. When my mum gets wine, it's much sweeter, and I never liked it. But this is great."

Catia's mouth curves into a small smile of approval. She gives one short little nod.

"Your mother probably drinks South African or Californian wines," she informs Kelly. "Those are more fruity and sweet. In Italy and France, we prefer dry wines. We will do wine tasting and learn about it during your stay here. I am glad that you are interested."

"I didn't know I was," Kelly says slowly, "but I am now."

"Try to sniff it," Catia says, picking up her glass and lowering her nose to the rim. "See what the bouquet is."

Kelly copies her enthusiastically. I sit back, relieved that Kelly's potential meltdown has been averted. Opposite me, Ilaria and Elisa are making desultory conversation, looking bored; beyond them, two pairs of french windows, closed now, give a floor-to-ceiling view of the deep blue Italian evening outside, shimmering with the orange and red glow of the setting sun. I shiver in anticipation of something I can't picture, but that I sense is waiting for me in the velvety night air.

It's my future out there, waiting for me. I don't know how or why I know this, but I do. My life is starting, finally. Though it's lonely, in a way, to be surrounded by people I only met for the first time today, it also means that I can re-invent myself, be whoever I want to be, without my mother always looking over my shoulder, or coming up with some wonderful fun idea for the two of us to do together that somehow stops me from having ideas of my own.

The little woman is bustling in with an armful of dinner plates, our main course arriving. I smile at her, and she flashes a quick smile back as she slides mine in front of me: it's a dinner plate neatly arranged with a few slices of cooked meat, dressed with a couple of spoonfuls of sauce, three small boiled potatoes, and some slices of a white vegetable I'm not sure I recognize.

"This is roast pork with herbs, fennel, and potatoes," Catia informs us. "The fennel is very good for the digestion, so we often eat it with pork, which is a rich meat."

Nodding dutifully to show I've taken this in, I can't help wondering if Catia's didactic tendencies are going to extend to every aspect of our lives; is she going to pop in when we're getting ready for bed, to check we're resting our heads on our pillows at the right angle?

I'm vaguely aware of some Italian being spoken around

the table. It's only gradually, as I come back to reality, that I look around and realize that the atmosphere has suddenly become so tense that I understand, for the first time, the expression about cutting it with a knife. There's a pall so heavy hanging over the table that it's almost palpable.

"Umm . . . ," I mutter to Kelly. "I missed that last bit."

But it's Kendra who answers me.

"Catia was telling us," Kendra says with an artificial sweetness in her voice that makes all the hairs on the back of my neck stand up in fear, "that the word in Italian for pork is 'maiale.' The plural is 'maiali.' Which means 'pigs.'"

I suck in my breath, realizing exactly why there's so much tension in the room. Catia, Leonardo, and Andrea don't, of course: they're looking at us, puzzled, Catia's fork and knife poised in midair, waiting to take a slice of the main course.

But we can't explain. We can't tell Catia that Elisa, her daughter, and Ilaria, Elisa's friend, walked past us while we were sunbathing today and called us pigs. They could so easily deny it by saying that they were talking about what we were having for dinner; none of us speaks enough Italian to remember or repeat more than that single word.

And yet all four of us know, with absolute certainty, that Elisa deliberately looked over at us and used the word "pigs."

It's odd how loyalties shift and change so dramatically in the course of a few hours, or a day, like sands blowing over the desert, washing away ridges that were there before, flowing into new formations. I've seen it so many times at school: friendships breaking up, new ones being formed, best friends turning to deadly enemies and back again at the speed of light. Earlier today, I was loathing Paige and Kendra with everything I had, because they laughed at me and Mum when she was having her sobbing fit all over the security barrier at Heathrow. I was sure they would be horrible, and determined to pay them back somehow for adding to my humiliation.

Now, in an instant, they're my allies. Shoulder to shoulder, the four of us massed against the detestable Italian girls who are sitting across the table from us, smirking, knowing that we can't challenge them on what they called us, because it will only make us look paranoid. I meet Elisa's big dark eyes; she widens them still further in amusement, purses together her thin, pink-painted lips, and tilts her head to the side mockingly, her big gold earrings swinging. Ilaria, to her right, raises a hand to her mouth to stifle a giggle.

You mean bitches, I think savagely. *I'll get you back if it's the last thing I do.*

Elisa reaches for her wineglass, her bracelets tinkling in a way I'm finding increasingly irritating. She picks up the glass, and then, unforgivably, she turns her head to look at Kelly; the most vulnerable of the four of us visiting girls, the one who's visibly most socially insecure, least happy in her own skin. Elisa raises the glass to Kelly; and, holding it so that her outstretched arm blocks her mother's view of her face, she mouths *"maiali"* again, directly at Kelly.

Tears form in Kelly's eyes. Pushing back her chair, she jumps up and blunders from the dining room; I hear her sob as she runs out the door and up the stairs. There's an awful pause.

"Ma che cosa—" Leonardo looks at us, his handsome face open and concerned, as ignorant as boys usually are of the

74

evil machinations of nasty girls. "What happens? Why is she sad?"

I'm already half out of my chair, wanting to go after Kelly, but Catia's basilisk glare has me snapping back into the seat like a well-trained dog.

"She is homesick, I'm sure," Catia decrees. "I will go to see her after we have eaten. Now we will finish our dinner."

We all bend our heads over our plates and tuck into the pork in silence. *At least,* I think wryly, *we'll all remember how to say "pork" in Italian.* Forking some potato into my mouth, I meet Paige's eyes across the table. They're narrowed, her jaw set tight; she looks not only furious but determined. Paige is clearly as resolved as I am to make Elisa pay for insulting us all. I can't see Kendra; Leonardo's in the way. But there's no doubt in my mind that she's just as bent on revenge as Paige and I are.

Elisa may have ridden roughshod over other girls who've done this summer course, made their lives a misery, I think angrily. *But she's met her match this time. How dare she make Kelly cry—ruin her first evening away from home?*

I stare at Elisa until she looks back at me. And then I raise my glass to her, and, just as she did, with my arm blocking her mother's view of my lips, I mouth *"maiali"* right back at her, watching with satisfaction as she bridles in fury.

You've got no idea what you've started, I convey to her very clearly. *It's war.*

I Do Not Do Megamixes

"Kelly?" I push open the door of our bedroom hesitantly: it's utterly dark and silent inside the room. "Are you all right?"

Stupid question, I tell myself immediately. *You're an idiot, Violet. Of course she's not all right.*

"Kelly?" I say again. "We're all going out for coffee and ice cream in the village. Leonardo and Andrea are taking us. We were hoping you'd want to come."

I hear Kelly shift on her bed; the springs creak a little.

"No thanks," she mumbles, her voice thick with tears. "I just want to be alone."

"Oh, come on." I'm not sure if it'll make her feel worse if I insist, but I really don't want Kelly to feel abandoned while we all go out to have fun.

It sounds as if Kelly's face is buried in the pillow. "I just want to be alone, Violet. *Please*," she mumbles again, so miserably that all I can do is take her at her word.

"Well . . ." I hesitate. "Don't be too upset, okay? We all think Elisa's a total bitch and we're not going to let her get away with it. I had a word with Paige—she's sure Elisa tries this on every year with the girls who come on the course. She probably doesn't like the competition."

Nothing but silence answers me. Kelly's said all she wants to say.

"Well, if you're sure . . ."

I'm desperate to rush off: I dive into the bathroom, reapply perfume and lipstick, grab my lip gloss for emergency repairs, and run downstairs again, scared that they might have decided I'm taking too long and gone without me. I'm not friends with Paige and Kendra, and I have no idea what they're like with boys yet, whether they share well with others. They could easily have chosen to take the two boys for themselves, swept them off to the village, assured them that I'm going to stay behind and look after Kelly. I could miss out on all the fun, and they could say, wide-eyed tomorrow morning, that it had been just a misunderstanding, they'd thought I'd decided to stay upstairs with poor Kelly.

So it's with a huge wash of relief that I see the four of them clustered in the hallway where I left them, chatting and laughing, the American girls' colorful print dresses standing out brightly against the white-painted walls.

"How is she?" Kendra asks as I join the little group and we head out the front door.

"Not great. I hate to leave her, but she said to go. When

Catia went up before, she was crying. Catia just thinks she's homesick."

"Well, we know better," Kendra says, a martial light in her eyes. "Ugh, that Elisa *totally* needs a reality check."

We're outside now, walking around the house to the parking lot; Leonardo clicks his keys and a light flashes on a small Fiat. We pick our way over the gravel—we're all wearing sandals with heels—and climb into the car, boys in front, girls in the back.

"We'll get her back," Paige hisses to me as the car pulls away. "She's got *no idea* who she's messing with!"

"Shh," Kendra says, nodding at Andrea and Leonardo in front of us: Andrea's already swiveling around, smiling at us.

"So!" he says, as the car bumps over the dirt road and we all squeal and hold on to each other, the seat belts ineffective against potholes. We're all lightly tipsy on the unaccustomed wine with dinner. "We go for *caffè* and gelato, and then we go to dance? *Sì?*"

"Ooh! Dancing! Cool!" Paige says happily, and I brighten up too: I love to dance, and have a pack of friends who all live in central London, near decent clubs, so we go out a lot. I'm relieved I didn't wear high-heeled sandals tonight, though I thought about changing them when the idea of going out to the village came up; luckily, the ones I have on are strappy silver kitten heels, broken-in enough that I can walk miles in them and dance all night if I want to.

But it's exciting just to be out in the warm Italian night, the smooth, velvety air on our skin as we pile out of the Fiat in front of the village bar. It has a big garden in front, with a tall, wide canopy hung with white canvas over long trestle tables, and a low wall on which lots of boys are sitting, checking out all the new arrivals. Fairy lights twinkle from the posts holding up the canopy, to the trellises along the far wall, and the bar beyond is brightly lit, neon strips in the ceiling bouncing light off the shiny tiled floor and the glass cases of cakes and ice cream.

My heart is racing like a high-speed train. Everyone turns to look at us as we walk into the garden, all the boys on the wall swiveling theatrically, leaning over to stare at us, unashamedly goggling, low whistles following us like a vapor trail. Andrea and Leonardo are smug as peacocks as they shepherd us in, throwing comments over their shoulders at the boys who toss questions at them; I hear the words *"inglese"* and *"americane,"* whose meanings I know, but that's all I understand. I feel suddenly very vulnerable, in a strange country, where the boys can say whatever they want about us and we won't know what they mean. I'm really glad that I'm not alone, that Paige and Kendra are with me, strong, confident girls who don't look like they'd be pushovers for the first boy who comes along.

But wow. The *boys*. I couldn't blame any girl for being a pushover in this country. Once we're settled at an outdoor table, positioned in the center, under a big light—*like trophies Leonardo and Andrea are showing off*, I think in amusement—drinking strong bitter espresso from small china cups and eating fresh, sharp lemon sorbet that comes in real half-lemon shells, I can snatch glances around me at the display of sheer male Italian gorgeousness, taking it in with disbelief.

Boys with short curly hair, boys with shaved heads, boys with long tousled hair. Boys with earrings, or silver chain necklaces, or big leather watchstraps hanging from their wrists. Boys in tight, bright T-shirts over snug ripped jeans or equally snug white trousers. All of them with tanned, smooth skin; lean, muscly arms; sexy, confident stances. None of them seem shy; none of them are remotely embarrassed about staring at us openly as they stroll past, or lounge against the walls, or cock their hips and lean on nearby tables.

There are other girls here, of course; pretty, thin girls in miniskirts and lots of makeup. But they're all a very similar type, and the girls at our table definitely are not. Paige is the only tall, fair-skinned blonde; Kendra the only girl darker than a Mediterranean tan. I'm less unusual, and I accept fairly humbly that I'm not the star attraction, though the way I'm dressed clearly marks me as "not from around here."

Elisa and Ilaria have come down to the village too. They're standing at the bar, drinking Campari and playing with unlit cigarettes, deliberately ignoring our table. I sneer at them, but they're talking to the burly bartender and don't notice. Boys are whooping as they play table football over by the wall, bouncing the table, spinning their players, making extra noise to draw attention, trying to stand out, get the girls to notice them; there's a palpable sense of excitement and possibility, of flirting and laughter. Guys keep coming up to our table, ostensibly greeting Leonardo and Andrea, but not even looking at them; they squeeze in on the benches, flashing big smiles at us, shaking our hands. It's like a male beauty parade: they're showing off for us, opening their peacock tails to display the bright colors.

I glance at Paige and Kendra, who look just as wide-eyed and dazzled by all the attention as I feel. Paige, with her bubbly personality and blond curls, is literally surrounded by boys, and I can't tell if she likes any of them in particular. Kendra is flirting with Andrea and a friend of his, her technique the opposite of Paige's. Paige is loud, expansive, reaching out to draw more and more boys in; Kendra speaks softly, sexily, so boys have to lean in to hear her, entranced by her spell.

"I am sorry about my sister," Leonardo says to me, and I jump, realizing that again, I was lost in thought.

I'm not sure how to respond, and besides, having him talk directly to me is a bit dizzying; he's very good-looking, dark and lively and fun, with his sexy stubble and his self-assurance. *Italian boys are as confident as grown-up men*, I think; *English boys are really shy by comparison.* I'm not used to being chatted up by boys this happy in their own skin; *I like you, you like me, maybe we could have some fun together?* says his bright glance, straightforward and utterly charming.

"She is a *stronza*," Leonardo's saying. He grins. "It is a bad word. I don't know the English."

I grin back at him.

"Well, why is she such a *stronza?*" I ask, making him laugh.

"Good!" He claps. "You have a good accent! She is a *stronza*," he says, leaning closer to me, "because she does not like my mother to have the foreigners in the house. She does a cooking course, some yoga courses, it is not just the girls for the summer. But I say, my mother has to *fare soldi!*" He rubs his fingers and thumb together in the universal symbol for money. "It is normal! My father gives my mother Villa Barbiano, but not much money."

"Are your parents divorced?" I ask sympathetically.

But he looks amazed at the question.

"Oh no!" he says easily. "*Mai*. Never. It is not necessary. He lives in Florence, my mother in Villa Barbiano. But Villa Barbiano, it is expensive. She must have people here to make money. And Elisa is—" He struggles for the word and finally finds it. "Proud," he concludes triumphantly. "She doesn't like to have people paying to stay in the house. But, you know, she has her car, her pretty dresses. Nice things. She is okay. So I say to her, she must be nice to the people who come. But she doesn't like to be nice."

I can't help feeling with a tinge of amusement that it's easy for Leonardo to say—after all, he has the better side of the bargain. If the house were filled with four foreign guys every summer, he might well be grumpy about it, while Elisa would doubtless be relishing the attention. Still, that doesn't justify her being a total bitch to us.

I shrug.

"We're not so bad," I say cheerfully.

"Oh no!" Leonardo laughs. "Not so bad! You are much better—you are very nice! *Molto bella!*"

And he picks my hand up from the table and raises it to his lips, kissing it as he kissed Kendra's when he paid her a similar compliment. I didn't realize before that he looked straight into her eyes when he did it; wow, it's absolutely mesmerizing. It makes me feel hot all over. I'm more glad than I can say that I'm sitting down, because honestly I think I would go totally weak at the knees and grab at something for support if I were standing up when he pulled this super-seductive move on me.

Elisa was right about her brother, I think, having enough experience to recognize when a boy's flirtation skills are set to automatic pilot. Leonardo isn't homing in on me with any kind of special interest, he's just having fun with the girl he happens to be sitting next to at the moment. *Leonardo is a big slut.*

But I rather like it.

Just as I've reached that conclusion, and am smiling at my own observation, something happens that is the oddest thing I've ever experienced. There's no way to explain it but by some sort of extrasensory theory, and as a rationalist I don't believe in any of that stuff.

Well, not much.

Because while the most charming boy I have ever met in my life is holding my hand, staring into my eyes, his mouth warm and moist on my skin, I have that particular, prickling sense between my shoulder blades that tells me, inevitably and unmistakably, that someone is staring at me. And instead of ignoring it and smiling back as seductively as I can at the charming boy, as any remotely sensible girl would do under the circumstances, I'm compelled to turn my head in the direction of the stare.

There are plenty of boys clustered around the wall, laughing, shoving each other playfully, yelling, competing for the attention of the girls. But somehow I know that the one who's staring at me is the boy leaning against the post holding up the canopy, his shoulders square to it, his head ducked over the cigarette he's holding, a tiny red point flaring in the shadow as he pulls on the filter.

I shake my head and say firmly to myself, *Smoking's disgusting.*

I'm still looking, though. He's tall and slim, I can tell that much. And his hair, dropping over his forehead, is jet-black, as if he were a hero in a manga book, drawn with pen and ink, two or three thick glossy strands separating into perfect dark curves.

I snap my head back from the lurker in the shadows to the actual boy still holding my hand, only to see that Leonardo is looking over my shoulder in the same direction.

"Luca!" he exclaims, dropping my hand to wave at someone. *"Finalmente!"*

I am determined not to turn. Just in case it's the same boy. I don't want to look too interested, or too eager. *Besides, he might be really ugly. Or spotty. Or have some silly chinstrap shaved onto his face—*

"Eccolo!" Leonardo's saying happily, and it would be silly of me, by now, not to turn to face the person who's strolled over and is leaning aganst the side of the table.

I look up at him, and my heart stops for a moment.

"Luca!" Andrea says, echoing Leonardo. *"Finalmente!"*

"This is Luca, our friend," Leonardo says happily as I think:

Luca. Finally.

"Ciao," Luca says, nodding at us, his long legs stretched out, crossed at the ankles. He's wearing a dark blue shirt tucked into black jeans, and silver rings on a couple of his long fingers, the cigarette held loosely between them. His

inky hair tumbles over his forehead, and I see, with a shock like a knife to the chest, that his eyes, heavily fringed with thick black lashes, are the midnight blue of sapphires or deep seawater.

I can't speak.

"Hey!" Paige waves flirtatiously at Luca, one of those girl-waves where you open and flutter your fingers while flashing a brilliant smile. I hate to admit it, but Paige totally pulls it off. "I'm Paige. And you're hot!"

Oh my God. Paige is brave enough to tell him to his face that he's handsome, while I can't even say hello. I am completely pathetic.

"*Questa è Kaiindra,*" Andrea says, his arm resting on the back of Kendra's chair, as Kendra smiles at Luca and says hi.

There's a pause. I hold my breath. And then Luca turns his head to me and says:

"*E tu? Come ti chiami?*"

This means "What's your name"; I know that much. But he's looking straight at me. His cheekbones could cut glass, and his dark eyebrows, elegantly raised in a query, are two perfect ink-black arches.

"Violet," I manage to say. I'm so nervous that it comes out casual, dismissive, as if I don't give a damn about him. Which, actually, is no bad thing. He nods, taking a last drag on his cigarette and stubbing it out in the ashtray on the table, before he pushes off the table to stand once again.

"*Allora,*" he says, nodding toward the road. "*Andiamo?*"

"*Come no!*" Leonardo jumps up from the bench, pulling me with him. "We go to dance!" he says happily. "In Firenze!"

"I'm not so sure," Kendra says, looking up from her

conversation with Andrea, who seems mesmerized by her. "I'm not so crazy about dancing."

"Oh, *dai!*" Andrea pleads with her. I'm trying to pick up as many words as I can: *"dai"* seems to mean "come on." He pushes back his hair with both hands dramatically. "You must come! We all go! To make celebrate you come to Italia!"

Andrea's accent is the heaviest of all the boys who've talked our language so far, his English the most broken. It's very engaging, and Kendra can't resist his entreaties; despite herself, she breaks into a really pretty smile. Kendra is so poised most of the time, that when she lets herself go, it's actually quite adorable; her teeth flash white against her plum-glossed lips, and her eyes half close, lashes heavy on her cheeks.

She's adorable, I reflect, *when she's not laughing at your mum making a fool of herself. Be careful, Violet. You don't know these girls well at all.*

I catch myself. *Only one battle at a time.* I glance over at Elisa, who's standing in the doorway of the bar now with Ilaria, talking to some other girls, who are equally intimidatingly thin. Elisa's looking straight at our group, and I think she's staring at Luca.

I don't blame her.

Kendra is still hesitating.

"I don't know," she's saying. "It's getting kinda late already, isn't it? Maybe I'll just go back to the villa. . . ."

Paige and Andrea look panicky at this suggestion. Leonardo throws his arms wide.

"But how?" he asks. "No, we must all go together."

I've never been out partying in the countryside before, but this dilemma is bringing home to me the brutal reality that cars are few, as are designated drivers. Everyone needs to travel as a group. If Kendra goes back to the villa, we'll all have to go. The momentum will be lost. And the evening will end here.

Which means I'll barely have spent any time with Luca.

"Oh no, Kendra, do come!" I hear myself say, loudly and enthusiastically. I give a little jerk of my head over to Elisa. "We'll have so much fun out with the boys . . . come on, there's one for each of us!"

Luca's eyebrows rise again, his lips quirk in amusement, and I realize that he understands English very well; I'm mortified. *Now he'll think I'm a total party girl.* But quick-witted Kendra catches on immediately; she flicks her eyes sideways, taking in Elisa, who now has her hands on her hips, frowning as she watches us. Elisa says something to Ilaria, and they start to walk toward our group: that's enough to make Kendra's decision for her.

"Sure, okay, I'm in!" she says, jumping up with an athlete's speed, and taking Andrea's proffered arm. "Let's get going!"

The boys don't need telling twice; they shoot us off, probably afraid Kendra will change her mind again. We head for Luca's car, a big Audi, sturdier and more solid than I expected; Luca looks as if he should be driving a sports car, a convertible, something lean and long and low to the ground. This is a grown-up's car, something you drive to work. But it does fit six of us in; with much giggling, Andrea nominates himself as the one to sit in the back with the girls, squashing in between me and Kendra, dragging the seat belts over so we're all sardined together, buckled in.

I look out the window and see Elisa on the pavement, talking urgently to Ilaria, a frown on her face. That's enough to have me settling back smugly in the seat. I squeal as the car takes off, shooting off down the road so fast we're all plastered to the back of our seats with the g-force. Luca drives like the Audi is a race car, whipping it around the tight curves of the road till I feel dizzy. We're all clinging to each other in the back, laughing, our eyes wide with excitement; even Paige, who was carsick earlier in the day, seems relaxed enough, maybe because of the wine from dinner, to giggle with the rest of us as Luca fires the car like a heat-seeking missile up and down the hills between Chianti and Florence.

I'm sitting behind him. Which means I can stare at the back of his head, as much as I can see around the headrest. His black hair is silky, long enough to reach to the collar of his shirt; I can't see any of his skin, but I can make out the line of his shoulders, see the muscle move as the fabric of his shirt pulls over his arm, and the pleasure of being able to watch him like this, with no one realizing what I'm doing, is more intoxicating than the wine at dinner.

I have no idea why he has such a powerful effect on me. I've met lots of boys before, out dancing, at parties; for instance, my friend Milly's brother Ronan is great-looking and always flirts with me—we've kissed a couple of times. I've had a bit of a crush on him for years. He's blond, sporty, with a lovely open smile, much more the physical type I've always been attracted to. But now all I can see is Luca's face. . . .

I must not make a fool of myself, I tell myself with conviction. *I must not drool over him like some idiotic panting dog with its tongue hanging out.*

The Audi shoots around a big roundabout and dives into a warren of narrow streets, buildings rising high on each side: my first view of Florence. There are cream-painted buildings with shuttered windows, bright restaurants lit up briefly as we pass, Vespa scooters buzzing past us, weaving in and out of traffic in a way that would utterly panic me if I were driving. We cross a bridge, and all of us girls gasp in unison and crane our necks to the right-hand window of the car, pushing each other to get a sight of Florence by night—the dark velvety river lit up with glittering lights; narrow bridges farther down, the famous one with all the houses on it clustered tight together; a cathedral dome, terra-cotta and white, rising above the marble buildings, illuminated with soft spotlights, exactly like—

"Oh, it's like a movie!" Paige exclaims in delight.

"*A Room with a View,*" Kendra agrees. "I *love* that movie."

I do too; I think the bit where Julian Sands goes up to Helena Bonham Carter in the cornfield and kisses her is one of the most romantic scenes I've ever seen. I'm just about to agree, when Luca says, "Oh, yes. Italy is *very* romantic," so dryly that the words die on my lips. His accent's light, his English seems very good: "Lots of corruption, lots of bribes. Very romantic."

"Well, *he's* a load of fun, isn't he?" Paige says in my ear, giggling, as the car swoops down through an underpass, up the other side, and into a huge open-air parking area. Luca finds a space that's half legal and half not, the left-hand side of the car bumped up onto the pavement, and the other boys seem to consider this perfectly normal; they bounce the doors open and pile out, talking loudly, full of enthusiasm, laughing and joking as we follow them over to a big archway with a sign reading CENTRAL PARK. It's bordered with silver stands with red velvet ropes dangling between them, and behind them a lot of bouncers in black trousers and black bomber jackets over white shirts are hanging around, looking bored.

"Central Park!" Paige exclaims loudly. "Oh my God, like in New York City! That's so funny! You know, Kendra?"

"Yes," Leonardo says to her, amused, "but that is just a park. This is a club, in the middle of Florence. Better than just a park, *si?*"

"*Si!*" Paige repeats enthusiastically, nodding for emphasis. "Much better!"

"It's kinda quiet," Kendra says, which is just what I was thinking. "No line at the door."

"*È presto,*" Leonardo says to us. "It's early."

I file away the word "*presto*" for future use as Paige says:

"Really? But it's past eleven!"

"We do not usually go dancing in Italy till midnight, past midnight," Luca says over his shoulder as he goes to talk to a couple of club promoters, a hypertanned guy in a shiny shirt and a girl in what's basically a bikini top over sprayed-on metallic trousers. I feel a rush of jealousy as he puts a hand on the girl's bare waist, leaning in to kiss her on both cheeks. She laughs and touches his shoulder intimately, and the jealousy rises in me like bile till I have to look away, furious with myself for having this kind of reaction about a boy with whom I've barely exchanged a word.

I'm just going to throw myself onto the dance floor, I tell myself firmly. *Distract myself by getting all hot and sweaty and too tired out to even remember his name.*

Luca turns to us and gestures with his arm, waving us all over; apparently he's got us in free because he knows the promoters. We pile past the bouncers, feeling very cool indeed, and Luca hands us each a black card.

"It is for drinks," he informs us. "You give it to the barmen when you want a drink and they will put a stamp on it. Then we pay when we leave, okay?"

"You must keep it safely," Leonardo chips in. "If you lose it, you pay fifty euros."

Our eyes widen as we stow our cards safely in our bags. Mine's a small cross-body; again, it's madly lucky that I grabbed this one, as it's perfect for dancing. And dancing is all I'm going to be doing. I can hear the bass line already. Not pounding up from the floor or bouncing off the walls, because the floor is stone, and there are no walls. I see why it's called Central Park: it's almost all open to the air, like a beach party in the center of town. Wooden posts hold up trellised roofs draped with white canopies, palm trees between them, their trunks lit up by lights at their base, bright green fronds glowing verdant against the white fabric.

The boys know exactly where they're going, leading us along stone paths as we gawk. I've never seen anything like this club; it's amazing. Paige is oohing and aahing as well, exclaiming loudly at how gorgeous it is. Kendra, of course, is too cool to stare around or make a comment, but I bet she's secretly just as impressed. We reach a long bar, illuminated pillars like mother-of-pearl radiating light; a whole ceiling with little inset lights is built above the bar; translucent glass gleams behind it; and the bottles shine lights themselves, the colored liquids inside bright flashes of ruby and sapphire and chartreuse on the radiant glass shelves. Tables stretch out onto a terrace beyond, open to the black velvet night; stars glitter in the sky, tiny and distinct, and I can see the bridges in the distance across the dark ribbon of river, the streetlights of Florence turning the sky over the city pale mauve with their reflected glow.

Everything in Italy is as beautiful as a picture, I think. *There's something about this country that makes me want to capture what I'm seeing, paint all the sights, show other people how lovely it is. . . .*

They're heading for the bar, Leonardo raising a hand in greeting to a bartender dressed all in black; but I don't want another drink—not yet, anyway. And I'm much too restless to sit down with them and make halting Italian-English conversation; my limbs are twitching with excess energy I need to burn off.

"I'm going to dance," I say to Paige, nodding my head in the direction of the throbbing bass line pounding from beyond the bar. "I'll see you back here, okay?"

I dash off before anyone can say anything, or decide to follow me. I need, very badly, to do my own thing, to move exactly as I want to, without having to accommodate my dancing style to anyone else. It's been a long, stressful, confusing day. My mum, of course, has been sending me screeds of guilt-inducing texts to which I've sent only short, unsatisfactory responses. Elisa needs dealing with, Kelly needs looking after, and Luca is making my head spin. Time to forget about everyone for a while and pound some holes into the dance floor.

And that's exactly what I do. There are already quite a few people dancing and the DJ's playing a disco remix that, though a bit cheesy, gets my feet moving straightaway. Besides, it's Italy! Florence! In an outdoor club, under the stars! The usual rules don't apply—I don't have to worry about looking cool, whether a band's in this week or already out. I can dance to anything that keeps me moving, and I do; it's mostly Europop, some R&B, silly, sexy, and fun, songs that make me giggle when I hear them come on, and keep me spinning around.

I realize quickly that Italians don't dance like we do in London. Back home, we take no prisoners, or at least my lot don't; we throw ourselves around, we do silly choreographed moves to cheesy songs, we chest-pump, we pogo to the rock songs and swing our hair back and forth. We get sweaty.

Which seems to be completely contrary to the Italian way. Most of the boys and the girls are basically standing and wiggling a bit, smiling, throwing back their hair, shaking their hips; nothing that would do more than bring a light glow to their glossy, tanned, olive skin.

I know there's an expression "When in Rome," which means that when you're in a foreign country, you should do what the locals do. But I'm too wound up, too buzzed by all my new experiences today to be able to restrain myself. I need to let off steam. When the DJ plays some Pink,

I actually pogo, my heels bouncing off the shiny wooden dance floor, my arms flailing, a silly smile plastered on my face; I wish Milly and Lily-Rose were here, singing the words back at me, because we know every Pink song by heart: *So what? I'm still a rock star! I've got my rock moves! And I don't need—you—tonight!* But even without my girls, I'm representing London here in Florence, showing the Italians how it's done. A few boys try to dance with me, put themselves in front of me with what's supposed to be sexy hip swivels—or worse, imitate my moves with a stupid grin, which is the single worst thing you can do while someone's dancing. I can't believe anyone would think it's cool to copy someone and expect them to like it.

But I'm on fire. I ignore them all. I'm really good at that; I have the technique of ignoring annoying boys on the dance floor down to a fine art. I spin and I twist and I never meet their eyes. I dance faster than them, harder, my arms flying out to my sides so they have to jump back to avoid being hit, so they can see that I don't want to dance with them or anyone, and eventually they give up and turn to another girl instead, leaving me free to do exactly what I want, lose myself in my own world.

I have no idea how long I rule the dance floor; the DJ's brilliant at mixing one song into the next so seamlessly that there's never a pause when I can catch my breath, realize how long I've been going. What actually stops me, finally, believe it or not, is a *Grease* megamix. I was having a lot of fun with "You're the One That I Want"—though I'm missing my girls more than ever, as *Grease* songs really need a couple of girlfriends to sing along with—but as it cuts off halfway through, rolling over into "Greased Lightning," I realize the full horror of the situation. My feet finally come to a halt.

I do *not* do megamixes. And "Greased Lightning" is a really silly song anyway.

And suddenly, I realize that I'm knackered. Catching my breath, wiping my forehead, deftly swerving to avoid some idiot boy who reaches out to try to catch me as I go past, I walk off the dance floor, feeling hot all over. On the far side, a breeze is lifting the long white muslin drapes that hang around the dance floor like an Arabian tent, hooked back here and there, looped around the palm trees; I head for the gently blowing wind, lifting my hair off the back of my neck; half of it has tumbled down with all my gyrating, and my neck's all sweaty. I'm holding my hair up, pulling a couple of kirbigrips out of my curls so I can pin them back onto the crown of my head. I feel released, happy, the tension all gone, my limbs loose and easy, my mind clear.

The cool breeze caresses the back of my neck. I take one of the grips out of my mouth and anchor it through a handful of curls; I'm just about to do the same with the other one when a shadow moves behind a white fall of muslin like a ghost, one long-fingered hand, ringed with silver, reaching up to pull back the curtain.

It's Luca.

They Have Pizza in Italy!

The curtain billows gently in the breeze behind him as he steps out to meet me, his hair jet-black by contrast with the translucent white fabric. I jump, gasp, and nearly swallow the grip that I'm still holding between my lips; quickly, I pull it out before it goes down my throat and chokes me. It's wet with drool. *Lovely, Violet. Really attractive.* I shove it into my hair, anywhere, praying it will stay and not fall on the floor, still dripping with spit.

Luca's smiling down at me. His face is half in light, half in shade, from the spots playing across the dance floor, his blue eyes gleaming.

"You like to dance," he observes conversationally.

"Yes. . . ."

Safe question, safe answer. Well, at least I didn't babble. But he doesn't say anything else; he's just looking me up and down, and I feel incredibly awkward under his scrutiny. I'm sweaty, catching my breath; my eyeliner's probably running. I desperately need to escape into the dark night beyond the dance floor, where the breeze will cool me down and the shadows will hide my shiny face.

"I want to get some fresh air," I say, and move around him, stepping off onto the stone slabs and promptly sinking with one heel into the narrow space between them.

"Oops!" I say idiotically, ignoring the hand that Luca is stretching out to help me. The last thing I need right now is to touch him, for all sorts of reasons. I keep walking, pulling my heel out from between the paving stones; mercifully, it comes out without catching or ripping off. I honestly think that even if it did, I would keep going; I'd walk on a sandal without a heel all night, balance on my toes, pretend nothing had happened, and think it a fair price to pay for my flight into the comparative darkness of the chill-out area, where Luca can't see the sweat on my face.

He's following me. I can hear his leather-soled shoes on the stone. And I have no idea where I'm going. I feel ridiculous. Luckily, ahead of me I see a terrace with tables, and I walk toward it as if I'd planned to head there all along.

"You want a drink?" he asks. He gestures over to the right, and I see the white gleam of the long bar, the translucent milky-white pillars shining as if we're underwater.

I don't need to drink any more alcohol tonight. Especially in the company of Luca. "Maybe some water. I'm really thirsty."

He nods, turns, and walks toward the bar. I watch him go. Tall, lean, with a nice firm bum in his black jeans. *Exactly what I like in a boy.* And then I feel my face flaming, because this isn't just some boy at an airport, or viewed from a car. This is real. *He's* real. He'll be back in just a few minutes, and I won't have the faintest idea what to say to him. . . .

Turning away, I frantically dab at my face with the backs of my hands, trying to matte myself down. I consider, momentarily, running off to the loo to do a better fix-up job on myself, but what if Luca comes back and doesn't find me here? I can't go over to the bar and tell him I'm going to the loo and to wait for me, because the mere thought of trying to communicate the word "toilet" to him makes me wish for the ground to open up and swallow me whole. What if he doesn't understand? What if I have to do some sort of mime to explain? I'd rather *die.*

So I pat my face down, pull out the lip gloss from my handbag and reapply it, pray that some of my perfume is still clinging to my pores—hopefully canceling out any sweaty stink—and surreptitiously lift the bodice of my dress and flap it back and forth, cooling myself down as much as possible.

"Violetta!" I recognize Luca's voice: light, husky, and with an edge of humor, as if he's perpetually amused by a joke that only he can understand. Hearing him say my name—and in Italian!—is paralyzing. If I were with a girlfriend, I'd probably burst into hysterical, juvenile giggling; as it is, I bite my tongue, hard, take a deep breath to calm myself, and after a few moments, manage to glance around as casually as I can, spot Luca standing by a high bar table, and even raise a hand in acknowledgment as I walk toward him.

There are lots of these tall round tables dotted around the terrace, with no stools drawn up to them; square tables with white-backed chairs are farther down, closer to the edge of the terrace, but Luca hasn't chosen one of those. I wonder if this means he doesn't intend to stay long, just have a quick drink with me and then head off.

"Italians stand up a lot at bars," I comment, taking the glass of water Luca's pushing toward me. It's fizzy, with ice and lime in it, and I drink it very gratefully.

He smiles. I notice that one corner of his mouth lifts higher than the other when he does so, in a little quirk that sets off his handsomeness precisely because of its irregularity.

"Italians like to show off their clothes," he says. "They like clothes that are signed." He hits his brow theatrically with one hand. "*Firmati,*" he says. "That is how we say 'designer.' They like designer clothes. If you stand up, people see them better."

Ha! I bet every single piece of clothing Elisa was wearing today is designer.

"But your style, it's very English," Luca observes, and he reaches across the table to snag his index finger under the big strands of fake pearls around my neck, lifting them for a moment, then letting them fall back to my collarbone again. For a split second, his finger touches my skin, and he might as well have brushed me with a lit match.

"Very . . ." He snaps his fingers, searching for the word. "*Eccentrica,*" he says finally.

"Oh God!" My face drops. "It's that bad?"

"*Cosa?*" He looks confused. "Bad?"

"In English, 'eccentric' is sort of like 'mad,'" I explain.

"If you're really posh, especially. You could be a raving loony who eats bats for breakfast, and as long as you have a title, they'd call you eccentric and think it was charming."

Luca, clearly, hasn't understood all of this. But he's thrown his head back and is laughing so hard that I see people beyond us turning to look in curiosity. He looks absolutely gorgeous when he laughs, his mouth curving up, tiny lines creasing around his eyes; his usual cool demeanor is wiped away, and he looks younger, sweeter, much more approachable.

"Bats for breakfast?" he says, when he manages to speak. "*Pipistrelli per colazione?* You are not eccentric, Violetta *mia*, you are mad." I'm bridling, when he adds: "I like this very much. You are not boring."

"Wow," I say as coldly as I can. "Thanks a lot."

My brain is racing at the fact that I think "Violetta *mia*" means "my Violet." Which is, doubtless, just the way they talk in Italy, but sounds . . . I can't even *think* about that. I push it to the very back of my brain to be pulled out much later, when I'm alone, and turned over and over like a precious stone glinting in my palms.

I can't meet his eyes. They're full of amusement, bright and blue; it's almost as if I'm afraid of being hypnotized, like a rabbit looking at a snake.

"You like music," he says; not a question, a statement, and I nod. "I see you sing to some of the songs when you dance," he adds, and although this makes me want to scream inside my head—*He watched me dancing? Oh no, did I look insane?*—I manage to shrug as if it's a matter of complete indifference to me that he saw me flailing my arms like a madwoman on the dance floor.

"You like Italian music?" he asks, sipping some Prosecco.

"I don't really know any," I admit. "Just opera, I suppose."

He laughs. Luca does seem to find me very amusing. "I like music a little more modern than that," he says. "Vasco Rossi, you know him? He is our rock star. I think you will like him to dance to. And Jovanotti. Maybe I will play you some songs of his. He writes very beautiful songs. About love, politics, the world, all in the same song."

"That's very difficult," I say frankly. "I mean, lots of people try that but mostly it just comes off really pretentious. Like Coldplay."

"Ugh! I hate the Coldplay!" he says. "The singer, he tries to look so serious when he sings, but instead he just looks like a sheep."

"I know!" I say enthusiastically. "With that curly hair and that silly expression he makes . . ."

I try to imitate it, and Luca laughs again, his eyes bright blue with amusement.

"And the words are silly too," I say. "They don't make sense."

Luca leans forward, propping his elbows on the bar table, and I think he's going to ask me something, maybe what some particularly nonsensical Coldplay lyrics mean: but instead he starts to speak in Italian, so smoothly, the words so soft and liquid, that I swiftly realize he's quoting some lyrics. The words flow over me, winding around me like velvet:

" 'Ci sono trenta modi per salvare il mondo, ma uno solo perche il mondo salvi me—che io voglia star con te, e tu voglia star con me.' "

I gaze at him, and now I do feel hypnotized. I have no

idea what he's saying—he could be reading the phone book in Italian and I'd stare at him across the little bar table, unable to take my eyes from him.

"That is from a song by Jovanotti. Shall I translate for you?" he asks gently.

All at once, I panic. What if the words are so lovely I can't bear them? It's as if he's casting a spell over me, and I need to break free before it settles so tightly around me that I'm completely in his power. I manage to drag my eyes from his, and with a huge wash of relief, over his shoulder I see a whole group of people sitting at a table at the brightly lit end of the bar, where the party is: a big crowd of boys encircling a blond head and a darker one. Paige and Kendra have a lot of admirers.

"Oh, look!" I point over to them, my voice unnaturally high. "The girls! I should probably go over and say hi— they'll be wondering where I am. . . ."

"They don't look very *preoccupate*," Luca remarks, casting a glance in their direction. "In fact, they are very busy without you."

He's quite right. But I need to get away from this tête-à-tête; it's too intimate, too like being on a date with him. I can't think why he's singled me out. Maybe he wants to practice his English. But I'm sure that any moment, some gorgeous, pin-thin girl in designer labels will come up and drape herself around his neck, and he'll introduce his girlfriend, and she'll pull him away, and I'll be left standing alone at this table with a half-finished glass of water and a humiliated smile plastered to my face.

Anything's better than that.

"I should probably just go and tell them I'm okay . . . ," I mumble.

I set down my glass and take a couple of steps around the table, heading toward Paige and Kendra. And then, I feel the lightest of clasps surround my wrist. Like a bracelet closing around it: delicate, almost weightless, a question, not a command. A fine gold chain that I could shake off instantly if I wanted to, keep walking without breaking stride.

But I don't want to. I stop at the touch of his hand on my bare skin, my heart pounding in shock. I turn to look up at him, meeting his blue eyes, half hidden by his black lashes. I swallow hard.

"I would not go over to them if I were you," he says softly.

"Why?" I frown, not understanding: *Is he saying that Paige and Kendra are cross with me? But they can't be . . . I haven't done anything to them.*

"They are busy with the boys," he says, his long fingers still encircling my wrist. "And those boys, they will not be as . . ." He considers, looking for the right word. "Interested in you," he finishes.

"*What?*" I drag my hand away, furious now. "What's wrong with me?"

I'm burning up with anger, and I wish I hadn't asked that question: it makes me sound so insecure. Before I can correct myself, however, he's saying:

"Italian boys, in a club in the summer . . ." He shrugs, smiling. "They like foreign girls. Foreign girls are more *facile*—more easy. And they look different. It is exciting to be different—not like their sisters. You may be English, *eccentrica*, but your face, your body—you look like an Italian girl, from the south. With many brothers, who carry big knives. So you are not different, and maybe not easy. They will think they will not get what they want from you."

I'm gawping at him in shock as he nods toward the table where the American girls are sitting.

"The blond one," he adds, "she is funny. Like a toy for a little girl, come to life. The Barbie, and also the one who cries when you pull the string in her back. *Una bambola per ragazzine.*"

I flash instantly and disloyally on what he means: Paige *does* look like a cross between Barbie and a little girl's doll, one with round cheeks and big eyes and enviably cascading blond ringlets.

"She looks easy," Luca continues. "Because she likes too much to be liked."

I glance back at the girls' table. Paige is throwing her head around, blond curls bouncing, as she whoops with laughter at something Andrea is saying. The boys are standing behind her chair, leaning on its back, too close to her, in her personal space, and she's letting them get that near, something I wouldn't do with boys I'd just met an hour or so ago. Reluctantly, I see why Luca's made that observation: Leonardo's waving his glass around, and his hand is coming pretty near Paige's fabulous bosom. Too close again.

"But the black girl," Luca observes, "she is more difficult for a boy. Not so easy. She puts a high *valore*—value—on herself."

It's true: Kendra is sitting up straight, elegant, like a goddess, her posture excellent, the boys around her staring at her worshipfully instead of trying to snuggle up to her while she's laughing.

"She is . . ." Luca kisses his fingers to Kendra. "*Bellissima.* The African beauty, so elegant. *Sofisticata.* Her"—he nods at Kendra—"the boys, they will follow her everywhere in Italy. *Molto elegante.*"

If there's anything more annoying than a boy praising another girl's beauty to your face, I can't think what it is. Besides, I also don't like the way he's judging Paige and Kendra and me. It's so cynical.

"I think you're really rude," I say angrily. "And superficial."

Luca shrugs once again.

"I tell the truth," he says. "*E la cosa più importante nel mondo.* The most important thing."

"You can know what you *think* is the truth," I snap, "but no one's making you say it out loud."

Like that Italian boys won't fancy me, I think bitterly. *He couldn't have told me more clearly that he isn't interested in me if he'd written it on a big sign and held it above his head.*

Luca leans toward me, an expression of intense interest on his face.

"So," he starts slowly, "if I am thinking that I want to kiss you, I should not say it out loud?"

Oh, he's completely messing with me now. Taunting me. I feel tears of shame and rejection rise to my eyes.

"*Please,*" I manage to say in as withering a tone as I can manage, "I thought you were all about telling the truth. And now you're nothing but a big liar."

His lashes lift as his eyes widen. His lips part and I watch, hypnotized now, as he says softly, so softly that I find myself tilting toward him to catch every word:

"Violetta, *cara mia*, you are wrong. I am not a liar."

He doesn't reach out to take hold of my shoulders, or take my hand to pull me in. He's so sure of himself that he simply leans down, so close I can feel his breath scented with Prosecco warm on my face, for a split second, and then his lips meet mine.

His confidence is breathtaking; when I've been kissed in the past, the boys always touch you just as they're about to do it, make sure you're willing, put an arm around you, hold your hand. It gives them a moment's grace, a few seconds of self-protection, so if they've misjudged the situation—if you pull away—they won't be left standing there looking like a fool, with their head craning toward you and their lips pursed like one of those baby dolls he mentioned that blows kisses when you pull the string in its back.

Luca, however, doesn't lay a finger on me. He simply kisses me. And not in a soft, tentative, exploratory way; his mouth is long and narrow, his lips hard and insistent. It's not the kind of kiss I'm used to at all.

I lean in. My back arches, my head tilts up, and I meet his insistence with equal fervor. I can't help it. You'd have to lasso me around the neck and yank me away to stop me from kissing him back. Even if this is some kind of awful joke, even if he's kissing me to somehow lure me in and make a fool of me, I can't help it.

Our lips part; our bodies are pressing together now. I'm really glad I'm wearing heels, even if they're not that high;

Luca's much taller than I am. And then I feel his hand in the small of my back, his fingers splayed out, lifting me toward him, and his other hand slides around my neck, tilting me up more. It's the most incredibly intimate sensation I've ever felt; a spark flares up in the pit of my stomach, like the head of a match scratching along the rough powdered glass and phosphorus of a striking strip on a matchbook.

Ripping, tearing the flame into life. Not pretty, not romantic, not the kind of kiss you expect under the stars with white muslin curtains blowing in the distance. Not at all. Luca's tongue is in my mouth, mine meeting his eagerly, so eagerly I'd be embarrassed if he weren't dragging me to him now with a powerful flexing of his muscles. And I'm gripping his upper arms, feeling the biceps swell, long and lean, like tensile steel rather than the big plump muscles of more solidly built, sporty boys.

My brain is racing. It has to. If I stop thinking, I'll be completely lost, overwhelmed with sensations I don't know how to process. Right now, feeling Luca's body all down the length of mine, his tongue warm and wet, all the excitement bursting up in me, all the emotions swirling around, plug right back into the kiss, making it more and more intense with every moment that passes. It's as if we're creating a cyclone around us, wrapping tighter and tighter, spinning us around with enough energy to lift us right off our feet.

I'm clinging to Luca not just to pull him closer, but for support now too: I don't trust my ability to stand up on my own.

And that realization jolts me back to some sort of reality.

I'm in public, in a club in Florence, snogging a boy who I met only a couple of hours ago, so madly that I'm weak at the knees . . . in full view, if they looked over, of his friends and two girls I barely know. . . .

My eyes snap open, and I drag my mouth away from Luca's, gasping for breath. I find my feet under me, pull back from him, and promptly grab the edge of the table to steady myself. My hair's fallen down again; I can feel it tumbling down my back. My lips are wet. I raise a hand to wipe them dry, aware that my eyes are stretched wide with shock. I literally cannot believe what just happened. I feel like someone just gave me a violent electric shock.

Luca looks equally disheveled. His hair's tumbling forward in straight black lines, his blue eyes wide, his lips redder from kissing me so hard. He looks as amazed as I am.

"Ammazzati," he mutters.

I'm still too close to him. I can feel the force field between us. I take another step back, still gripping the table's edge, because I see his expression change unexpectedly. His blue eyes darken, and his mouth twists cynically.

"So," he says, his tone sarcastic, almost bitter, "you are a success in Italy, Violetta. *Congratulazioni.* You spend only one day here and already you are kissed by a boy! Your friends will be envious."

My blood boils. He's making it sound as if I asked him to kiss me, as if I'm the kind of girl who would flirt with him and lead him on just so I could get a first notch on my belt, to score one up on Paige and Kendra and Kelly. I stare at him, furious, and then he raises his hands and claps his long clever fingers together, once, twice, as if he's applauding me for getting kissed. *Against the odds, because, as he's already pointed out, Paige and Kendra are much more attractive to Italian boys than I am—*

The clapping is insufferable, the last straw. He's mocking me; he's deliberately ruining everything that just happened between us. I don't understand why, but it makes me so angry that, to my absolute amazement, my hand raises, my open palm slapping his cheek with more force than I even knew I had, a smack that seems to echo all around the bar.

We stare at each other for a moment, both of us in shock. I don't say a word. I don't trust myself to come up with anything sufficiently articulate. All I can do is swivel on my heel and walk away, toward the table where Paige and Kendra are sitting. It takes all the courage I have, because people are glancing our way; I don't know how much they saw, but the noise I made slapping Luca has definitely attracted attention.

I'm cringing inside. I've never slapped anyone in my life. I didn't know I was capable of it, and I hate that I just did it.

But if it happened all over again, a voice in my head tells me, *you'd react just the same way. You'd slap him, you know you would.*

I'm startled by my own behavior. Luca brings out dark things in me I didn't even know were there.

Stay away from him, the voice advises, and if it wouldn't make me look like a lunatic, I'd nod fervently in agreement.

"Hey!" Paige calls out, turning in her chair, wooden legs scraping on stone, boys jumping aside as she waves enthusiastically at me; she's a bit tipsy, her gestures even larger now. "You all danced out?"

I start to answer, but she's already racing ahead eagerly:

"We thought we should maybe get going, 'cause it's getting late, but we'll stop and get some pizza on the way home." She throws her arms wide, palms up. "Apparently they have pizza in Italy! Who knew?"

"*Allora,*" Leonardo says, pushing back his chair and holding out his hand to Paige to help her get up. "We go to get pizza, yes? Because the pizza, we have it in Italy too!" He and Paige fall over each other, roaring with laughter.

"It was funny the first time," Kendra says dryly to me. "But that was, like, a while ago."

Still, Kendra looks like she's had a really good evening too. She's not tipsy or merry, like Paige, but she's glowing, her skin luminous and plumped out by compliments. It's obvious that the two American girls have been the belles of the ball tonight, surrounded by handsome Italian guys who've been competing for them, exactly as we all dreamed of spending our summer in Italy. Even as Kendra stands up, Andrea and two other guys jump to attention, jostling each other in their attempt to be closest to her. Kendra's pretending not to care, but I can tell by the gleam in her eyes how much she's loving it.

"So, you have a nice time with Luca?" says a sharp, high voice right behind me.

I turn to see Elisa.

"Luca likes to kiss the girls." Elisa seems to be confiding, but also manages to smirk at the same time, which is sort of impressive. "Many girls. *Molte ragazze*. Every summer, the foreign girls. Very many."

Cold spreads across my rib cage as if she's held an ice cube to my breastbone. But Elisa isn't the first mean girl I've met in my life, and I've got plenty of experience dealing with them.

"Don't be jealous!" I say, tilting my head to one side and giving her my best faux-sympathetic smile. "He's free now." I glance sideways and spy at Luca, who's standing by the bar table, finishing his Prosecco as coolly as if he's entirely unaffected by what just happened between us. "You could go over and see if he'll kiss you. Though I warn you, I'm a hard act to follow."

I spoke slowly and clearly, but I don't know how much she understood; enough, anyway, to make her eyes and mouth narrow into slits.

"*Stronza*," she hisses, tossing her head and walking away, swaying like a giraffe on the impossibly spindly heels.

I shrug dismissively, and see that Ilaria, who's been waiting a short distance away for Elisa to drip her poison into my ear, registers this gesture. They made enemies of us the moment they called us "*maiali*," they declared hostilities first: I've lost nothing by showing Elisa that I can take her on and beat her at her own nasty game. It might have been nice to have made some friends with Italian girls, but they wouldn't let us, so now they've made their beds and they can lie on them.

"Luca!" Leonardo calls as our group masses together and starts to move across the bar. "*Si va, eh? E ci si ferma per una fetta di pizza—abbiamo anche la pizza in Italia, sai!*"

He cracks up, and Andrea does too: they're clearly bringing Luca in on the whole "pizza in Italy" joke. I realize suddenly that Luca is our designated driver, and I stiffen at the thought of spending any more time in his company. But it's such a bustle of activity as we stream out of the club, divide up into different cars, and head in a convoy through Florence, that there are always people between us. The boys at the table, Leonardo and Andrea's friends, follow along, and Elisa and Ilaria are on the fringes too: when we pile out at the little open bar on a roundabout next to the Arno river, lights still twinkling over the bridges and along the riverbanks, there are at least fifteen of us, laughing and joking, a big jolly group. I make sure I'm close to Paige and Kendra. I do notice ruefully that Luca's right: the boys surrounding them barely pay any attention to me. They're too busy calling "Payyge! Kain-dra!" and teaching the girls Italian words, teasing them at their pronunciation, showing off their own basic English.

Luca, as seems to be his way, stands off to the side watching the show, propping his shoulders against the side of the bar, drinking an espresso. I don't look at him. I don't want to feel the rush of emotions that will come if I accidentally meet his eyes. I concentrate on eating my slice of Margherita pizza, greasy and delicious, which really hits the spot.

It's great, too, to have something to do with my hands. I take small elegant bites so I don't look like the pig Elisa called us. By the time I've polished it off, taken a handful of napkins from the dispenser, and wiped my hands clean, we're all piling back into the cars again. An enthusiastic peck on each cheek from the boys, European-style, which adds up to more kisses from boys in this one night than in the whole rest of my life to date, one sparkling-eyed, dark-haired, floppy-fringed boy after another leaning in to kiss me in a waft of pizza breath and aftershave, even if I am the also-ran in the Hot Foreign Girl stakes.

Luca's already in the driver's seat, and the atmosphere is so boisterous as he starts up the car that I don't have to say a word to him. The car twists and turns up a sweeping, majestic avenue lined with overarching cedar trees, which opens out into a huge square overlooking Florence, with the dome of the Duomo terra-cotta against the night sky, glimpses of the Arno river twisting through the city. A stunning statue of David is lit up in the center of the square, making all of us girls exclaim in surprise, oohing and aahing in wonderment.

"How romantic!" Paige sighs, seeing the dark shapes of entwined couples leaning on the stone balustrade at the far side of the piazza, looking down at the panorama below. "*Super*-romantic!"

"I bring you back here," Leonardo promises, swiveling around from the front seat. "We come back soon, we visit Piazzale Michelangelo in the night. . . ."

Paige claps her hands like a five-year-old and says, "I can't wait!"

She likes too much to be liked, Luca remarks dryly inside my head.

"I bring you," Andrea, sitting between Kendra and Paige, says to the former in a very hopeful tone. "You like that, Kain-dra? You like to come with me?"

Kendra smiles but says nothing.

She puts a high value on herself, Luca comments.

For a moment, I let myself look directly at him, the pro-file and shoulder I can see over Paige's body; he's staring straight ahead, his eyes never leaving the road, and yet I have the eerie feeling that he knows I'm glancing at him, and that he knows, too, that I'm hearing the observations he made earlier this evening about the two girls. *You are not different, and maybe not easy,* he said about me. And then he kissed me, and that match scraped across the striking strip, and I was as easy as that. As lighting a match.

I squinch my eyes shut so I don't look at Luca anymore. He's playing music in the car, a soft guy's voice singing in Italian. It's even nicer not knowing the words; I can let the music sweep over me, be soothed by it without listening too closely. Suddenly, the sheer weight of the events of the day overwhelms me, and I snuggle back against the padded seat, comfortably squashed against Paige's big warm side. I doze, rocked back and forth by the motion of the car, all the way back to Villa Barbiano.

I'm half asleep as we climb out of the car on arrival, yawning and tripping on the gravel. Luca doesn't get out. He waits until the last door's slammed to back up and turn around.

"*Ciao*, Kain-dra!" Andrea calls from beside Luca, lean-ing out of the car window, waving goodnight. "*A presto! Ciao*, Paige!"

"*Ciao*, Violetta," Luca says, to my surprise, and I whip around to see if he's looking at me, but he's already pulling away, the headlights swiveling over the gravel.

I turned around so quickly that I stumbled, but Paige is nice enough to hold out an arm to me, and we climb the stone stairs at the side of the house, Leonardo still chattering under his breath to the other two girls as he produces the house key from his pocket. Catia hasn't stayed up to see if we're safe home, I notice. Our first night here, and we're out till past one in the morning, quite unsupervised: she's not exactly in the running for Chaperone of the Year. The girls are saying goodnight to Leonardo. Of course he lives here too with his mother and most uncharming sister. I head straight up the stairs. I want nothing more than to kick off my shoes, rip off my dress, chuck myself into bed like a sack of potatoes, and pass out cold. I'm so completely overwhelmed by everything that's happened to me in the last eighteen hours, I've half forgotten we've left Kelly behind.

All the lights are off on the top floor of the villa. I pick my way across the antechamber by the faint moonlight throwing slanted pale oblongs over the stone floor, and gently ease open the door to our bedroom, not wanting to wake Kelly. But as I do, I hear something that sounds like a dog whimpering, faint and almost imperceptible, buried under piles of blankets.

Kelly hasn't succeeded in crying herself to sleep. Or she woke up when she heard me come in.

I'm ashamed to admit it, but my heart sinks. I can't cope with someone else's misery. I just want to curl up, fall asleep, and—hopefully—relive certain key events of tonight as they tumble through my dreams. Actually, Kelly isn't acknowledging my presence. I click the door shut behind me and stand there, debating what to do. I can nip quietly into the bathroom through the connecting door, wash my face, brush my teeth, strip my clothes off, and climb into bed, pretending that I haven't heard the tiny stifled sounds of misery that she's making. Get a good night's sleep, hope she eventually does too, and wake up tomorrow with a head not hazy and clouded with exhaustion.

I'll be able to help her much better tomorrow morning, I tell myself. *Right now, I'm no use to man or beast, as Mum always says when she's knackered.*

And Kelly probably wants me to pretend I can't hear her, the voice adds. *She hasn't said anything, has she? It'd be a kindness, really, to let her have her cry-out in peace and quiet.*

I've convinced myself to ignore her misery. Turning toward the bathroom, I take a couple of cautious steps—it's nearly pitch-black in here—and my foot knocks painfully into something on the floor that I'm sure shouldn't be in the path to the bathroom door, and wasn't here when I left to go out for the evening. Biting back a gasp, I bend down, rubbing my toe. My hand brushes against the outline of the obstacle, and with a sinking heart I realize what it is.

Kelly's suitcase. We shoved our cases under our beds after we'd unpacked, and now hers has not only been dragged out again, but—I slide my hand up the side, my fingers catching briefly on the rip in the fabric—yes, it's newly full of clothes once more. I realize she's pulled out from the drawers and off the hangers all her stuff after I went out, and dumped it back into the suitcase with the broken wheel.

Packed, because she's probably decided to leave tomorrow.

I close my eyes in exhaustion, kneeling there on the stone floor. I picture Kelly, with the cheap matching set of luggage, the case that broke the first time she used it, which she told me she saved up to buy from the local cheap market, so she'd have brand-new, smart-looking luggage for her Italian adventure. I compare her to me, with my own suitcase and carry-on, battered now from all my travels with Mum, but which cost, I know, a lot more than Kelly's did. I think of Paige and Kendra, with their huge cases stuffed with expensive clothes and makeup; Paige said this afternoon at the pool that she'd made her parents buy her a whole new set of electrical beauty items—hair dryer, straightener, tongs, hot rollers, epilator—ones that'd work with the European voltage. I imagine how Kelly must feel, not socially confident enough to withstand Elisa's nastiness, not rich enough to feel she can compete with the rest of us, not privileged enough to act as if she can take the luxury here for granted. Yet she managed to get herself here to be part of an Italian summer program: that means she's got a strong wish to be here.

I remember her lugging that suitcase through the Pisa airport, the wheel coming off and rolling into the crowd, her face pink with embarrassment and humiliation.

I take a deep breath, stand up, pull off my sandals, and pad over to her bed.

They Love Us Over Here!

"Kelly?" I say gently, my bum sinking into the mattress. "You don't sound happy. Want to talk about it?"

Kelly goes absolutely silent, so long that I panic, thinking I've done completely the wrong thing; that she's now pretending to be asleep, and wants me to go along with it. I'm just about to lever myself off her bed and sneak off to the bathroom when she heaves a deep breath in, letting it out on a flood of sobbing that's an unignorable cry for help.

"I shouldn't have come!" she wails, and from her muffled voice, I realize that her face is pressed right into her pillow. "I shouldn't have come! I'm a bloody idiot—stupid, stupid, *stupid* . . ." She hits her fist feebly against the mattress. "My gran tried to tell me, but I wouldn't listen—she *said* I'd be a fish out of water, she *said* no good comes of trying to act posh when you're working-class, 'cause everyone just laughs at you and makes you feel *horrible,* and she was right, she was *bloody right!* I hate myself and I want to *die.* . . . I'm fat and stupid and everyone here thinks I'm common. . . ."

"Oh, *Kelly!* Don't say that! You're being so harsh."

I scrabble around and manage to locate one of her hands by dint of finding an arm and working my way down it. The window doesn't have curtains, but shutters, and they block off any crack of light. Kelly's hand is limp, but I wind my fingers through hers, which feel like damp, knuckly sausages.

"Look, Elisa's mean and angry, and everyone knows it," I start. "All she wants to do is wind us up and make us feel bad, and we mustn't let her. She's a nasty snob—she's got a chip on her shoulder because her mum's got to rent this place out for courses to make ends meet. She's not rich either."

I fill Kelly in on what Leonardo told me in the bar, about his dad and Catia effectively being separated because they won't get a divorce, and Catia having to make Villa Barbiano support itself.

"He explained that Elisa was proud. She didn't like having paying guests in the house," I finish. "That's why she's such a bitch with us."

Kelly huffs a sodden, heavy exhalation into her pillow.

"Spoiled cow," she mutters. "She's got a big stick up her bum."

"Even her brother said she was a *stronza,*" I tell Kelly. "I don't know what that means, but it can't be nice."

I remember Elisa calling me the same word in Central

Park, her eyes malevolent; obviously, *"stronza"* must be equivalent to "bitch." Very useful: I store that word away in my memory and also decide to check a dictionary.

"You shouldn't get all worked up about Elisa," I say, giving Kelly's hand a comforting squeeze. "We'll all gang up on her and make sure she doesn't get out of line with us."

But Kelly doesn't respond with a squeeze of her own; instead, she pulls her hand back and shifts away from me, swallowing hard.

"It's not just her," she mutters, turning over to lie face-down. "It's everything. Dinner tonight, all the food and everything . . . I got the plate wrong, I picked up the one underneath when I shouldn't have, I didn't know which fork or knife to use, even the pasta was complicated! Grating cheese at the table, with everyone looking at me . . . being *waited on*! I've never had anything like that happen in my life, I felt like everyone was looking at me and laughing . . . I made a stain on the tablecloth with my fork. . . ."

I have to stop her and this litany of self-accusation.

"You were very good at the wine-tasting bit," I say, breaking in. "Catia was impressed. I saw she was."

At least this stops Kelly listing everything she did wrong. She falls silent, and though her breathing's slow and bubbly with snot, she isn't actually crying. *Which has to be an improvement,* I tell myself grimly.

"I really want to go to a good uni," she says eventually, in a thin thread of a voice. "Oxford, or the London School of Economics. But it's *so* expensive now with the tuition fees, my family just can't afford anything like that. I have to get a full scholarship, and there's so much competition. My school said I needed to have an advantage, you know, show I've got extra skills. I did Latin A-level and I was good at classics and history, so my Latin teacher thought a summer course, Italian art and learning the language, would, you know, impress the interviewers. Do something the posh kids do. Learn to talk their language." She huffs another long sigh. "I found this course online, and it sounded perfect."

I wince as I say as nicely as I can:

"But isn't this really expensive too? I mean, I don't even quite know what it costs"—I'm embarrassed to admit that, as it shows how privileged I am compared to Kelly—"but I know it's not, um, cheap."

In other words, I'm thinking, *So how can you afford this, if you can't manage tuition fees?*

"I had money saved up from holiday jobs," she says, turning over to lie on her back now, her voice coming a bit clearer. "That wasn't tons, but it was a start. And my teacher went and talked to the head, got the school involved. No one's ever gone on to somewhere like Oxford or the LSE from my school." She sniffs. "It's a real armpit. Total sink school. But there's this new head, she's trying to reboot it, and she got very excited at the idea of a student her first year not only getting into an Oxbridge university, but hopefully managing a scholarship as well. So she rallied everyone, all the governors, and they held raffles and fund-raisers to help come up with the dosh to send me here. Plus she got some of the governors to make donations. They wanted me to prove I could do it for everyone in our school."

"That's so nice," I say, impressed. "You must be majorly brainy to have them go to all that trouble."

"But—" Kelly heaves herself up to a sitting position, stuffing her pillow behind her. "It's *so much* pressure. Now I've *got* to get a scholarship, don't I? 'Cause they've spent loads of time doing fund-raising, and sent me off to Italy for two months!"

She sniffs again, snot bubbling in her nose.

"I was excited. I didn't want to think about what my gran was telling me," she confesses. "One part of me knew she was right, but I just shoved it to the back of my mind and told myself I'd manage. And then as soon as I saw all of you, I knew I'd made a mistake. I tried so hard to get some nice clothes, I bought those suitcases—but you lot were all so posh and *rich*. You're so *confident*. I knew you could tell that my clothes were dirt cheap—and when my suitcase broke, I could've *died*, and I knew it was wrong anyway—it looked really pricey on the stall, but when I saw it next to your stuff, I knew I'd got it wrong, it looked so *manky*—and I just want to go home! I want to go home *tomorrow*, I packed everything up—but I'll be letting everyone down, they'll be so disappointed, I can't face telling them I'm too bloody common for a summer in Italy."

I think she's going to cry again, and I stand up, taking a deep breath.

"Hang on," I say. "I'll be right back."

I pick my way across the bedroom, my eyes sufficiently adapted now; shielding my eyes with a hand and squinting, I click on the overhead light in the bathroom. And when I return to the bedroom, I leave the door open, letting some illumination flood in, thinking that it can't do Kelly's spirits any harm.

"Here," I say, sitting back down next to her and handing her a facecloth that I've dampened in the sink. "Wipe your face."

She obeys dutifully. I take it back from her and give her a handful of tissues instead; she blows her nose, making a whole series of yucky, gurgling, honking noises.

"Look," I say firmly, chucking the facecloth onto the stone windowsill. "Here's what we're going to do. Tomorrow morning, you're going to get up and unpack your suitcase all over again. And then you're going to get dressed, go downstairs, and get on with this flipping course, okay? If your school thinks you can get a scholarship to Oxford or the LSE, you're cleverer than me, and you're *definitely* cleverer than Paige. So you're ahead of at least two out of three of us already in the brains department. As for all the manners, every meal you're going to sit next to me, or across from me, and copy what I do, so you'll know what forks and knives to use, all that sort of thing. If I see you doing something wrong, I'll kick you or give a signal or something. I've learned all this from my mum. It's not hard at all. It's just getting someone to show you. You mustn't just give up and go home, you *can't*. Not over stupid stuff like manners and clothes and things, when you've worked so hard to get here."

I pause. Kelly's still honking away; I hope she heard me over the nose blowing.

"How does that sound?" I ask.

She sniffs.

"I suppose I could try . . . ," she says in a small voice.

"It'll be fine," I say encouragingly. "You're really clever, you'll pick all the social stuff up very quickly. There isn't much in it, honestly."

"When do you take your napkin off your plate?" she asks, still in that small voice. 'Cause I looked around when the pasta came, and everyone else had their napkins on their laps already, but I didn't."

"Pretty much straight after you sit down," I say. "Whether it's on your plate or under your fork, you sit down, then take the napkin off the table and spread it out on your lap. Oh." Something else useful occurs to me. "And when you have different kinds of cutlery around your plate—you know, two forks on one side, and maybe a spoon and a knife on the other—you always start on the outside and work your way in. The outer is for the first course, and the inner is for the second."

Kelly heaves a long sigh.

"Thanks, Violet," she says. "I'm really glad you're here too." And I feel her stretch out her hand, reaching for mine. I meet hers, and we clasp our fingers together.

"You'll be fine," I say softly. "Promise."

Kelly squeezes my hand tight. "I hope so," she says.

I close my eyes. I'm so tired I could burst into tears myself. Kelly sounds okay, at least for tonight; her crisis has been averted. My whole body sags in exhaustion. *Another minute, and I can go and brush my teeth, wash my face, finally crash into my own bed—*

"Oh *wow!*" exclaims a loud voice, and our bedroom door flies open; a big dark shape looms up in the doorway. "Wasn't it, like, the *coolest* night out *ever?* Kelly, honey, you *totally* missed out—you should've come, there were enough boys for everyone! Violet, you've been telling her all about it? Oh my *God*, we were like the *stars* of the night! They *love* us over here!"

Kelly may be taking etiquette lessons from me, but she should definitely take a confidence course from Paige, who'd make Wonder Woman look shy and retiring.

"Don't turn the light on!" Kelly says quickly, and I realize she doesn't want Paige to see her tearstained face.

Paige steps forward and crashes into Kelly's case.

"What's *that*?" she asks as I say swiftly:

"Over here! We're over here, on Kelly's bed."

"Yay! Girl talk! Kendra's crashed, but I wasn't ready to go to sleep yet, I'm all buzzed—"

Paige lands heavily on the end of Kelly's mattress.

"So!" she says happily. "Did Violet tell you everything? About the bar we went to, and the club, and all the boys?"

I nudge Kelly, and say, "Oh yeah. Everything," because otherwise Paige will launch into an entire catalog of every single event that happened tonight, and we'll be up till dawn.

"Cool! Oh, and did Violet tell you she had a fight with Luca? What *happened*? I didn't see, but Kendra says she thinks you, like, *slapped* him or something? I didn't want to ask you in the car, but did he, like, *grab* you? Oh my God, if he grabbed me, I *so* wouldn't slap him! I'd kiss his face off! He's *totally* cute! I mean, he's a bit gloomy, but he's *definitely* hot. . . ."

No one but Elisa seems to have spotted me and Luca snogging. I sag with relief. Elisa's scarcely going to start confiding in the foreign girls she despises, so my secret's probably safe.

"Who's Luca?" Kelly asks, nudging me back. But it's Paige who answers.

"He's gorgeous! Kinda grumpy, though. Tall, dark, and handsome and sort of brooding. He drove us to Florence."

"You went to Florence?" Kelly hisses to me.

Paige is burbling on, thankfully for me not hearing Kelly. "He was at school with Andrea and Leo, and they said Elisa's got a crush on him." She giggles loudly. "I think she was really pissed that Luca was hanging out with Violet. Yay Violet!"

"Elisa said to me that Luca's a bit of a slut," I say.

"Oh, I bet he is!" Paige exclaims. "He's so sexy! Did he try to kiss you, Violet?"

"I wouldn't trust a word Elisa says," Kelly mutters as Paige rolls over her like an army tank.

"He lives nearby, like on a hill or something," she says. "Oh yeah, and get this—he's a prince! Or his dad is, which means he will be one day! And he lives in a castle! How cool is *that*?"

There's a sudden tightness in my rib cage, a lightness in my head, a dizziness in my limbs as I hear myself ask:

"It's not the Castello di Vesperi, is it? I read that was close to here."

"That sounds like what Leo said," Paige says. "But I dunno—Italian all sounds the same to me. Anyway, they're all going to take us out again this weekend, to some fabulous party a friend of theirs is throwing in his house in the countryside that sounds, like, *super*-glamorous . . . I can't wait!"

I don't believe it! My heart sinks. *That would make Luca the son of the family I've come here to find out about. If he actually lives at the castello—he could take me around, show me the place, tell me about the family history, help me find out if the way I look is because I'm some kind of distant relation. . . .*

Oh my God, as Paige would say. After what happened between us. I really doubt that Luca's going to be remotely helpful to me. His moods change so fast, he's capable of making things even more difficult for me, because it amuses him. Or to make me feel bad, because I slapped him in public.

I close my eyes. As if things weren't complicated enough, I've not only pissed off the boy who might be my passport into the Castello di Vesperi, I've snogged him, too.

And, I think dismally, *worst of all, I slapped him.*

Next time I see him. I'll have to apologize. He mocked me, he was a sarcastic bastard, but I'll still have to apologize for slapping him.

My feelings toward Luca are so complicated they make me think of a marionette with hopelessly tangled strings. But the prevailing emotion as I finally drift off to sleep is resentment: he came after me, he kissed me, then he taunted me and managed to put me in the wrong.

Stay away from him, I think again. And I know it's the best advice—if I can only take it.

Molto Particolare

"*Questa è una rosa,*" Catia says in a bored tone, holding a flower up in the air so we can all see it. "*Cos'è questo fiore?*"

"*Questa è una rosa,*" we all dutifully chant as she adds it to the bouquet she's forming in her hand.

"*Questo è un tulipano,*" she continues, holding up a plump pink tulip and adding it in turn. "*Cos'è questo fiore?*"

"*Questo è un tulipano,*" we chorus.

This has been going on for some time now. It's like watching paint dry with a call-and-response segment to add audience participation.

"*É questo è un mazzo di fiori!*" she says, holding up the bouquet to indicate that it's finished. It really is very elegant. I wonder if we should clap. "*Cos'è?*"

We all stumble over the response—all of us but Kelly, who rattles back *"Questo è un mazzo di fiori"* as easily as if she'd been babbling Italian in her cradle.

"Brava, Kelly," Catia says, nodding approvingly. Kelly goes pink with pleasure. "You can also say *'Questa è un bouquet.'"* She gives the last word a very Italian spin. "As I have already said, Italian uses many foreign words now. Like *'fare il footing,'* which means to go jogging. Or—"

But Paige snuffles with laughter at Catia's pronunciation of "footing," which she says by pursing her lips together on the "foo," drawing out the vowel and sounding, honestly, pretty silly. Kendra digs Paige in the ribs, hard, to make her shut up, drawing an "Oof!" of shock from her.

"It *is* a little ridiculous," Catia says to our surprise as she places the bouquet in a glass vase. *"Il footing."* She shrugs. "Why not *'il jogging,'* after all? *'Il footing,'* it makes no sense."

She makes a dismissive gesture, as if she's throwing something away. It looks so cool I long to copy it.

"But to learn a language, you must be prepared to make a fool of yourself for a while. You must make mistakes, have people correct you, even laugh at you sometimes. *È normale."* She shrugs again. "But it's the only way to learn. You must go out, talk to Italians, not to each other. That is why I encourage you all to make friends with my son and my daughter, to meet their friends and learn and improve your Italian."

Paige, irrepressibly, giggles again: it's not improving her Italian that's the first thing on her mind, and from the lowering look Catia casts in her direction, she knows that as well as the rest of us. But Kendra and Kelly nod seriously, accepting her authority.

"Now you will all make your own bouquets," she says, indicating that we should come up to the dining table, where a range of flowers are laid out along its length on an old cloth placed there to protect the polished surface: roses, tulips, lilies, big brightly colored daisylike flowers that Catia says are called gerberas, and fernlike greenery to soften them. "You may choose what you want and which vase to use, then I will judge them. Remember to arrange them in your hand first, like I did. It is better not to put them in the vase until the bouquet is done."

Paige is already at the table, her head tilted to one side, pink tongue poking out a little in thought as she selects her flowers, exuding confidence from every pore.

"Her mom's in the Junior League," Kendra mutters to me and Kelly. "She's all up in this whole Martha Stewart stuff."

We nod: we don't quite understand all the terms Kendra's using, but we get the gist. Paige's mum is a lady of leisure who does lots of charity lunches and flower arranging. Kendra's mother, I get the sense, is a high-powered executive who pays someone else to do her flowers and tells them beforehand exactly what she wants. Certainly, the rest of us approach the bouquet-making challenge with much less assurance than Paige; Catia strolls out onto the terrace to sit on a dark brown wicker armchair, pulling out her phone, clearly in no rush for us to be finished. To our surprise, we actually get quite absorbed in the task. Silence falls, broken only by the sounds of us clipping the ends of flowers, muttering quietly to ourselves as we pick our vases, or flinching as we snag our fingers on rose thorns. Thirty minutes fly by; Paige is done first, though she fusses happily around her bouquet once it's in the vase, fluffing out rose petals, making every flower look as full and blooming as possible.

Weirdly, as we eventually step back and look at what the others have done, I realize that our bouquets are perfect reflections of our characters. I don't know if the other girls see it too, but to me it's blindingly obvious. Paige's is big and luxurious and rich, a riot of bright pink roses and fluted white lilies, plumped out with glossy green leaves, tied together with twine concealed inside the faux-rustic ceramic vase to keep it in perfect shape. Kendra's is spare and elegant, pale pastel tulips in a narrow white glass cylinder. Kelly, who was frowning in concentration the whole time, made a very conventional bouquet, everything carefully measured and in perfect alignment, the kind of thing that would get you an A grade simply because of its perfect execution.

And mine . . . well, I don't know what Catia will think of mine. One thing it definitely isn't is conventional. Paige's blond brows shoot up in incredulity as she looks at it: she's too nice to make a comment, but she doesn't need to; her expression says it all.

"*Allora?*" calls Catia, so slim that I can see the terrace wall between her legs in her tight white jeans as she walks. Bangles jingle on her wrists as she slips her phone back into her pocket. "*Avete finito?*"

"*Si,*" we sing out. Catia takes in the four vases placed on the dining table, and her eyes flicker. Dark, deep-socketed, heavily ringed today with brown eyeliner, they're very expressive; they turn down slightly at the outer corners, which makes her look a little mournful, like a sad clown.

"*Allora,*" she repeats, which seems to be a very useful

word, meaning something between "all right" and "well, then." "Paige, very nice. You have done this before, yes?"

Paige nods, blond hair bouncing.

"*Si vede.* I can see that. *Molto bene.* Very fun, very American. Kendra"—she takes in Kendra's vase—"*veramente elegante. Molto japonese.* It is a very Japanese style."

Kendra's eyes light up; she allows herself a rare, wide smile, showing dazzlingly perfect teeth and lots of pink gums.

"My mom has a lot of Japanese art," she says. "She'll change the scrolls over for the different seasons. So that's sort of influenced me. I like things quite simple."

"Very nice." Catia nods. "The tulips are not right for what you try to do, but the style is there. You need different flowers, that is all, which you did not have today. "Kelly—" She moves along the side of the table. "You do not, I think, care about flower arranging."

Kelly looks absolutely mortified. I grab her hand, nervous that she's going to freak out like she did last night and run from the room. Catia's holding up her hand in reassurance, though.

"I mean," she says, "that you have done a very good job with something you are not naturally drawn to. I'm right, *si?* You see this as a job to be done, and you have done it. I think you did not see it as something you artistically had a plan for."

Kelly relaxes; I loosen my grip on her hand. She even manages a self-deprecating smile.

"I'm *not* artistic," she admits. "I just tried to make something that looked balanced."

"It does look okay," Catia says, smiling at her. "It looks very professional. Like in a hotel—not personal."

This would pretty much be the worst thing that anyone could say to me about my own vase—I know exactly what Catia means, those stiff, conventional flower arrangements that sit on semicircular tables on hotel bedroom floors when you get out of lifts, probably placed underneath a gilt-framed oil landscape painting. But, looking at Kelly's face brighten, I understand why this is a good thing to her. It means she's done something that fits into the world she wants to join. "Conventional," "formal," "traditional" are all good words to her, and it makes total sense that they should be. If you feel like an outsider who hasn't grown up knowing when to put your napkin on your lap, or that you start using your cutlery from the outside in, then making a bouquet that could go in a vase at a four-star hotel is pretty much perfect proof that you're doing things along the right lines.

"*È Violetta,*" Catia says, looking at my vase, and my heart jumps, because I instantly remember Luca calling me Violetta last night. I think I remember every word he said to me in the order of utterance, which is depressingly pathetic. I'm distracted by my memories of Luca, so it takes me some time to realize that Catia hasn't yet passed judgment on my arrangement.

It looked a *lot* better when I pictured it in my head. I wanted to try to do something with the gerbera daisies, whose bright orange and fuchsia inspired me; they're so glaringly colored that they almost look fake. I cut them to different lengths, messing about with them; none of the other girls went near the gerberas. I know they're not elegant, but there was something crazily alive about them that drew me to them instinctively. I got the big glossy lily leaves that Paige used so successfully in her bouquet, but I pierced holes in them with the scissors and pulled some of the gerberas through them to look as if the flaming orange flowers were bursting out of the bases of the leaves.

"It's not, exactly—" I begin unhappily.

"Hmm!" she comments, reaching out to swivel the vase. "As a bouquet, it is not very good. In fact, it is very bad." She tilts her head to one side, pulling her mouth down at the corners. "But," she says finally, "it is interesting. Maybe even *artistico*."

"I'm really looking forward to the painting classes," I hear myself saying, locking on to the word "*artistico*." "There are so many amazing views around here, I'd love to be able to paint them."

I am surprised at myself. I was never that keen on art before—making it, that is. St. Tabby's was a very trendy, fashionable school, so we did all the latest kind of modern art projects: papier-mâché sculptures on chicken wire, installations with silly titles, conceptual stuff, making machines to paint randomized dots on paper. Our art teacher was always making us go to Tate Modern and look at artworks that were sculptures that the artist had blown up with dynamite and then hung from the ceiling, or rooms that were completely empty apart from lights turning on and off. She had long explanations for why they were good that none of us remotely understood. I can't remember ever doing anything as basic as sitting down with some paints and a bunch of flowers and trying to get on canvas what you see in front of you.

Which is all I want to do right now. Nothing too ambitious or intellectual, nothing that comes with seven pages of complicated catalog notes about why the lights are going on and off in the empty room. I'd just like to try to paint some flowers. Or a stone wall. Or some grass. Something really basic.

To see if I have any talent at all.

"*Molto particolare,*" Catia says, turning away from my vase. A tiny sigh escapes her lips; I may be paranoid, but I can't help interpreting it as relief that she doesn't have to look at my gerbera mess a moment longer.

"*Molto particolare?*" echoes a high, familiar voice, and all of us girls tense up immediately as Elisa comes into the room, wearing a linen shirt over a pair of beige shorts so tiny that only someone as thin and elegant as her could get away with them; anyone else would look like a stripper in search of a pole. "*Cos'è molto particolare?*"

"Elisa—" Catia starts, not looking best pleased at this interruption, but Elisa, black kohl like a sooty finger circling her eyes, a small cup of espresso in one hand, her phone in the other, wanders in, her leather sandals slapping lightly on the tiled floor. She takes in the scene at a glance, and yawns widely without even bothering to cover her lips. I see her pink tongue, the red-ribbed roof of her mouth.

"Ugh, *che noia,*" she says, looking down the dining table. "Flowers are so boring."

"Elisa—"

"Ah, I see it!" She's staring at my arrangement with a nasty little smile. "*Veramente particolare!* You know what this word means?" She looks straight at me, and I feel very large and under-made-up by comparison with her Italian chic. "*'Particolare'?* It means strange, or odd. You say this word when you don't like something but you don't want to be rude."

"Well, that's not something *you* ever have a problem with," Kendra snaps back, and even through my upset at Elisa's meanness, I admire Kendra's quick wits.

Catia clicks her tongue crossly.

"It means 'special,' or 'particular,'" she says to me reassuringly, but we all know that Elisa's hit the nail on the head. "And Elisa, if you don't like flowers, you can leave us, please."

"Oh, *stai zitta,* Mamma," Elisa says, shrugging exactly the same way her mother does. She walks across the room and out the french windows, where she collapses as if boneless onto the wicker chair, lifts her phone, and sips her espresso while dialing a number.

"It's like 'darling,'" Paige says suddenly. She looks at our bemused faces. "My grandmother's from Georgia," she explains, "and there, if you want to be mean to someone, you say her bag or her hair or something's 'darling.' It's the worst thing you can say. Like you're paying a compliment, but it's really the opposite. Or," she adds, warming to this theme, "if you're talking about someone and you say 'Bless her heart!' that means you think she's a total moron."

Catia decides, visibly, to ignore Paige's comments and her daughter's horrid behavior. Instead, looking suddenly very tired, she says:

"There will be a light lunch in the kitchen for you all at one o'clock. Please tidy up all the flowers you have not used and put them in the big buckets with water; I will arrange them later. You may take your own arrangements to your rooms if you wish."

Kelly cradles her vase in her hands, obviously looking forward to placing it in our room, a symbol of her success. I start to disassemble my daisy disaster, throwing the pierced leaves into the compost pile and placing the flowers back in the bucket for Catia to do something prettier with them.

"It was just an experiment—I didn't want to keep it," I say to reassure the other girls, who are looking at me with appalled stares, perhaps worried that I've taken Elisa's nastiness too much to heart. But I'm not just saying this to make them feel better. My arrangement didn't work, but I learned, at least, what not to do.

"You shouldn't pay any attention to what she says," Kendra says firmly, nodding at Elisa sprawled out on the terrace chair. "She's just a nasty bitch. Ignore her."

Elisa hears this, as she's meant to.

"And you," she calls to Kendra, swiveling on her chair to face inside the dining room, "you think you are so pretty, so beautiful, because all the boys want you. Well, they only want you because you are different. They think you are *esotica*. Exotic."

Kendra looks as if Elisa just slapped her in the face, and Paige draws in her breath sharply.

"Are you *kidding* me?" Paige snaps at Elisa. "What did you just call her?"

Her hands clenched into fists, Paige marches around the

table in Elisa's direction; skinny Elisa flinches at the sight of 140 pounds of super-confident, sporty, protein-fed American girl heading toward her with fury in her eyes. I nip around the table from the other side and head Paige off before she backhands Elisa like Serena Williams hits a tennis ball, and sends her flying across the terrace and into the olive grove beyond. I'm not an etiquette expert, but I can't help feeling that knocking our hostess's daughter over a stone balcony might not be considered the most appropriate way to celebrate the first full day of our summer course.

"Paige, leave it! She's just jealous," I say swiftly. "Ignore her. She's having a go at us because she's pissed off that Luca likes foreign girls—he doesn't want her."

Elisa grabs her cigarettes and her phone, jumps up, and, sneering at us all, storms off the terrace, muttering "*Vaffanculo!*" as she flees the wrath of Killer Barbie.

That's right—run away. To me, "exotic" sounds nice, like a compliment: out-of-the-ordinary, glamorous, exciting. But Kendra clearly hasn't taken it that way, nor did Paige. I want to ask them why, but it's Kelly, of all people, who saves the moment by saying meditatively:

"You know, we should make a note of all the mean things Elisa says to us in Italian. That way, we'll learn *all* the best swearwords."

The Elisa Cerboni
Alternative Italian Course

"*Stronza!*" Paige says cheerfully to me as I emerge from swimming a length underwater, pushing my hair off my face.

"*Stai zitta!*" I respond promptly, propping my arms on the edge of the pool, relishing in the sensation of the warm sunshine against my cool, wet skin.

"You better make sure Catia doesn't hear you," Kendra advises, sitting on a lounger fiddling with her phone. "This is *not* the kind of Italian our folks are paying for us to learn."

"Hey, we'll just tell her we've been taking the Elisa Cerboni Alternative Italian Course," Paige says. She's painting her toenails cotton-candy pink; she has an entire little manicure set laid out next to her lounger.

"I still can't believe she told her mum to shut up. In front of all of us," Kelly says, shaking her head.

That, it turns out, is what *"Stai zitta"* means; what the dictionary couldn't help us with, a free online translation service could. Kendra exchanges an equally disapproving glance with Kelly.

"I know," she says. "I can't even *begin* to think what would happen if I talked to my mom like that, even in private. Let *alone* in front of a whole bunch of people!" She shudders in horror.

"She'd whup your ass!" Paige carols in a funny accent; it sounds like she's doing some film imitation that Kelly and I don't recognize. "With a big ol' stick!"

"She pretty much would," Kendra agrees. "My mom doesn't mess around."

"Mine wouldn't even notice," Paige says happily. "We're a *biiig* family," she informs me and Kelly as she leans over her legs and very carefully starts to add a second coat of polish, twisting the little brush expertly against the edge of the bottle every time she does a new nail, loading the brush with exactly the right amount of candy-pink viscous liquid. "Five of us—three boys, two girls. And we're all loud. My mom doesn't listen to a word anyone says—she hasn't for years."

"It sounds lovely," I say wistfully, picturing Paige and her family in one of those gigantic American kitchens, a central island in the middle the size of a car, five huge blond boys and girls tearing in and out, making themselves American food—but what? Peanut butter and jelly sandwiches, I decide, that's what they always seem to be eating on TV—

with a huge blond mother and father presiding over the chaos. I'm texting my mum—I emailed her last night before dinner, and I've already got back screeds of endless texts.

Right now, the idea of having a mother who doesn't listen to a word one says is very appealing indeed.

"I know what you mean," Kelly's saying to Paige. "There's three of us girls, my mum, and my stepdad, and my nan lives with us too. That's my grandmother," she adds, as Paige must have blanked on the word. "It's a really small house, so you never get a moment's quiet."

"My brothers are *soooo* noisy!" Paige says. "There's, like, never a moment when you don't hear a ball bouncing off something or them shooting something in a video game, or dive-bombing each other in the pool—"

"You have a *pool?*" Kelly asks, her tone incredulous, and as Paige launches into a description of her family's split-level ranch, I reach for a swim float, wrap my arms around it, and push myself into deeper water, floating happily, closing my eyes, as the conversation ebbs and flows over my head. If Kelly and Paige are getting on, I can basically stop worrying about Kelly from this moment forward: the way Paige defended Kendra today, she's like a lioness with people she cares about.

I can't summon a drop of empathy for Elisa getting her knickers in a twist—or, as Paige would put it, bent out of shape—because her mum needs to take in guests and do summer courses to pay her way. I mean, she still lives here, in what's pretty much paradise. So what if she doesn't have Villa Barbiano all to herself? Elisa could try making friends with the girls who come to stay—then she'd have people to visit all over the world, instead of making deadly enemies of them.

A big bumblebee buzzes past me, fizzing with purpose, and lands heavily in one of the lavender bushes planted as a hedge at the deep end of the pool. It's joined by another, and they bumble from one tiny mauve flower to the next, sucking up nectar, their black and yellow fuzz very dark against the gray-green leaves and the pale stone wall beyond. *Lavender honey*, I think, watching them through my lashes; if I painted this little scene, that's what I'd call the painting, *Lavender Honey*, and let people work out why I'd given it that title.

My float turns in the water, and I turn with it, my legs trailing, and then paddle a little to bring myself to the infinity edge of the pool, looking over the brimming stone curve to the landscape beyond. It's so beautiful you don't quite believe it.

Just below me, to my right, is Catia's ornamental English rose garden, which she walked us around this morning before our flower arranging and Italian lessons. It's a riot of color, because late June, she said, is prime time for roses: salmon pinks, yolk yellows, flaming reds, clear bright whites, all planted in neat little beds, curving around in a complicated formal design. I want to sit there when it's not quite so boiling hot, maybe at dusk, so I can watch the colors fade as the sun sets and night falls, making everything look like a faint shadow of itself.

I shake my head in amusement at the way my thoughts are drifting, water dripping down my forehead from a loose strand of hair. Since I've come to Italy, I keep finding myself framing images, seeing how colors and light work together. I'm planning to study art history, so of course what my teacher calls "the visual arts" are what I want to specialize in. But picking up a brush, loading it with paint, trying to capture even a little of the loveliness in front of me—that's an entirely new desire.

The image of the painting from Sir John Soane's Museum pops into my head: *Portrait of a Young Lady.* That's why I'm here, after all—because I accidentally came across a portrait of a girl who's my mirror image. And now, the idea of painting itself is beginning to obsess me. . . .

I get a craving to look at the picture on my phone. I do that a lot. I've transferred it to my laptop too, of course, but I've kept the original photo on my phone, and I look at it very often, as if it's a sort of talisman, reminding me that I came here because I have a mystery to solve. I spin myself slowly around in the water and kick toward the shallow end, the float tucked under my tummy, too lazy in the heat and the relaxation of floating to bother to do anything as strenuous as haul myself out of the deep end. Walking up the stone steps out of the pool is like wading through toffee, slow and languorous, the weight of water dragging at my legs. By the time I flop onto my lounger, adjusting the top bit to shade my face, and pick up my phone to look at the photo, I could fall asleep.

Paige and Kelly stopped chatting a while ago; I think they're dozing. But Kendra is still *click-click-click*ing away at her phone.

"Blimey, Kendra," I say on a big yawn, scrolling through

my photos, "you've been texting for hours! Aren't your parents going to freak when they get the bill?"

"I'm not texting," Kendra says, and there's a grimness in her voice that makes me sit up and pay attention. "I'm reading through the texts that the boys from last night sent me, and then I'm deleting them all."

"You're *what?*" Paige heaves herself up, awoken by this information. "You're *kidding!* I, like, *never* delete a text a guy sent me! Like, *ever!*"

"You heard what Elisa said," Kendra replies. "When she said they only wanted me 'cause I'm exotic, I remembered right away that one of them even called me that last night. I *hate* that word."

"I'm sorry," Kelly says simply, "I don't understand why it's so bad. I don't think Violet does either, honestly."

Paige pulls a face.

"It's kinda racist," she says frankly. "You know, saying she's different. I mean, she's *not* different. She's just another American girl."

"I *won't* be their exotic summer treat," Kendra interjects. "Like they're looking at something in a zoo."

"Oh *no*," I say, really distressed. Not only at how upset Kendra is, but also, as Paige says, at the waste of deleting nice texts from a whole raft of admiring boys: from the amount that Kendra's been clicking away, her phone must have been absolutely flooded with messages and invitations. I mean, I may have been kissed last night, but it didn't exactly end on a high note, and no one asked me for my phone number so they could deluge me with texts. It's incredibly frustrating to think that Kendra's got what we all fantasize about—loads of hot boys avidly pursuing her—and is rejecting them all.

Particularly because this entire situation has been caused by Elisa. I hate her having this much power over us.

I open my mouth to say all this, but Paige gets there first. Swinging her legs vehemently over the edge of the lounger, which creaks in protest, she pushes herself to her feet, stomps over to Kendra, and grabs the phone from her hand.

"Are you *kidding?*" she bellows. "You're doing this 'cause of *Elisa? Please!* Violet was totally right earlier, that girl's so jealous she can't think straight! She saw you and me yesterday with all those boys hanging off us and she went away and spent, like, all night figuring out the meanest, crappiest thing she could say to get you all wound up like . . ." She waves her arms around in frustration. "I dunno, what gets wound up?"

"A yo-yo?" Kelly suggests.

"Right! A yo-yo! A fricking yo-yo! And it *works!* You're doing just what she wants!" Paige stabs a finger at the screen of Kendra's phone. "These are *hot Italian boys! Prime Italian boy-meat!*" She throws her arms wide. "What the *hell*, girl? You are *so not* giving this all up! You think I care that they're chasing me 'cause I'm blond and have big boobs and all the girls here look like they weigh a hundred pounds, max? So *what* if they like me 'cause I'm different? I got more attention last night than I *ever* did back home, 'cause back home tons of girls look like me, and here I'm exotic prime meat too!"

"USDA prime exotic?" Kendra asks, her mouth beginning to curve in a reluctant smile.

"*Hell*, yeah!" Paige bangs her chest with Kendra's phone. "Damn right! I'm USDA prime exotic fillet steak! What's that one your dad likes?"

"Chateaubriand," Kendra says.

"Yeah! That one! I can never pronounce it, but that one!"

Paige is panting for breath in her enthusiasm for convincing Kendra to change her mind, her hair—clipped on top of her head because she blow-dried it this morning and didn't want to get it wet—beginning to fall down in big curls.

"Look, Kendra," I say, trying to pick my words as carefully as I can, "I can totally see that it must be horrible to have people make decisions about you based on what you look like, because it's not about you as a person."

I was worried that she might snap at me that being black's completely different from anything she thinks I might know or say.

"Some boys will *always* want you for some bit of you, not the whole thing. You know, some boys will like Paige because she's blond with ginormous boobs"—Paige sticks her chest out and does a comedic wobble of them, which makes all of us giggle—"or Kelly because they like redheads—"

"Fat chance," Kelly mutters gloomily.

"—or *anyone*," I continue quickly, "for all sorts of stupid reasons. But you find out very fast when you hang out with them, or snog them, what they're really like and what they're really after."

"Like the ones who just go for your bum straightaway when they're kissing you," Kelly chimes in. "And then keep trying to get their hands around to the front, no matter how much you slap 'em off."

"I *know!*" Paige howls. "I mean, I've got my jeans zipped up 'cause I like them that way! Stop trying to unzip them! Pigs! I'll do that myself *if* I'm good and ready, which is *nowhere near* the first date! And besides, I *hate* them touching my tummy! It isn't even flat when I'm lying down—I *never* want anyone to go near my tummy!"

"It only takes one, anyway," Kelly says, reaching for the sunblock: she's so pale she's understandably paranoid about burning. "That's what my mum says. It only takes one boy that you really like and you feel you can trust."

The image of Luca floods into my mind, and despite the heat of the day, I shiver from head to toe. If I'm being honest, I have to admit I don't even know whether I like him, let alone trust him; but my body's telling me that he's the only one I want.

I've been thinking about him so much, turning over and over in my head all the words he said to me. I wonder whether his telling me that I looked too Italian for the other boys to be interested in me was a way of making me feel grateful, that he liked me enough to talk to me, even to kiss me. Was it some sort of awful ploy to weaken my defenses so I'd let him go farther, do things I wouldn't normally let a boy do, because I was afraid that if I lost him, no one else would be after me? That I'd spend this whole holiday—*Summer study course,* I correct myself—this whole summer course watching the other girls be chased by gorgeous boys, while I'd turned down the only one who'd deign to fancy me?

Is that what he was doing? Playing a psychological game with me, trying to soften me up so I'd let him do whatever he wanted, just to keep him? I shiver again, my head spinning, as I remember that kiss last night, how it made me feel things I've never, ever felt before. Do things I'd never done before, like snog him passionately in the middle of a crowded bar—*or slap him in the face.*

Kendra and Kelly and Paige are giggling together now; they're all sitting on the edges of their loungers, leaning forward in a cozy little group, telling stories about boys, ones they like, ones they don't, ones who try to get you drunk, ones who don't do anything but you wish they would. I shut my eyes and lie back on the lounger and remember what it was like to feel his hand splayed out on the small of my back, his biceps lean and flexing under my palms, his body pressing tightly into mine. . . .

I took the time to look up online that songwriter Luca mentioned. It took me ages just to work out how to spell the name Jovanotti, and it took forever to find the lyrics:

"Ci sono trenta modi per salvare il mondo, ma uno solo perche il mondo salvi me—che io voglia star con te, e tu voglia star con me."

And then it took me even longer to translate it. Those online search translations are pretty rubbish when it comes to sentences. I had to work my way through it, painstakingly. But it was worth it.

"There are thirty ways to save the world," Jovanotti says, "but only one way for the world to save me—if I want to be with you, and you want to be with me."

I can't help it. I came to Italy trying to find out about a painting and its connection to myself, but instead, all I can think about is Luca.

The Yellow Brick Road

The castle walls loom above us, stark and gray. Set on a grassy mound, which raises them even higher, they're just as intimidating as they were built to be; forbidding, almost sheer sheets of stone, so tall we need to tilt our heads back to see the crenellations between which the archers would kneel to fire down arrows on the besiegers. Or pour boiling oil on their heads, or push them off their ladders so they crashed to the stony ground below and broke their backs.

It's a sunny day, but the graveled area where Catia parked the jeep is in what's probably perpetual shade, surrounded by a thick rank of tightly massed cypresses, their dark foliage cutting off all direct light. The castle towers dominate the landscape, forcing us to look at it; we've been chattering away on the drive in high excitement, but as soon as we step down from the jeep, we fall silent, standing there in the shadow of the castle, staring up at its walls. Feeling very small and fragile and mortal by comparison with its solidity and endurance.

"'Abandon all hope, ye who enter here,'" Kelly murmurs, and Catia, hearing her, taps the fingers of one hand into the palm of the other in approval, a clap performed by an Italian too elegantly restrained to actually make much noise.

"*Molto bene*, Kelly," she comments. "A Dante quotation! You have been doing your homework from our class yesterday, I can see."

Unsurprisingly, Catia is turning out to be a strict teacher. The afternoons spent by the pool are now supposed to be used for homework time after morning classes; we've done Dante and Petrarch, the famous Italian poets, started Italian art history—lots of icons at the moment that all look exactly the same to me, but are painted on gold backgrounds, which Paige oohs and aahs over—and are studying Italian verb conjugations. Though we don't have formal tests, Catia will fire out questions in classes, fully expecting us to be able to answer from reading through the bound printouts she's handed to us the day before. I'm doing all right, Paige is frankly struggling, but Kendra and Kelly are the stars of the group. A competition is developing between them that isn't always friendly.

I see Kendra dart Kelly a resentful glance, and Paige blurts out rather sullenly:

"Jeez, Kelly, you are *such* a brainiac."

I'm sure that isn't meant as a compliment; Paige accompanied the comment with a roll of her eyes at Kendra. But Kelly, who has none of Paige's advantages, who'll have to make her way in life entirely on her own brainpower, not Mummy and Daddy's money and social status, takes it as one, and beams with pleasure.

"Can you tell us where that quotation comes from?" Catia asks. Kendra opens her mouth to answer, but Kelly gets in first:

"The *Inferno*. When all the doomed souls are going into hell," she says quickly. "It's written above the gates."

"*Eccellente!*" Catia comments, and her approval provokes Kendra to raise her immaculate eyebrows and drawl:

"Kelly, better not tell Luca next time we see him what you said about his ancestral home, eh?"

Kelly flushes red with embarrassment.

"I—I didn't mean—" she stammers, but Kendra's already turning to exchange a smile with Paige, having scored a point off her academic rival.

Why do we have to do all this sniping and bitchery? Kelly and Kendra are both really clever—one of them doesn't have to win over the other to prove that.

Sometimes I think hanging out with boys would be an awful lot simpler. And then I remember how much they like to make fart jokes, and I change my mind again.

"We will certainly not say that to the principessa," Catia says firmly, "who is waiting to show us around the castello. Come, we go in this way."

She leads us along the wide gravel drive, to a high arched gateway whose ancient wrought-iron gates are pushed wide open; it doesn't look as if they've been closed in decades. The Castello di Vesperi isn't expecting an attack any time soon. Still, the gates are wicked-looking things with spikes on top, presumably in case anyone tries to scale them and climb in that way, and as we walk inside, into the stone courtyard, I notice that all the girls instinctively glance back over our shoulders, as if we're checking that we know where the exit is. The walls are just as imposing from this perspective, casting deep shade over this side of the courtyard. It reminds me, unavoidably, that they're this high, this looming, not just to keep invaders out, but to keep prisoners in.

Inside the fortifications, a car is parked, a battered old white Fiat Panda, square as a children's toy, along with a sleek Mazda. I can't help noticing that Luca's car isn't there, and this is surely where the family leaves their cars; I was secretly hoping we'd bump into him on this visit. I've made a huge effort with my hair, my makeup, and my clothes. A mixture of disappointment and relief floods through me at the realization that I'm unlikely to see him today. Relief, because Luca stirs up all sorts of incredibly confusing feelings in me, and I have more than enough to cope with—meeting his mother, trying to find out as much as I can about the castello's history and any clues that might lead to the unknown girl in the portrait who looks like me—without the powerful distraction of my attraction to Luca being thrown into the mix.

It's definitely for the best, I tell myself firmly, and I try very hard to believe it.

A long strip of pavement rises to one side, curving around in a wide semicircle, leading to a cluster of buildings at the center. Catia starts up the path, and we all follow. I can hardly believe I'm here, at the castello. It's so weird that this is Luca's home but maybe also connected to me. . . .

"It's like the Yellow Brick Road," Paige mutters irrepressibly. "Look out for the monkeys!"

The castello is a ridiculously imposing building. The jeep had to climb a steep, winding road to reach it; it stands on its own hill, Catia said, on the historic border between Florence and Siena, and was a battleground for centuries as the two cities waged perpetual war with each other. I can sense all the years of history here, am imagining battles fought, arrows flying, blood seeping into the stones beneath our feet. I may be letting my Gothic ideas run away with me, based on my love for historical novels, but as I look at Kendra and Kelly, I'm sure their thoughts are running on similar lines. They look grave and solemn as we round the wide sweep of pavement and finish at an enormous pair of double doors made of thick oak, so heavily embossed and decorated with ironwork bosses and shields that I can't imagine how much they must weigh. Or indeed, how many men it's going to take to heave one open to let us in.

Catia pushes a brass button recessed into the wall, and a high, eerie electric bell reverberates beyond, sounding as if it's bouncing off acres of stone corridors inside. We wait for a minute or so, and then the four of us girls jump out of our skins as an awful creaking noise starts up from the doors, and a smaller one, cut into the larger left-hand door, swings open. It's cunningly concealed, so we didn't notice it was there, which is a shock in itself; and the woman who stands there, small, with a heavily lined face, wearing a black dress and shoes that look like orthopedic clogs, is equally scary-looking; she's positively glowering at us. We cower back. I'm paralyzed with fear that this tiny, evil-faced apparition is Luca's mother.

"*Buon giorno, Maria!*" says Catia, the only one of us who isn't intimidated by the grimacing dwarf. She rattles off something quickly in Italian, to which Maria shrugs, raising both shoulders and then letting them fall so heavily I can almost hear her bones creak. She turns away, leaving the door open, and Catia gestures for us to go inside.

"I just told her she needs to oil the hinges," Catia says firmly. "It is ridiculous, that noise. It will give everyone terrible headaches."

Catia runs a very tight ship; everything at Villa Barbiano is oiled and dusted and polished within an inch of its life, her cook and maid bustling around in a perpetual flurry of activity. Here at the Castello di Vesperi, the atmosphere is a lot more laissez-faire. Maria—who must be the housekeeper or maid; there's no way Catia would greet the owner of the castello by lecturing her about oiling her hinges—is definitely not as keen as Catia on proper house maintenance. We're walking down a high corridor, what's probably a priceless carpet beneath our feet, but there's definitely a stale, old smell in the air; the brass up-lighters meant to illuminate each picture hanging on the paneled walls aren't gleaming as they should be, and the heavy gilt frames themselves are equally dull.

"Well, I guess we found the monkey," Kendra says dryly to me, and I can't hold back an answering huff of recognition. With her lined and creased face, her dark, beady eyes and gruff demeanor, Maria does look very like a monkey. A mean, evil monkey who'd rip the food out of your mouth, scurry up a tree, and perch on a branch to eat it, throwing the bits it didn't want at you with a nasty laugh.

We emerge into a majestic hall, with a wide central mahogany staircase straight out of a period film, or one of my favorite historical novels. It's illuminated by stained-glass windows that throw diamonds of blue and red and green light over the wooden floors, and I can see dust mites gleaming golden, turning over in the shafts of sunlight that pierce the gloom. A gigantic chandelier hangs from the center of the ceiling. It must be four feet around, and it's the most extraordinary thing I've ever seen: like an explosion in a glass factory, curlicues of white- and pink- and gold-edged glass, fluted and twisted and curling around each other, enormous and vulgar. It doesn't go with the rest of its surroundings at all.

"Oh, I *loooove* the chandelier!" Paige gushes predictably. Kendra, who's come to a halt next to me, rolls her eyes.

"You *would*," she says as we stare up at it. "It looks like something from a mall in Dallas. Or a Disney cartoon."

"So?" Paige is unabashed. "I love Disney cartoons!"

Directly below the chandelier is a circular table, big enough to seat eight people around its circumference. Curious to see more, I walk closer and gasp when I realize the top, set on a carved wooden base, is a slab of shiny, streaky dark green stone that looks as if it's been cut from one huge rock, though that can't be possible. Set into it is an elaborate design that looks like a family crest, in black and dark red and mother-of-pearl, all pieces of stone cut to fit and slotted in so smoothly that when I run my fingers over the surface, I can barely feel the joins.

"Ah, Donatella! *Eccoci!*" Catia says, and I look up to see the figure of a woman on the landing above, or really a balcony that runs the length of the stone wall, split in the center by the wide staircase. It must be a nuisance to have to walk along the balcony to get down the stairs, but it does allow you to make an amazing entrance as your guests stand below, looking up at you as you descend the stairs like a queen.

Or at least, in this case, a princess.

"This is the Principessa di Vesperi," Catia says as the slender woman makes her way down the stairs toward us. The light is behind her, so I don't see her face at first, just her slim figure in a Chanel jacket over a silk T-shirt with a double string of pearls at her neck, narrow blue jeans, and Ferragamo pumps, those quilted navy ones with bows on the toes that so many posh women wear. Her black hair is too big for her head, blown into a rigid bob by an old-fashioned stylist. Led by Catia, we shuffle around the gigantic green table to meet the principessa, finding ourselves lining up to say our names and shake her hand as if we really were being greeted by the queen: Paige actually does a tiny bob, like a modified curtsy, when she takes the principessa's outstretched hand. I look down at my own fingers and realize with horror that the tips are gray with dust from the table; I wipe them swiftly on the side of my leg before holding out my hand, but she's seen the gesture and shakes her head.

"I'm sorry, the table is not clean," she says to me, and I feel my face go red as I mumble some apology for having inadvertently pointed it out. "It is beautiful, though, yes? It is my own family *stemma*."

She shakes her head, looking cross with herself that she doesn't know the word in English.

"Coat of arms," Catia interpolates, and the principessa nods gratefully.

"This table came with me when I came 'ere to live, many years ago. I begged my father to let me bring it," she says. "I always love it, even when I am a little girl. It is malachite, the green stone."

"The carving's amazing," I say, because she's looking at me expectantly.

"If you like," she says, "there is a *museo* in Florence that shows many examples of this kind of work. Maybe Catia can take you. It is called *Museo dell' Opificio delle Pietre Dure*. They 'ave many *mosaici*. I go often, I find it very interesting."

Her Italian accent is much heavier than Catia's, and the name of the museum is so complicated that, mouthing it to myself, I get hopelessly stuck. Also, she looks very like Luca, and that's weirdly hypnotizing. I recognize his high cheek-bones, his pale skin, the black of his hair, his blue eyes, and his slim build, though Luca is lean, tensile muscle while the principessa seems surprisingly fragile. Her hand in mine was thin, all bones under her heavy gold rings, and the skin of her face is drawn too tightly over the high cheekbones, as if they might actually slice through it.

She's frowning now as she looks at me. I feel myself blush-ing again, not sure what I've done; then she says something in Italian to Maria, who clops forward in her cloglike shoes. To my horror, Maria grabs my shoulders with hands like claws and swivels me around so my face is illuminated by one of the shafts of white light that pierce through the clear panes in the stained-glass windows.

The principessa shakes her head as if in shock. Maria, squinting closely at me, her ancient skin creased so deeply it's cracked like leather, mumbles a stream of Italian that sounds like a string of curses. Both of them seem transfixed by the sight of my face. I hear the name Monica repeated as they look briefly at each other, then back at me. Maria's fingers are sunk into my shoulders, gripping me so hard it's as if she's digging right down to the bone. She's much stronger than she looks; I don't dare to move because I know she'll just clutch me harder with those claws.

It's Kelly who comes to my rescue.

"Hey, you could be hurting her!" she says bravely, stepping forward, confronting Maria. "Let her go, okay?"

The principessa, white as a sheet, issues a quick command to Maria that has her, finally, releasing her death grip from my shoulders and stepping back. I can't help wincing as the blood rushes back to the dents she's made with her fingers; I rub myself to help the circulation. The principessa says quickly:

"Mi scusi, I am so sorry. You are all right?"

I mutter a yes to be polite, though really, I'm not at all okay. I'm in shock, cursing myself as much as Maria probably just did. Because in all my scheming to get here, to the castello where the picture of the girl who looks like me once hung, one thing never occurred to me.

If I look like a girl who might have been a di Vesperi ancestor, from hundreds of years back, there might be other portraits still here that look just as much like me. Or, even more powerful, that resemblance might still be present in its descendants.

Which means that a member of the family, recognizing my face, might have as many questions for me as I have for them. And the first one is blindingly obvious: Who is this girl? How on earth does a girl from London, with a Scandinavian mother and a Scottish father, end up looking as if she'd walked out of an ancient Italian family portrait?

A Genetic Atavism

"*Mi scusi,*" the principessa says again, now more composed. "But it is very strange. What is your name?"

"Violet," I say. "Violet Routledge."

"I do not know this name," she says. "Row-ti-laydge." It takes me a moment to realize that she's attempting to pronounce my surname, she mangles the word so much. "But you see, Violetta, you resemble very much Monica, the sister of my 'usband, when she was at your age. There are some photographs, and a picture. I show you."

She walks over to a grand piano on one side of the hall; it's so big, this space, that I hadn't even noticed the piano was there. It's closed, a silver candelabra standing on top of it, and along its ebony lid are arranged a whole raft of family photos, all in silver frames, the way the aristocracy displays its photographs; for some arcane reason, it's considered common to hang them on the walls. I see one of Luca; he's a few years younger, scowling at the camera, his black hair hanging in inky strands over his face, his expression somehow so characteristic that it makes me smile, makes me want to reach out and touch the face in the photo.

Oh God. I really do have it bad for him.

The principessa is reaching out for a photograph right at the back of the collection, her thin wrist snaking elegantly between the frames.

"*Lascia stare,*" Maria snaps at her. "*Non lo fare.*"

"*Zitta, te,*" she responds autocratically, and the four of us girls exchange a startled glance; we just heard a princess tell her housekeeper to shut up.

"*Ecco!*" The principessa lifts up a large photograph in an ornate frame and shows it to me. Everyone else cranes in too. "This is my 'usband"—she has some problem with her h's—"and 'is sister on 'oliday, so many years ago. In Capri."

I was expecting the principe to look like his son, but he doesn't. Luca takes very much after his mother. His father is stocky and dark, strong-featured, with an imposing nose, square shoulders, and a very hairy chest. His hair's longer than is fashionable now, cut in layers that almost come to his shoulders, and he's wearing very short terry-cloth swim trunks. He's sitting on what looks like the back of a yacht, on one of the long padded seats, his arm around his sister, whose hair is tumbling all around her face in frizzy curls.

She's dressed in a white caftan with wide sleeves, trimmed with gold rickrack, and she's smiling at the camera, one hand lifted to push her hair back, while her brother is staring straight at it challengingly. *If Monica's my age in this photo,* I think, *she's really confident, poised, and sure of herself, her legs crossed elegantly. She definitely looks much older than seventeen.*

"Their clothes! *So* seventies!" observes Paige, mistress of the inappropriate comment.

Fortunately the principessa ignores her. She's looking at me now; I'm very conscious of her eyes on me as I stare at the photograph and at Monica's face. Almost reluctantly, I recognize my dark slanting eyes, which narrow into slits in photos when I'm smiling into the sun. My arching eyebrows, my smooth, sallow skin, my full cheeks, and my pouty mouth. It isn't quite like looking into a mirror, as it was with the *Portrait of a Young Lady*, but the resemblance is definitely present.

"You seem to have the di Vesperi face," she says softly.

"*Senti, Donatella,*" Catia says sharply to her friend, "it's simply the same type, but not the same. Small dark Italian girls. Lots of girls around here look like her."

Just as Luca pointed out, I think, wincing. *In Italy, I'm two a penny.*

Catia reaches out and takes the photograph from the principessa's hand, returning it to its distant place among the others.

"You're making too much of this," she says firmly. "Goodness knows why."

Catia is taking the principessa's elbow, turning her away from the piano, guiding her to the foot of the staircase.

"We really should get on with the tour," she says, briskly now. "There's so much here the girls will be interested in."

Behind them, I see Maria nodding vehemently, her gaze fixed approvingly on Catia.

"Sisi, brava, signora," she agrees. "Vado a preparare i bibiti."

Turning to us, she flaps the skirt of her dress like a farmer shooing geese, indicating in no uncertain terms that we should follow our hostess and be quick about it. We scramble to do as she says: Maria is someone you definitely don't mess with. My shoulders are still sore.

"So!" Catia beckons us up the stairs; they're waiting for us on the balcony. "I will tell you a few facts about the castello as we walk around. The castle you see now is not the original one—that was built in the nine hundreds. It came into the possession of the di Vesperi family in 1167, but because it is placed so strategically, at the edge of the territorial boundary between Florence and Siena, who were almost always at war in those times, it was a very important defense for Florence. You can see its position is very good, on this hill. Hard to attack, easy for the occupiers to see what is happening for miles around and to report back to Florence what the Sienese soldiers are doing. So it became a target for the Sienese, and in 1478 it came under a huge attack by them and the Aragonian army from Spain, who were fighting together, and they bombarded it for weeks— can you imagine?—and finally demolished it. It was razed to the ground."

"Razed?" Paige asks, looking baffled.

"Like a razor," Kendra says, miming shaving her face. "All smooth, nothing left."

"Jeez," Paige says, as Catia continues:

"But then the war ended, they made peace, and Florence gave money to the di Vesperis to help rebuild."

"That was nice of them!" Paige says happily.

"They didn't give them the dosh 'cause they were *nice*," Kelly says. "They did it 'cause it was strategic. They needed a castle here so they could defend the border and have a vantage point to see what the Sienese were up to."

"*Esatto*," Catia says, beaming, and Kendra looks cross; Catia didn't say *esatto* when Kendra helped Paige with the definition of "razed." Kelly and Kendra are clearly used to being the brightest girls in their respective classes, the teacher's pets. Now they're battling to win the lion's share of Catia's attention and approval.

Unlike me. I was never the teacher's pet. Apart from anything else, it was exhausting enough always having my mum hover around me at home; the last thing I'd want is a teacher doing it at school. I'm steady, a good student, but I never aspired to be the girl at the front of the class with her hand up and the fanatic gleam in her eye of someone who knows the answer to the question and is longing to spit it out.

"This was a working castle, of course, when rebuilt," Catia continues as we proceed along the balcony and into a high long room running along the far side of the building. Its red damask walls are hung with paintings clustered tightly together, in gilded frames so opulent and curlicued that they're almost works of art in their own right. "But the principe at that time, Bettino was his name, he took the opportunity to build also a lovely house here for his family, a proper mansion, not just a medieval castle. As a result the house is very grand but also most comfortable, even today for the generations who follow."

Catia does a sort of acknowledging wave and smile at the principessa, like an official announcement that she's paid a compliment to the family.

"We are *very* lucky to be allowed to visit it like this," Catia adds, and we all compose our expressions to ones of gratitude. "The public is *never* allowed inside—the house is not open for any kind of tours. The di Vesperi wine is famous, of course, but that is sold from the *cantine*, the wine cellars, which have a separate entrance from the other part of the *fortezza*, the fortress. We will visit those today as well as the house. They are part of the old dungeons, which we will also explore. You may be interested to know that as well as making wine, the Castello di Vesperi also produces oil, *vin santo*—a kind of sweet wine like sherry, *marmelate*—jams, and honey."

Lavender honey, I think, remembering the bumblebees by the pool yesterday.

"And this, as you can see, is the family portrait gallery. We will start with Bettino di Vesperi. . . ."

My heart tightens. Will I see what I'm looking for?

Catia is standing under a huge oil painting of a man in armor looking very serious indeed. I stare up at him, her words suddenly very far away and indistinct, like the buzzing of bees in lavender bushes. I'm wondering if I'm looking at one of my ancestors; as her words flow on—clearly, Catia has done this tour every year with her summer course girls, perfecting her tour-guide information—I look from face to face eagerly, up and down the line of portraits. Looking for the girl in the picture from Sir John Soane's Museum. Looking for myself. I'm both afraid and excited.

"*Buona sera!*" comes a high, familiar voice, and we swing around to see, to our great annoyance, Elisa, walking down the carpet that runs down the center of the portrait gallery as if she were on a Milan catwalk. She's in tight white linen trousers trimmed with gilt coins, and an equally tight khaki silk shirt, almost entirely covered with pockets and shoulder tabs; clearly the safari-meets-military-chic-in-San-Tropez look is in this summer. Her heels are three-inch-high wooden studded platforms, and her hair is artfully tousled and anchored by a huge pair of D&G sunglasses. I can tell they're D&G because each arm is decorated with a gigantic logo. Luca was definitely right about Italians liking to show off their designer labels.

"Elisa!" her mother says, looking very surprised. "*Non ti aspettavo, cara.*"

Elisa flicks her fingers at her mother in a gesture that's half acknowledgment, half dismissal, and strides up to the principessa, who takes Elisa's face in her hands and kisses her on both cheeks.

"*Piacere, Elisa,*" the principessa says fondly. "*Ma sei venuta a trovare Luca? Mi dispiace, lui non c'è oggi. E andato a Firenze.*"

"*Lo so, lo so,*" Elisa assures her, and she casts a malicious glance at us girls. "The princess asks if I come to see Luca, and I say no, I know he is in Florence. That will be a disappointment for all of you, *non è vero?* I'm sure you took a long time to get dressed up, hoping to see him."

We're all seething, but of course it's completely true.

Elisa has a horrible way of hitting the nail bang on the head. I'm not the only one who agonized over the choice of clothes today. I settled on a jersey tea-dress, black with a print of cherries on it, and sandals with red heels to echo the cherries: black and red suit my skin and my hair. The dress has a sweetheart neckline, sort of sexy without showing cleavage, which would be a big no-no when you're meeting a princess. My hair's pinned up and smoothed into curls, my lashes are mascaraed, and my cheeks have a hint of blush.

We've all made much the same decisions, thinking along the same lines, choosing pretty dresses smart enough for a visit to a castle, but body-fitted and attractive enough in case the son of the princess just happens to be there. Paige took hours just to do her hair, and it's amazing, like something out of a shampoo commercial, lustrous golden waves you want to reach out and touch.

Elisa's eyes narrow in amusement as she looks us up and down. Clearly, she thinks she's a great deal smarter and chicer than we are. *And she's probably right*, I reflect gloomily, smoothing down my skirt. Elisa is wearing what is the height of fashion in Italy right now, and she knows it. Somehow, she's managed to make herself appear much older, much more knowing. *We look like the teenagers we are*, I think. *Elisa looks like she's well into her twenties, all grown up.*

"I only come to the castello to see my friend Luca, to have parties," she continues, smiling nastily. "Never to hear the history, like a tourist. So I think it will be fun to pretend to be a tourist."

Having put us all down thoroughly, she turns on her heel, wraps her arm through the principessa's, and strolls away with her a couple of steps, making the point that she's an always-welcome guest, and we're . . . not.

Catia's frowning deeply. Eventually she relaunches into her information blitz, but we're all visibly distracted. The other girls, when not casting glances of loathing at Elisa, were made curious by the principessa's outburst on seeing me. They wander around, pointing out various women who they think resemble me. Everything begins to blur together after a while; the faces, though above Elizabethan ruffs to huge crinoline skirts to Regency slip dresses with tiny puffed sleeves, are very like mine. *But then, I do look Italian,* I think. I see Luca's father's features again and again—the square build, the commanding nose, the tight dark curls—but I don't see Luca at all. He really does take after his mother's side of the family.

"Here," Kelly says, stopping next to me as I look up at a painting of a woman sitting on a bench outside the castello, a delicate fan in her hand. Two children play in her wide brocade skirts—a little boy with a top, a little girl with a doll. "Now, that little girl looks just like you, Violet."

I elbow her crossly at being compared to a chubby little four-year-old.

"No, honestly! She's got just the same hair as you! And the eyes go up at the outside corners, like yours do—"

"Hey, look at this one!" Paige calls from the other side of the gallery. "I think I found Violet here—though this dress makes her butt look like the side of a house—"

I stick two fingers up at her as Kelly, giggling, runs over to join her and Kendra.

"One thing's for sure," Kendra's saying sarcastically, "I'm

not going to spot anyone who looks like *me* in these pictures. I guess they didn't have any slaves in Italy, right?"

"Or anyone like me," Kelly joins in, not to be outdone. "No redheaded Irish maids with freckles either."

"I think your freckles are *sooo* cute," Paige gushes. "I used to draw ones on my nose with one of my mom's eye pencils and pretend I was Pippi Longstocking when I was little. Ooh! I should get a red wig and go as her for Halloween this year! What do you think? Wouldn't that be hilarious?"

Their voices fade; they're following Catia, the principessa, and Elisa into a salon beyond the gallery, and I hear Catia's voice raised, describing the rococo furniture and marble fireplace. Hopefully they won't miss me for a while. Tears have been pricking at my eyelids ever since the principessa showed that photograph of her sister-in-law, Monica. It's suddenly overwhelming, this confirmation of my suspicions that I may truly have some tie to the di Vesperis. That's why I'm not doing a great job of finding my image in these portraits; I'm wondering whether, in all truth, I really want to.

Maybe you should just forget this whole thing, I tell myself. *You've got a mum who loves you with all her heart, and a dad who's—well, he's a good dad and he loves you too, even if he did move halfway across the world so you never see him anymore. But you're still so much luckier than lots of the girls at school, with their parents they never see, or being pulled back and forth with horrible custody messes in all the divorces.*

So what if you look like the di Vesperis? One of them could be connected to someone in your family, from ages and ages ago. You could be a throwback from them. I think of what happened with one of Milly's dog's puppies. He was all black and gray when the rest of them were all white, and apparently it was the genetics remembering when the breed was black and gray as well as white, at least a hundred years ago. The breeder said it happened sometimes, and that's what she called it: a throwback.

You're a throwback. A genetic atavism, if I remember what Milly's mum called it. It doesn't mean anything, really. You should just let the whole thing go.

These words are such a comfort to me, are so sensible, that I feel myself sag with relief as I say them to myself. I turn to leave the gallery having firmly decided to put all of this behind me, the portraits, the history, the past. By this time I can't see anyone in the salon; they've covered the rococo furniture and marble fireplace and moved on. I hear voices echoing from farther down the corridor, which is surprisingly poorly lit, and follow them slowly, in no hurry to catch up. I have made the right choice. The Castello di Vesperi doesn't mean anything to me anymore. I've made an official decision. I absolutely do not care anymore about how I might, conceivably, be linked to them.

Lots of kids have fantasies about being adopted, I know. There are loads of novels about it. You have a fight with your parents and you storm out and you find out that really you're Harry Potter the wizard, or the heroine of *The Princess Diaries*, and your life's really different from how you thought it was. Honestly, I never had those fantasies: I love my mum and my dad. The only thing I wanted, secretly, was just a little bit more space from my mum, and now I have it. Guilt washes over me when I think of Mum. *Forget the painting that started all of this,* I tell myself firmly. *I'm forgetting the whole thing. I'm going to concentrate on an educational Italian summer. And when we get back to Villa Barbiano the first thing I'm going to do is upload some pictures to my laptop and sit down and write Mum a really long email about everything that I've been doing.*

Well—I think of Luca—*almost everything. . . .*

I'm strolling down the corridor, the voices fainter and fainter in the distance, and lower now, as if they've gone down a flight of stairs. Sure enough, at the end of the corridor is a large wooden door, wide open, and I realize why the corridor seemed dark: they've left the door ajar to show me which way they went. A stone staircase with uneven flags leads downstairs, a lamp above it turned on, like a hotel light with a green shade, much more modern than the ancient staircase.

For a moment I pause, because the treads look so bare, the walls equally so, raw stone instead of the carpeting over wooden boards in the corridor. Then I remember what Catia said half an hour ago: *the old dungeons, which we will also explore.*

My spirits lift. Nothing like Gothic, gloomy, possibly haunted locations to make you feel better about your own bad mood. With luck, the dungeons will have barred windows, ancient cobwebs, rusted chains, gruesome tales of prisoners down there for years whose hair had gone completely white when they were finally released. . . .

I trot down the steps without a moment's hesitation, calling:

"Hey! Wait for me!"

I'm about six steps down when everything goes horribly wrong. The light above me goes out, leaving me in the pitch-darkness. The door slams. I gasp in shock.

A gust of wind blew the door shut, I tell myself firmly. *But why did the light go out?* Trying not to panic, afraid to go forward in the dark, I dash up the stairs again and push at the door.

It doesn't yield. Just as I put my weight on it, I hear the unmistakable click of a metal lock sliding shut. It's not a key turning, it's a latch lowering into its hook. And then I hear someone's footsteps walking away.

I beat on the door with both my hands, and yell: "Come back! Let me out! Let me *out!*"

But nothing happens. And then I realize: whoever's locked me in was hiding behind the door all along, waiting for me to go down these stairs so they could shut me in. It was a trap, and I fell right into it.

The Thin End of the Wedge

I yell my head off. I yell, and I rattle the door as best I can, though that isn't very much, as it's almost flush with the wall and fitted exactly to the doorframe. God knows how much of my yelling is making it through the heavy wood and the two-feet-thick stone walls. When this realization dawns on me, my shouting trickles away. I stand there in the dark, the only illumination the faintly outlined rectangle of light around the door. Breathing heavily, I begin considering my options.

I can't get out this way. And I don't want to go down those stairs by myself in the dark.

I know it wasn't wind that blew the light out; that only happens in nineteenth-century ghost stories, where a character's exploring a ruined abbey and her candle suddenly goes out and she feels a cold hand on the back of her neck . . . *Gah! Stop it! The last thing you need is to scare yourself!* I slap my hands up and down the side of the wall where the door opens, looking for a light switch. I go right up to the light fitting, standing on tiptoe, and feel all the way around it in case there's a little button or switch to turn it on. But though I feel the bulb, still warm from recent use, and the shade, and the metal plate they're fastened to, I can swear that there's no switch. I suppose it's unlikely there would be one in this little staircase; it's probably in the corridor outside. But I don't stop until I'm absolutely, one hundred percent convinced that there's no way of turning on the light above my head. Pride alone drives me on; what an idiot I would look to be found here in the dark, when I could have just turned on the damn light.

I sit down on the cold stone and try to calm my racing nerves.

They'll find you eventually, I tell myself, doing my best to ignore all those scary old legends about people getting walled up and starving to death, like the bride in the castle who hid in a chest in a game of hide-and-seek on her wedding night and then couldn't get the lid up again, and the wood was so thick that no one heard her screaming and pounding at the sides, and anyway it was airtight so she passed out really quickly and they searched the whole castle but didn't think to look in the chest and she was only found years later, her skeleton curled up in the mass of her wedding dress, white lace and white bone, the dark, empty sockets of her eyes staring sightlessly up at the poor person who found her. . . .

Stop it, Violet! Not helping! Not helping at all!

I draw a deep breath. *They'll definitely find me. They'll work out where they saw me last, and come back for me, and I'll hear them and make enough noise so they'll know where I am.*

There's plenty of air in here; I'm not going to suffocate like the bride in the chest. Not for ages, anyway. It's awful, but I find myself wishing I smoked, just because it would mean I'd have a lighter on me, or matches, something that would allow me to see in the dark. I reach out, and my fingertips touch the walls. The passage is narrow enough that I can pick my way down the stairs without falling, if I keep touching the walls; there's no drop I could tumble down. And though the black void beyond is frightening, I also don't want to sit here waiting pathetically to be rescued.

The thought of action, any kind of action, instantly makes me feel better. I might as well see how far the staircase goes. What if it leads outside and I could escape instead of sitting here like a lemon? I picture a door opening onto green grass, sunlight, the blue summer sky, and the image works like a charm. Shuffling along each stone tread, making sure I know where the next step is so I don't fall, I slowly work my way down.

My ears are still pricked for any sounds from above, in the corridor. If they've noticed they've lost me, they won't be searching in silence; they'll be calling my name, and that I'm sure I'll hear. And going up fast is much easier than going down. I can shoot back up the stairs if I hear a search party on my trail.

I'm not counting the steps, but I must have gone down twenty or so when my right foot, sliding forward in what by now is a practiced movement, hits not the expected edge of the step, slippery and curved from years and years of use, but something that rattles and gives, just slightly, as the toe of my sandal comes into contact with it.

A wooden door.

I practically throw myself at it, patting it frantically with my open palms, searching desperately for a handle, a latch, a big iron key sticking out of a keyhole, ready for me to turn. I run my hands up and down, up and down, making sure I'm not missing a square inch of wood, covering it all, every bit of it, right up to the hinges on the other side.

To no avail. There's nothing here. No lock, no latch, no big wooden bar that I can lift out of its bracket.

Despair slams into me like a tidal wave. I've done so well, made it down the stairs, been brave enough to go searching in the dark for an escape route. And all for nothing. My shoulders sag; tears prick once more at my eyes. I feel overwhelmed by exhaustion and misery. No matter how much I keep telling myself that I'll be found, that I'm not going to rot away in this stupid passage, it's very hard to keep my spirits up—because down here there really isn't any light at all, not a sliver. And it smells really damp. Like a dungeon.

My legs go weak. I slide down the wall and plop onto a step, slumping forward, drawing in long breaths that are meant to calm me down but instead are coming out dangerously like sobs.

I mustn't cry, I tell myself furiously. *I'm going to be rescued, and when I am, I am* not *stumbling out of this bloody passage with my eyes all red and swollen from sobbing, looking completely pathetic. I am* not *going to let whoever locked me in here see how much it's affected me.* And because what I really want to do is curl up in a ball, hug my knees, and have a cry, I do the opposite: I sit up straight, biting my tongue to stop the tears, and lean my head against the wall behind me, tilting it up in another effort to make sure I don't cry, a trick my mum taught me. She says it's impossible to cry when you tilt your head back and look up at the ceiling.

Click. Something knocks against the stone behind my head. For a split second I think it's someone signaling to me, tapping from the other side of the wall, some other prisoner—*Yeah, or a skeleton knocking with its bony knuckles, I suppose!* I tell myself, mocking my overactive imagination.

Because of course it's not some signal, from this or the other side of the grave. It's my silver hair clip at the back of my head, which has just tapped against the stone.

And as soon as I realize that, I jump to my feet and head back up the stairs, not even bothering to feel the wall on either side of me. I was right: going upstairs in the dark is an awful lot easier than going down. Anyway, my hands are fully occupied, fumbling in my curls to undo the silver clip, feeling the shape of it, turning it over to work out how best to use it.

Of course, it's not real silver, but that doesn't matter. What's important is that it's strong, very hard to bend, and that its shape is long and narrow and pointed. It's hinged at one side, and each piece has small teeth down it to catch and hold the hair, but I don't think they're going to be a problem; they're really very small. Bracing myself, I pull the sides of the clip away from each other, exactly the opposite of how you're supposed to use it, forcing the ends to rub against the spring lever that holds them together, trying to break them apart. The teeth, the metal edges, dig into the soft flesh of my fingers; the more I pull, the more painful it becomes. I'm wincing, telling myself not to give up, but I'm beginning to get scared that I'm going to cut myself, and the two pieces are utterly refusing to break apart. I can't see in this dark why that might be. Maybe the spring's just too strong for me. But this isn't going to work. I'm not going to be able to separate them.

Okay. Plan B. I'll just have to use the whole thing. Even if it is a bit bigger than I wanted.

Taking the wide part of the clip in my hand, I work the narrowest part, the other end, into the chink of light that I can see between the stone wall and the wooden door. The thin end of the wedge. It doesn't want to go—as I thought, it's a bit too big. Furious now, determined not to be defeated, I pull up my skirt, raise my foot, put my sandal sole onto the end of the clip, and kick it as hard as I can, one hand braced against the wall so I don't stagger back with the impact and fall down the staircase.

Whack! Something gives—whether it's my sandal or the clip or the door I don't know, until I straighten up again and see, triumphantly, that I've forced the door to yield a fraction. The clip is definitely deeper into the crack between the door and the wall. I feel around, making absolutely sure I have it in the right place: yes, I do. The door has actually splintered around the clip. I can feel the chips of wood coming loose, and smile as I lift my foot again and repeat the maneuver, slamming kicks into the clip once, twice, till it's halfway in. Far enough for what I want to achieve, probably as far as it'll go.

Then I bend over, take hold of the clip with both hands, and wobble it up and down, up and down, feeling for the metal latch on the other side. I've driven the clip in just below it; if I manage to get enough traction, then I'll be able to lift the latch with it, please God—lift it out of its socket and up, enough so I can push open this bloody door.

The clip stops in its upward movement. I've found the latch. My heart soars. Carefully now, going slowly to get the right angle, I keep going, putting what feels like all my weight on the clip now, forcing it down against the wood of the door and the extra heft of the latch that's resting on it, levering the latch higher and higher, hopefully high enough for it to clear the socket and fall free—

And then everything seems to happen at once. The latch lifts off the end of the clip; I hope with everything I have that it hasn't fallen back into its socket but is hanging free. I'm about to push the door when it flies open, light streaming in, blinding me; I stagger, losing my balance, because most of my body weight has been shifted forward. I tumble forward into the corridor, the clip dropping from my hands.

What just happened? I think frantically. The next second, I crash straight into something. Some*one*. Hands grab my upper arms as I collide with a lean body. I'm steadied, and I blink frantically, my eyes trying to accustom themselves to daylight after being in the dark for so long.

I don't know who I expected to see, but it wasn't him.

It's Luca. Hair falling over his face, his blue eyes staring down at me, his handsome features expressing complete disbelief.

Kissing Is Nothing at All

"Violetta!" Luca exclaims. *"Ma che cosa—che cazzo ci facevi—"* He catches himself and stops, his lips parted, before starting again in a language I have more hope of understanding. "What is happening? Why are you in the *passaggio segreto?"*

He looks at me incredulously. My hair's falling down again, and I'm sure I must look completely manic with shock.

"Someone locked me in there," I say weakly. It sounds so mad, as if I'm the stupid heroine of a horror film, the idiot who went downstairs to the basement—when everyone knows that's *exactly* what you never do—and fell into the trap the villainess set for her. "They left the door open, and when I went in, they shut it and latched it."

"Cosa?" His eyes go even wider. "But no, I have not

understood you. It is not possible that—" He looks me up and down. "*Vieni qua,*" he says. "Come here." He turns me, guiding me along the corridor a few steps to a window seat set back in the paneling, with a faded old velvet cushion. He must have realized how near to collapse I was, because I crumple onto it almost bonelessly, more grateful for soft fabric beneath me and the daylight filtering in behind me than I can say.

Luca sits down next to me; the seat isn't that wide, and his thigh presses against mine as he positions himself so we're facing each other.

"You will not hit me again?" he asks solemnly, and I writhe in shame at the memory.

"I'm really sorry about that," I mumble. "I shouldn't have slapped you."

"It was not nice," he says with that half smile that twists his mouth with a hint of cynicism. "But I was not nice, either."

"No, you weren't," I blurt out. "But I still shouldn't have—"

"Then we agree," he says. "Sometimes I am not very nice. I am sorry too."

He reaches one hand out, and I think he's going to stroke my hair or pull me toward him; my breath catches in my throat. What he actually does is pick a big, gray, dusty cobweb off my hair, show it to me, his mouth quirking further in amusement, and then drop it to the floor, dusting off his hands.

"It did not suit you," he says seriously. "*Meglio senza.* Better without."

"Ugh! Are there any more?"

He tilts his head and surveys me.

"No," he says. "No more *ragnatele*. So please, tell me again why you were in that place."

"I told you!" I say. "I lost the group and tried to catch up. Someone left the door open, and when I went down the stairs, they shut the door and turned off the light!"

I glance back to the door, hanging open still; beside it I see a small brass plate, half concealed by a painting, that is clearly the light switch.

"But it is not possible," Luca says, frowning. "It is not possible that someone does that."

"How else could I get shut in there?" I ask, cross now. "You saw that I was locked in! I had to put my hair clip into the doorjamb and lift the latch to get myself out!"

"No," he says infuriatingly. "*I* get *you* out. I come down the corridor and I see movement on the door to the passage, very strange. Why is it moving like that? I ask myself. Is there a ghost? So I go up and I see the *serratura*—"

"Latch?"

"Latch—it is going up and down—"

"Just up! I was lifting it up!"

"And so I unlock it and open the door and an English girl falls into my arms." He shrugs. "It is a surprise, but a nice one."

"I unlocked it!" I protest.

"No," he says firmly. "I unlock it. I save you."

"I didn't need you!" I snap. "I was doing it by myself—I didn't need you to come along!"

"*Bene*," he says, taking my hand and lifting it to his lips,

182

a gesture so unexpected that I goggle at him, wide-eyed, my mouth gaping very unattractively as he kisses my fingertips. "You are very modern. You save yourself. We agree this story."

"Because it's true!" Narrowing my eyes, I snatch my hand back from him. "Don't make fun of me!"

"But—" Luca stops, and looks as if he's thinking something over. His face is too close for me to be comfortable looking directly at him, so I drop my gaze down his body, to the hand he dropped to his lap when I pulled mine away.

I drag my gaze away so I'm looking at my own feet in their red sandals. Leather straps crisscross my toes. My toenails, mercifully, are freshly painted, red to match the sandals. Having the beautifully groomed Paige and Kendra around is definitely raising my game.

The silence drags on, and I can't bear it. Any moment, the other girls and Catia and the principessa will come back, looking for me, and I'll just be sitting here with Luca, not saying a word. Which would be ridiculous. Almost at random, I hear myself say:

"I thought you were in Florence. Elisa said you were."

"I was in Firenze, *si*," he says absently. "But Elisa sends me an SMS to say she is here, visiting my mother and Signora Cerboni. So I come back early."

Did he come back for Elisa, or to see me? Did he realize that if Catia was here, we all were too? I'm dying to ask, but it would sound so flirtatious that I'm not brave enough.

"An SMS?" I ask instead. "What's that?"

He mimes texting on a phone. "*Un messaggio*," he says.

"Oh, a text."

He nods. "So when I come back, I go through the kitchen, and there is Maria making a tray with drinks and biscotti for all of you, and she says '*Guarda*, Luca, there is a girl here with Catia Cerboni who looks just like your aunt Monica, *figuriamoci*.' She says my mother was surprised, because you look like my family."

"Did you think that when you saw me?" I ask but he doesn't answer. Then I add, "*You* don't. Not your dad's family, anyway." And then I worry he'll be offended, but he smiles instead.

"I know," he says. "My mother is from the north, from the Veneto. In the north people look more like me. Taller, more pale, blue eyes. I am just like my *nonno*, my grandfather. That makes him happy. But you—" He shrugs again. "I say to you before you look like an Italian girl. I did not think you look like my aunt Monica."

He stares at me, and it's the hardest thing in the world not to blush or look down. Especially because his expression is so pensive, as if he's considering some complicated mathematical equation.

"You do not look like my cousins, though," he says. "Monica's children are very different from you."

"Do they live near here?" I ask.

"*Si e non.*" He pulls a face. "Yes and no. They live in Firenze with their father. My aunt Monica, she runs away years ago with an *amante*, a lover. She is maybe in Thailand, we think."

"You don't know?" I ask, horrified, and he shakes his head. A lock of hair falls over his forehead, and he reaches his hand up to push it back, the one with the silver rings on it. His black eyebrows wing up at the outer corners, straight lines, as if drawn with a ruler; I noticed that before, but by daylight everything seems clearer.

"She does not come back to see her own children," he says. "It's very sad."

"Oh, that's awful," I say. "My dad's living in Hong Kong now, but he rings me, and emails me, and we Skype, and I see him at least once a year. It would be horrible if he just disappeared."

"Your parents are divorced?" Luca asks, and I nod.

"I live in London with my mother."

"You are lucky," he says unexpectedly, and there's an edge of bitterness in his voice that takes me aback. "I wish my mother and my father were divorced. But here it is not very common. Not for *gente come noi*. People like us. For a long time, divorce in Italy is very difficult, because of the Church. Now it is more easy, but still my mother will not do it."

"You want her to?" I ask, puzzled.

He jumps to his feet. "Yes," he says, biting out the word. "Of course. My father, he lives in Milan, in the family palazzo. He pretends to work but really he is a playboy." This last word sounds so different with his Italian accent that it takes me a while to understand it, particularly because it's so old-fashioned. "He goes to parties with models and to the Cannes Film Festival, he has many girlfriends, all young, all stupid, like the ones who dance in bikinis on television, on the news."

Girls dance in bikinis on the news? I think, completely confused, but Luca is pacing back and forth now, scowling, and I don't want to interrupt him.

"It is embarrassing," he spits out. "For my father to be like this. And he was always like this. Always there were girlfriends. *Capisci?*"

I know this means "Do you understand?" and I nod, because I do. He means that even when Luca was young, maybe even as soon as his mother and father got married, his father was never faithful.

"*Da fare schifo,*" Luca says savagely. "Disgusting." And there's an expression in his eyes that I recognize, a twist to his mouth. *After we kissed, that's how he looked,* I realize. *Just before he applauded me. He looked . . . bitter.* It makes me nervous; I inch back on the window seat, watching him, concerned that he might turn on me again as he did before.

But his mouth softens, and he says sadly:

"My poor mamma."

"That's why you want her to get divorced?" I ask carefully.

He nods. "But she won't. No woman in her family has ever been divorced. And she loves Chianti, this castello, she says she wants to stay here. She helps to run it, the vineyards. She loves to grow things. She does not like the city."

"But she could go somewhere else in Chianti," I suggest. Clearly, it appears that there's enough money to buy the principessa a lovely estate if she wanted.

Luca throws up his hands.

"*Esatto!*" he says in frustration. "This is what I say too! Ugh, *mi fa incazzare a bestia.*" He glances at me, black brows drawn tightly together over blazing blue eyes. "It makes me very angry," he says.

"*Mi fa incazzare a bestia,*" I echo, and Luca's expression

changes in a flash, from furious to open and laughing. He jumps toward me and puts one hand over my mouth.

"No!" he says, laughing. "You must not repeat! Bad words! *Bestemmie!* I must not teach you bad words!"

His fingertips are light against my lips, more a caress than a constraint. The bracelet dangles off the knobs of his wrist bones; I dart my eyes down and see that it's woven with black rubber in between the steel links.

I don't dare to move. I don't want him to stop touching me. But I can't just sit here like an idiot.

What I really want to do is kiss his hand, but I'm not brave enough for that. I wish I were.

And then Luca's hand moves, just a little, to touch my hair again. He winds his finger through one of my curls.

"*Che boccoli,*" he says, sinking again to sit down next to me on the window seat. Our knees touch. "I don't know the word in English, but my cousins have these too. Bigger, curly, like African hair. And my father. Maybe you *are* some kind of relative, Violetta-who-looks-like-Zia-Monica. A cousin. My pretty Italian cousin. You know, when I first meet you I say you look Italian."

He's leaning close to me now, and I've completely forgotten how to breathe. I glance sideways at his finger, long, elegant, very pale by contrast with my dark brown curl wrapped around it. "*Boccoli,*" he said. I must remember to look that up.

"I hope I'm not your cousin," I say simply.

"And see how dark you are."

He lets my curl fall and takes my hand, holding it up next to his, my skin much sallower.

"I am white from the north," he says. "My mother's Austrian blood. But you, the color of your skin is from the south, or at least *Centro Italia,* my pretty Italian cousin."

"I don't want to be your cousin," I say again, nearly in a whisper.

"Why? Because we have kissed?" Luca's still holding my hand, but his eyes go darker, almost cynical. Almost bitter. "A kiss means nothing. Don't you know that yet, Violetta? Kissing," he says, so close now I can feel his breath on my face, so close I can almost feel his lips against mine, "is nothing at all. . . ."

I know I should pull away. Even before anything happens, he's told me it means nothing to him. I should push back, get up, go and find the group.

But if he doesn't kiss me now, I will go insane.

Our hands twine together. Our heads move in unison, tilting fractionally. Our mouths touch, our eyes close, our breaths merge. Our bodies edge even closer on the seat, wrapping around each other.

I'm completely and utterly lost in him.

Snogging in the Broom Cupboard

I reach up, kissing him, and wind his silky hair through my hands. Despite his dismissive words, his mouth is sweet on mine, his hands warm as he traces circles on my neck with his thumbs. I melt against him, feeling like a cat purring in delight.

He's so much trouble, a voice says at the back of my mind, trying to alert me to danger. *Look at what he just said to you right before you kissed! He told you it didn't mean anything! You're an idiot if you can't take a warning!*

I should push him away. Listen to the voice. But instead I pull him closer, twist my fingers even tighter in his hair, and give myself up to this endless series of slow, drugging, hypnotic kisses.

Don't do this! entreats the voice. *He's going to make you so unhappy!*

Luca's tongue slides into my mouth, slow, drowsy, intoxicating. I hear myself make a little involuntary moaning noise, and I'd be embarrassed to my core if he didn't echo it almost immediately, his hands cupping the back of my neck, his fingers caressing my skull now, as I caressed his. It's the most delicious feeling. Everything is exploratory; everything we do seems to feel better than the last thing, which was as wonderful as I thought it was possible to feel. I run my hand around his neck to the collar of his shirt, slide my fingers under to feel the skin I can't see, impossibly smooth, and one of his hands joins mine, covering it, to move my palm even farther under his shirt, at the open neck, sliding it to cover his collarbone, his skin so warm above and below mine that I gasp, and he does too.

"Violetta," he whispers into my mouth, "*Violetta, cosa mi fai?*"

I open my eyes just a fraction, to peep, and see his are still closed, his lashes trembling long and black on his cheeks, silky as his hair. There's something thrilling about seeing him like this, so carried away, when he doesn't know I'm looking; it feels illicit, almost like spying on him.

And I'm obviously not a very good spy, because I linger too long, watching his closed eyelids, a vein pulsing in his forehead, the color in his cheeks, like a wash of pink under the smooth pale skin, like blood seen through fine china. Luca senses something, perhaps that my attention has drifted from kissing him to watching him kiss me; he pulls back, his eyes flutter open, their blue shocking against his white skin and black lashes.

"Oh!" he exclaims crossly, the sound that Italians make a lot, and is actually more like saying "O!" because there isn't an *h* in it, and their mouths round perfectly when they're saying it. "*Non è giusto! You look at me! Cattiva!*"

"What does '*cattiva*' mean?" I ask.

"Bad," he says instantly, shaking his head in disapproval. "You are bad."

Our knees are pressed tightly together; we're mirroring each other, leaning toward each other from the waist. And I stare at Luca, his face tilted at just the same angle as mine. It really is as if we're looking into a mirror, or like a film I saw where one lover visits the other in prison, and though there's a big sheet of glass between them, they place their palms in exactly the same spot on the glass, as if they're touching, the closest they can get.

"You look so sad," Luca says very softly. "*Come mai?*"

"Violet! Violet, you're not *still* looking at the portraits, are you?"

It's Kelly, calling down the corridor, but it doesn't really matter who the voice comes from; it's enough that we're not alone anymore. We jump apart as if there were an electric fence instead of that sheet of glass between us. Luca's hands shoot up to his hair, pushing it back off his face, and I can't watch, because I want to push back his hair myself so badly.

I jump up and run to retrieve my silver hair clip, which, despite what it's been through in the last half hour, is surprisingly intact and working. I have a feeling that I've read in a book about someone being caught with her hair down, and now I fully understand the expression: hair loose implies that you've been up to something you shouldn't have been doing. I twist my curls into a spiral on the back of my head and spear them through with the clip, nearly stabbing myself in the skull in my frantic haste.

Kelly's thundering along the corridor now like a charging buffalo, Kendra a short distance behind her.

"There you are!" Kendra says as they pull to a halt in front of me. They both look flustered and cross. "We were totally freaking out," she says angrily. "Where *were* you?"

And then Luca rises up from the window seat, and their expressions change so fast it would be comical if I didn't know that I'll pay for this later.

"*Ohh,*" Kelly says, clattering to a halt a few feet away, a world of understanding in her voice, and Luca, looking amused at my obvious embarrassment, flourishes her a little bow and holds out his hand.

"I am Luca di Vesperi," he says, taking hers with a debonair smile.

I expect Kelly to crumble under this charm onslaught, but I underestimated her; she's made of tougher stuff.

"Of course you are," she says dryly, looking up at him. "I heard about you. What were you doing, showing Violet the family paintings? From your lap?"

"*Kelly!*" I plead desperately as Kendra muffles a giggle.

"I do not understand everything you say," Luca says to Kelly, his blue eyes gleaming, "but I think you are funny."

"Oh." This does disarm her. She coughs gruffly. "Well, thank you. We should be getting back. Your mum and Catia are doing their nut."

"Their *nut?*" Luca looks over at Kendra, who shrugs, an elegant rise and fall of her smooth shoulders.

"Don't ask me," she says. "It's like my dad said, the UK and the States are two countries separated by the same language. Everyone's in the Gold Salon. We should head back."

I shoot ahead with Kendra. The last thing I want is to be led back, the errant foreign girl distracted by the handsome son of the house, walking next to him like I've been caught out, just to make the point further. Kelly and Luca follow, and it sounds like he's getting a lesson in English slang from her; they're chattering away, and she's making him laugh a lot. Which in turn makes me jealous. I know that's ridiculous, but it does. I am pathetic.

We head down another flight of stairs, through a huge dining room boasting a mahogany table with at least twenty high-backed chairs that looks as if the last time it was used was centuries ago, through a sitting room with masses of occasional tables, silk-buttoned chairs, and embroidered screens, so maneuvering our way through it is like running an obstacle course for debutantes. Kendra navigates us expertly into another sitting room, this one with gold brocade walls and wide french windows open onto a stone terrace. The principessa and Catia are standing by a table in the center.

Catia is livid; I recognize the signs all too well from teachers at school when a girl in their form is naughty at assembly. She's making a heroic effort to control herself— as the teachers do in the headmistress's presence—but her jaw's set taut, her eyes are narrowed, and everything about her stance tells me that I'm going to be in serious trouble when she gets me back in the form room again.

"Where have you *been*, Violet?" she snaps in a small, tight voice that's much more frightening than a full-on shout would be.

"Oh, hey!" Paige bustles in from the terrace in a blur of color. "I was looking out at the garden. I thought you might have wandered out there. You really like flowers," she says with a wide, white smile. "And, like, nature. You're always staring at it."

I'm temporarily distracted by this: clearly, Paige is a better observer than I gave her credit for. I blink hard for a second before I say to Catia and the principessa:

"I'm so sorry—I was . . ." And then I trail off, realizing that I've been so distracted by Luca that I haven't given a moment's thought to how to deal with the fact that I was locked into the secret passage by someone. My head spins. Should I tell them? Would it be better not to, in case it makes me sound like a paranoid, delusional idiot? Even Luca, I know, didn't quite believe that I had actually been locked in; I could see the disbelief in his eyes as I told him what had happened.

I pause, my breath catching in my throat, a furious debate raging inside me, but Catia and the principessa are already looking beyond me and Kendra, to Luca and Kelly.

"Oh, Luca," his mother sighs in disapproval. *"Eravamo cosi preoccupate!"*

My heart sinks: I am suddenly very sad indeed. Because I can't help but recognize in the principessa's voice a resigned familiarity, which tells me that this is not the first time Luca has been dallying with a foreign girl visiting the castello, causing a fuss, only for the two of them to be eventually ferreted out, snogging in a broom cupboard or on a balcony. Or a window seat in a corridor opposite the door to the secret passage.

He likes to kiss the girls, Elisa informed me bitchily that night at Central Park. *Every summer, the foreign girls. Very many.*

Well, maybe, I think miserably, *she wasn't being bitchy at all. Even though that's how she meant it. Maybe she was actually being helpful, despite her worst intentions. She was warning me away from him.*

And he warned me too, didn't he? Kissing is nothing at all, he said, right before we went ahead and did exactly that.

I make myself remember the rule Milly and I instituted at St. Tabby's, when girls were having boy problems and spilled them out in mind-blowing detail. *What would you advise a girl who just told you what you told us?* we would ask, and if the answer was "Forget about him," "Dump him," or "Unfriend him immediately so you can't see what he's up to and be tortured every minute of every day," then the girl would have to bite her lip and admit that yes, she knew she ought to delete his number and move on.

It's easier said than done, though. Especially after a kiss like the one we just had. For the first time I understand those girls I thought were completely feeble, the ones who cling to boys who pick them up like a toy when they want to play with them and drop them from a great height when they get bored. Milly and I had rolled our eyes and folded our arms and sworn we'd never be that needy or weak.

I swallow hard and pray for the strength not to be like that with Luca. I'm determined not to be just the latest in a long line of girl-toys he plays with over the summer.

And then, I recall her words to me at Central Park as a thought flashes into my mind like a bolt of lightning: *Elisa. Where is she? The last I saw her, she was walking off arm in arm with the principessa, as cozy as anything.* I dart a glance around the room. No Elisa in sight: she isn't lounging on a chaise longue, enjoying my embarrassment, or talking on her phone on the terrace.

So where is she?

Is she the one who shut me in the secret passage?

I snap out of my preoccupation to realize that Luca and his mother are talking in rapid-fire Italian. The principessa gasps again, turning to me, one hand raised to her chest in the universal gesture of shock and disbelief.

"This is true?" she says to me. "Luca finds you in the *passagio segreto? Ma com'è possible?*"

Well, that's certainly made the decision for me. I can't hide it now.

"When I came along to join you all, the door was open," I say, speaking slowly so she'll understand me. "I thought you had all gone down there."

"What, down a small dark little staircase?" Catia interjects in a tone so sarcastic that each word drips with acid. "Why would we do that? Ridiculous!"

My own eyes narrow into slits of anger.

"Because," I snap, "*you* said that we were going to visit the dungeons. I thought that was the way down there and I was catching up to you."

She looks really cross that I have an answer for this, rocking back a little on her heels.

"But then why couldn't you get out?" Paige asks bluntly.

I take a deep breath.

"Because someone shut the door on me," I say.

The principessa sinks into an armchair, her blue eyes wide with surprise. Catia shakes her head.

"The door just got stuck," she says. "And you panicked and couldn't push it open again."

"No, the latch was down!" I'm really angry now at being disbelieved. "Ask Luca! He came along just as I was wedging it open again!"

"I let her out," Luca says, walking to the back of his mother's chair and leaning on it with both hands. He looks at me challengingly, and stupidly, I rise to the bait.

"You did *not*," I insist. "I got out myself, using my hair clip."

"Using your—" Catia throws up her hands incredulously. "This is the craziest story I've ever heard! Donatella"—she turns to the principessa—"it's clear what really happened."

She darts a quick, meaningful glance up at Luca. Obviously, she's implying that Luca and I bumped into each other and promptly started making out, then came up with the whole secret-passage excuse so I wouldn't get in trouble. I bridle indignantly, about to launch into my own defense, when Kelly, behind Catia, raises her hand and draws a line across her own throat, signaling that I should shut up. And Kendra, next to me, nudges me hard, telling me the same thing.

Frustration and anger rise in me like bile. I can see in Catia's eyes that she isn't going to believe me, no matter how much I protest. The girls are absolutely right.

I'm just working out why when Elisa strolls into the room.

"*Luca, ciao!*" she exclaims, walking toward him with her hands out, like an actress in a very bad film. She glances all around the salon, taking in the scene, and then says in English for our benefit:

"I hear your car, so I go to look for you. But I don't find you!" She kisses him on both cheeks, her hands on his shoulders, lingering as long as she can, pressing her thin frame up against him in a way that makes me want to rip her off him and send her flying. "You get my SMS and come back early from Florence to find me! How nice!"

"*Ciao, Elisa,*" Luca says rather dryly.

When did she "go to find Luca"? I want to know. *Before or after someone locked me in the passage?*

"*Ho chiuso la porta, Luca, ne sono sicura,*" his mother says, swiveling in her chair to look up at him. "*Le ho fatto vedere il passaggio, per curiosita, e poi l'ho richiuso.*"

Luca's dark eyebrows lift a little.

"My mother says," he informs us all, "that she showed you ladies the passage in her tour of the castello, but then she is sure she closed it again."

I look quickly around at the girls. That means everyone

knew about the passage, everyone who was with Catia. Any one of them, given the opportunity, could have doubled back and opened the door as a trap for me.

But why on earth would any of them play such a nasty trick?

Catia says, flicking her hand as if she's shooing an annoying fly away from her, "The wind opened the door and then it closed it again. Violet was silly to go inside, but she was never locked in, she just panicked. *Ecco tutto.* I should have noticed she was gone before, but it is such a pleasure for me to walk around your marvelous home, Donatella, that I was distracted. There is always something beautiful here that I have not noticed before. Like the mother-of-pearl inlay on the credenza in the *salotto* upstairs. Truly magnificent."

The principessa smiles at her a little uncertainly. I'm bristling with fury at being dismissed as a hysterical idiot: I glance at Luca to see if he'll defend me, insist that the door really was latched shut, but instead, reading my thoughts, he sticks out his tongue at me, and then, keeping it stuck out, closes his white teeth on it in a brief gesture that signifies all too clearly that I should bite my tongue and not say another word.

I fume. Almost literally. I wouldn't be surprised if smoke were coming out of my ears.

"*Allora*, shall we have our *brindisi* now?" Catia suggests, and the principessa nods.

"*Luca, il campanello, per favore,*" she says to her son, and Luca crosses the room to where a long golden woven cord is hanging near a doorway, suspended from the ceiling, ending in a matching tassel. He pulls it. No sound emerges, but obviously it's not supposed to; the bell rings in a far-off part of the castello, in the servants' quarters.

Paige sighs in ecstasy.

"How *cool*," she says, directing a melting stare at Luca. "I'd *love* to live in a place like this—just pull a cord when you need someone to bring something . . ."

"It is very old and falling down," Luca says depressingly, propping his shoulders against the wall and crossing his legs at the ankles. "And it costs so much to heat, in the winter we live in one small room."

"Oh, I'm sure that's not true!" she coos.

"*Si, invece*. In the peasants' houses, they have the big fire-place," he informs her. "With the stone *panchini*—" He looks at Catia, who provides him with the word "benches."

"*Ecco*," he continues. "With the stone benches to sleep next to the fire, to stay warm. Often I say to my mother, we need them here too."

Paige giggles.

"You need an American heiress," she says teasingly. "Like in the nineteenth century in England. Kendra and I saw the miniseries. These American girls with tons of money went to England and married the dukes and earls 'cause those guys needed money to keep up their stately homes, and the girls wanted to be duchesses. Or princesses," she adds pointedly.

"Subtle, Paige," Kendra says. "Subtle like a Mack truck."

Paige giggles again. "I'm just *saying*," she points out, tossing her blond curls. "I'd *looove* to be a princess."

"There are many princes in Italy," Luca says. "And almost all of them are very poor."

"Awesome," Paige says with relish.

"We're not all this bad," Kendra says to me and Kelly in an undertone. "Honestly."

"I think she's funny," Kelly says back. "I mean, she's only saying what everyone's thinking. I sort of admire her for coming straight out with it."

"Well, you're right about one thing," Kendra observes. "She's not the only one in this room thinking she'd like to be a princess."

And she stares pointedly at Elisa, who's tugging on Luca's arm as if it were the bell cord, a pack of cigarettes in her hand; she's trying to get him to go outside to smoke with her.

Kelly snuffles a laugh of acknowledgment, and though the entire conversation is setting my nerves even more on edge, I join in. We're a group, united enough to be intimidating, and Elisa senses the three of us staring at her, judging her; she swings her head around and glares back, her dark eyes glittering.

I'm as sure as I can be of anything that it was Elisa who sneaked back and shut me into the secret passage.

Good Daughter-in-Law Material

"*Ecco, signora!*" Maria, the housekeeper, bustles into the Gold Salon carrying a beautiful gilded wooden tray, topped with small crystal stemmed glasses, a matching decanter half full of a straw-colored liquid, and two china plates of biscotti— long and angled at each end, with almonds in them, so dry you could break a tooth if you don't realize that you're supposed to dunk them in your cappuccino first to soften them.

Luca takes the tray from Maria, who flaps and protests but is clearly very pleased at his courtesy. She supervises him carrying it across the room to a round table by the window, then shoos him away to preside over it, looking at the principessa expectantly.

"*Grazie, Maria,*" the principessa says, rising to her feet, visibly more relaxed now that the afternoon's visit has returned to something approaching its normal routine. *"Allora, cantuccini e vin santo?"*

She crosses with small, ladylike steps to the table. Maria starts to pour the glasses one by one, and we line up for the principessa to hand them out to us.

"This is *vin santo* from the di Vesperi estate," Catia informs us as we each take one; they're small, the size of sherry glasses. "Literally, 'holy wine.' It is sweet and not too strong. Traditionally the *cantuccini*, which are typical biscuits of the region, are dipped into the wine and then eaten when they get a little soft."

Elisa declines the biscuit, but the rest of us take one from the plate Maria hands around. She stops in front of me, and much to my surprise and embarrassment, she reaches out with the hand not holding the plate and pinches my cheeks, one after the other.

"Bella," she mutters. *"Molto italiana, Molto tipica, come nei anni cinquanta."*

Everyone looks at me. Maria's pinch is as forceful as her grip on my shoulders was earlier.

"She says," Luca informs me, "that you are beautiful in the Italian style. Like a girl from the fifties."

"Poi c'ha un po' di carne sulle ossa," Maria adds, looking me up and down with something very like a leer. *"Non come lei. È un stecchino,"* she adds, nodding vehemently at Elisa. *"Dovresti mangiare una volta ogni tanto."*

"Ah, she says that you have some meat on your bones," Luca says, visibly amused now at my expense. "But she says Elisa is too thin and needs to eat more."

I'm as red as a tomato. That evil old dwarf just practically called me fat in front of everyone! And Elisa, of course, is enjoying this tremendously; she throws back her head and laughs theatrically.

"*Che buffa, quella vecchietta,*" she says, and then, with an equally dramatic gesture, she looks out the open window onto the terrace and points. "*Luca, guarda! Pipistrelli!*"

We all look where she's indicating; it would be against human nature not to. Dusk is falling, the sky fading to a deep mauve-blue streaked with rays of bright pink from the red sun, setting behind the castello. But it's not the beautiful sunset that Elisa is staring at, it's the small dark shapes in the air, circling around the cypresses that line the northerly approach to the castello beyond the encircling, fortified wall.

"What are they?" Kelly asks.

"Bats," Elisa informs us smugly. "Luca loves bats. They come out at this time of the evening to eat the mosquitoes. We would always watch them when we were little." She links her arm through his, a favorite technique of hers, and saunters with him out onto the terrace. He doesn't look back.

"Eww!" Kendra says, shuddering and clamping her hands on her hair, as if a swarm of bats is about to fly in and try to nest there. "I hate bats!"

"I bet you've never even seen a bat," Kelly says pragmatically. "Anyway, they don't want us. They want the mosquitoes. You heard her."

"Come outside!" Luca calls over his shoulder. "It's very lovely out here!"

Kelly and Paige need no encouragement, and both shoot

out onto the terrace. Kelly wants to watch the bats; Paige wants to try to pry Luca from Elisa, as far as I can make out.

"The bats sleep in the *cipressi*," Luca explains, his voice carrying clearly in the still night air. "Because it is dark in there, and they like the dark. And in Italy, we have the *cipressi* always by the *cimiteri*—"

"Cemeteries," Elisa translates, still clinging proprietorially to his arm.

"So people think, oh, bats love the *cimiteri*, they are very *Gotici*."

"Gothic," Elisa prompts.

"Got-ic," Luca attempts. "But really, the bats like the *cipressi*. They are not really *Gotici*. They just like the dark inside."

"Well, that's a pretty good definition of Gothic," Kelly observes, and Luca turns to her.

I step back, farther inside the salon. Watching Luca surrounded by girls, all vying for his attention, Elisa attached to him like a nasty growth that will need extensive surgery to remove, is not my idea of a fun time. I drink some *vin santo*, which is stronger than Catia made it sound, definitely stronger than normal wine; no wonder they serve it in small glasses. But it really hits the spot. It warms me all the way down my esophagus, rich and sweet. I dunk my biscuit in it, feeling a bit common—but after all, Catia said to do it— and try a bite. Wow. This certainly beats dipping it into cappuccino.

Kendra has overcome her distaste for bats and ventured out onto the terrace too, not wanting to be left out. They cluster together, heads tilted back, watching the bats loop in circles and then dart swiftly among their invisible prey, the tiny insects that come out as night begins to fall. I see why Luca enjoys watching the sight; it's hypnotic and fascinating. How often do you actually get to watch bats, let alone when they're hunting for dinner?

But my view of the back of his black head, his white-shirted shoulders, is too much for me. Barely half an hour ago my hands were in his hair, feeling how soft and silky it was. The arm that Elisa's clutching was around me, pulling me closer to him. I never knew I was a jealous person before, and I'm shocked at how primitive I feel, seeing him bantering and laughing with a bevy of girls.

Catia and the principessa have retreated to a sofa and are sitting there, heads together, chattering away in Italian, sipping their wine. There's no space for me to join them, and their body language makes it clear that they're having what my dad calls a grown-up moment. So I finish off my biscuit and my wine, making them last as long as I can, and when I really can't stand there with an empty glass any longer, I put it down on a little table and do what all the wall-flowers and gooseberries do at parties: wander around the room, pretending I'm totally absorbed in the art hanging on the walls.

Out on the terrace, I hear laughter. They're obviously all having a lovely time. And since there's absolutely no point wishing that I were out there alone with Luca—his arm wrapped around my waist, my head on his shoulder, watching the bats circle while the sun sets and the red streaks fade from the sky as it turns a deep, velvety purple and the stars begin to come out and the moon rises behind the cypresses—since there's absolutely no point in picturing that *at all*—I find an album of watercolors on a marble-topped chest of drawers at the back of the room and start to turn its pages. It's a collection of paintings of fruit and sort of general vegetation, quite old, surely nineteenth century. Apples, pomegranates, quinces, lemons, oranges, each pictured on a white background, still on a stalk with their leaves attached, like a guide to recognizing them and their foliage. The pictures are very delicate, beautifully done, fine black-ink lines sketching in all the details with simple, clean strokes that look so perfectly executed that they must be the result of years and years of practice.

Well, I'm only seventeen, I find myself thinking. *I could start now, couldn't I?*

I've managed to distract myself so successfully from Luca and his group of admiring girls that I'm startled when I hear their voices, babbling loudly and happily as they come back inside. I close the book and turn around to see Maria circling with the decanter, smiling, topping up everyone's glasses, and I retrieve my own from the side table and accept a little more.

"*Mamma, io dovrei andare,*" Luca says, crossing the salon, the girls trailing behind him as if he were a rock star and they were his groupies.

"*Oh, Luca, veramente? Torni a Firenze?*" the principessa says, her face falling.

"*No, a Gaiole. A cena con Fabrizio.*" He bends down to kiss his mother on either cheek. "I go now," he says to his little court. "I have dinner with a friend."

There's a collective sigh at the thought of Luca going.

"I was going to say," Catia responds, "you could come back with us for dinner if you liked."

The girls perk up visibly, like flowers put in fresh water. I don't. I know Luca isn't coming.

"Ah, *per carità, Catia, no!*" the principessa protests. "*Semmai, cena qui, con la sua mamma—*" She stretches out one frail hand to her son entreatingly.

I don't understand the Italian, but it's obvious that they're all fighting over him. The principessa wants Luca to have dinner here; Catia wants him to come back with us, as do all the other girls but Elisa, who wants him to carry her off in his car, treat her to a romantic dinner, and then, probably, propose. And Luca knows all of this; I glance at him, and see a complacent expression on his face as he takes his mother's hand and kisses it, a gesture that brings more sighs from Kelly, Kendra, and Paige.

Well, I'm never going to be like that with him, I promise myself. I take a step back till I'm leaning against the side of an armchair, watching the scene play out as if it had nothing to do with me. *I'm never going to be part of a group of girls all vying to catch his attention, jumping up and down, practically screaming: Look at me, Luca! Look at me! The more I see that, the farther I'll walk away from it. If Luca wants me, he'll have to come and get me.*

And if he doesn't—his loss.

Brave words, I think sarcastically: even my *vin santo* tastes a little bitter going down, probably from the acid at the back of my throat, watching Luca flirt with the girls as he kisses them all goodbye on each cheek. *Let's see if you can stick to those brave words, Violet.*

Over the rim of my glass, I catch Maria's eye. She's busying herself behind the table with the tray on it, stacking the empty plates that held biscotti. But she's looking right at me, her beady little eyes sharp and dark, and I have the strangest feeling that she knows exactly what I'm thinking.

She must have seen so much go on here, I think. Luca's dad, the playboy prince with his girlfriends . . . the principessa, visibly lonely and unhappy, but clinging on to the castello as if it were all she had left . . . a family tragedy in miniature. Maria's gaze shifts away from me, and I follow it, to Luca, who's hugging his mother goodbye; she's clinging to him too, as dramatic as if he were leaving for a month instead of just going out to dinner with a friend called Fabrizio. (I understood that much. I was listening jealously to see if he'd name a girl he was due to meet.)

Luca waits patiently while she clutches him, kisses him, pats his cheek, muttering *"mio bellissimo figlio,"* "my beautiful son," something an English boy would loathe and detest with every fiber of his being. Luca doesn't seem to mind at all: Italian boys are clearly very used to being complimented in public by their mothers. Finally he detaches himself, kisses Catia goodbye, and looks over at me.

I realize I'm between him and the main door. I actually start to slip behind the armchair, as if I need a barricade between me and Luca; I'm frightened, physically frightened, of what might happen if he kisses me in public. Not that we might become overcome with passion, nothing that silly, just that I might give myself away, cling to him like the principessa just did . . .

"Violetta," he says softly, and before I know it, he's crossed the room to me with two brief strides of his long legs.

He takes hold of my shoulders, looks down at me. I brace myself. But he doesn't kiss me at all. He just says, equally softly, "*A presto,*" releases me, and walks out of the salon.

There's silence for a long moment as we all watch him go: then, like air whizzing out of a balloon, we all deflate. No more excitement for us. The hot boy has left the building.

"Time for us all to go," Catia says. "*Andiamo, ragazze!*"

"Enjoy your dinner," Elisa says, and I don't think it's just my imagination—I think that for some reason, she's directing this at me. She looks straight at me, with a mocking gleam in her eyes. "I stay here, I will have dinner with Donatella. To keep her company."

Maria, collecting glasses, nods approvingly, and the principessa looks touchingly happy not to be dining alone.

"Nice," Kendra mutters, just low enough that Elisa can't hear. "Way to show you're good daughter-in-law material."

"*Bene, bene,*" Catia says casually, but I detect a gleam of satisfaction in her eyes; she, too, knows what Elisa's tactics are, and approves of them. With practiced efficiency, she herds us into saying our goodbyes and thanks to the principessa; we don't even bother with a goodbye to Elisa, who has turned her back on us anyway. We flood out of the house, through the huge iron gates, to the jeep. Paige is talking nonstop, a stream of near-incoherent babble about castles and princesses and just having been kissed by a prince.

I wait, during all the drive back, and all the time I'm eating the minestrone soup that's our starter at dinner, for Catia to bring up the subject of me getting stuck in the passage at the castello. Ask me if I'm okay, speculate about how it could have happened, express concern that I might have been really upset. But she doesn't mention it at all, which I find telling. We go straight to the dining room when we're back at Villa Barbiano, and I don't have any time alone with the girls to talk over what happened. I'm not even sure how much I want to tell them anyway: my head's spinning, and I'm acutely aware that I met these girls only a few days before.

The cold truth is that I'm effectively alone, surrounded by near strangers. Kelly, the girl I'm closest to, seems lovely, and we've started to bond, but I couldn't honestly call her a friend yet, not after being roommates for just a few days. Paige and Kendra are fun and good company, but I have to remember that we've been drawn closer than we would normally be by Elisa's mean behavior; without that, we might still be circling each other warily, unsure as to how much trust we can place in the hands of girls we barely know. I remember Paige and Kendra sniggering as Mum made that scene with me at Heathrow. My first impression of them was that they were snide girls, quite happy to mock someone else's public embarrassment. I put that behind me, partly because we needed to maintain a common front against Elisa, but now the memory floods back—Paige commented on it, too, when we met for the first time at Pisa airport, actually rubbing it in.

Would she do something like shut me in a secret passage for a joke, a prank? Would she want me out of the way because she's obsessed with Luca's being a prince, hoped Luca would come back from Florence, and knew he and I had spent a lot of time together in Central Park? I thought neither Kendra nor Paige saw me and Luca kissing that night—they seemed too absorbed in their own flirtations—but what if one of them did, and resented it, and tried to make me look like an idiot when we visited the Castello di Vesperi? Or what if it's both of them together?

Or am I completely and utterly overreacting? Is there something wrong with me to doubt these girls?

I should talk to Kelly about who slipped away from the group when I stayed behind in the portrait gallery, I decide. Work out who could have had the opportunity to set that trap for me.

And then I think, *But that's assuming you can trust Kelly. How do you know it wasn't her? What if Kelly's jealous of you because you're English too, but you've got more posh social skills than she has? What if she wanted to take you down a peg by shutting you in the passage and giving you a scare? It was Kelly who came to find you, leading the way. Maybe that's because she knew where you were, and wanted to let you out, be your rescuer, make sure you were really grateful to her and would take extra care helping her out in the future. . . .*

I look around the dining table as we spoon up our minestrone soup, considering each face in turn. I'm seeing each of them from a different perspective, like the moment in films where the killer is unmasked and you realize with horror that it's someone you know and like, someone you'd never suspected, someone who's swinging a shiny hatchet sharply toward your unprotected skull.

Kelly, next to me, is still flushed from the excitement of the afternoon and evening, and from the *vin santo* at the castello and the glass of red wine we've been poured with dinner. She's carefully tilting the bowl of minestrone away from her, as I'm doing, the way you're supposed to tilt your soup bowl when you're finishing the last drops. I have no idea why, but it's considered polite, and Kelly's a quick learner; she saw me do it and followed me seamlessly. She senses I'm glancing at her and flashes me a quick smile, thinking I'm checking up on her soup-drinking etiquette.

Her smile's so open and unguarded. I can't believe someone could play such a nasty trick on me and smile at me like that. I look across the table, at Paige, whose big brown eyes are wide, her mascaraed lashes and dark brown eye pencil making them look huge; I can practically see the white all around her irises as she rattles on about the castello, the bats, the history, being in a real *castle* with a real *prince*, or at least a prince-in-waiting; she's been talking nonstop for so long it's like background music now, almost relaxing. But is Paige cleverer than she seems? Playing the dumb blonde could be a really good technique, not just to charm the boys, but also to make sure people underestimate you, so you can get away with things for which you'd otherwise be blamed.

Kendra, sitting opposite Kelly, is quite the opposite of the dumb blonde. She's sharp as a whip and cool as a cucumber. I doubt that Kendra's ever been underestimated in her life. Which is why I find it very hard to believe that Kendra would have done something as clumsy as shut me in a secret passage, running the risk of being caught as she locked me in. It doesn't seem to fit; if Kendra wanted to sabotage someone, I think she'd do something much more subtle. And much more effective.

And then I look at Catia, sitting at the head of the table, poised as always, with her streaked blond hair, her dark red lipstick, her big gold hoop earrings dangling almost to her shoulders. I simply can't see Catia making an excuse, slipping away from the principessa, pulling open that door, waiting behind it for me to come along, and then locking me inside the passage. It seems impossible. And why would she do something like that to one of her paying guests?

Because she wants Elisa to start dating Luca, says a sharp little voice inside my head. *And Elisa told her that you kissed Luca at Central Park. Daughters come first, way before paying guests. . . .*

My head's spinning. And not just from all this frenzied speculation. The room's going in and out of focus, and I'm finding it hard to breathe. My spoon clatters onto my soup plate, and I put both hands on the table to help me balance, telling myself I'm just having a moment of dizziness, overexcitement. My eyes close, because it's too much effort to keep them open. I slump back against the back of my chair, my muscles slackening.

I just need to rest, I tell myself. *I'm really tired for some reason . . . really, really tired. . . .*

And then an awful surge of nausea rises up inside me, jerking spasms in my chest. Unmistakable. Despite the weakness in my muscles, I manage to push myself up to my feet and stumble out of the dining room in the direction of the downstairs loo. I barely have time to make it there before I'm heaving into the bowl; I didn't have time to put the seat up first, and I have to contort my body extra-hard to get my face twisted over the water. The vomit sprays out of my mouth. I taste the *vin santo*, sour now with stomach acid, and another heave of vomiting is extreme. I start to cry in sheer misery and helplessness, fumbling for the toilet paper, trying desperately to wipe myself clean.

People are crowding behind me now, exclaiming in horror and concern. Someone—Kelly, I think—kneels next to me and holds back my hair. Voices rise around me, but I can't make out individual ones or what they're saying; I'm too feeble, too dizzy. Eventually I stop throwing up, because there literally isn't anything more in my poor abused stomach, and they wipe my mouth with a damp cloth and try to help me to my feet, but my legs won't hold me up, and I collapse again. Someone exclaims about my lips: they're blue, apparently.

That can't be good, I think. *Blue lips. Someone should probably call a doctor.* But I'm so dozy now, so knocked out by whatever's happening to me, that I can't really panic the way I suppose I should, or register much beyond whatever my body's decided to do next. Right now, that's lying down on the floor. The tiles are cool under my cheek. The lights are really bright, but I've closed my eyes now. I can rest. They've flushed the loo and the worst of the smell has gone. My stomach hurts, though, and I can barely breathe.

Someone's shaking my shoulders, yelling at me to wake up, but I'm a very long way away, as limp as a corpse, and I don't want to wake up anyway, because my stomach's really hurting now and I sense that the more conscious I am, the more pain I'll be in. *Leave me alone*, I say inside my head. *Leave me alone, I just want to go to sleep. . . .*

And despite the bright light in the ceiling directly overhead bouncing off the shiny white bathroom tiles, that's what I do. I flop forward onto whoever's shaking me, like a giant rag doll, and pass out as if there were a bottleful of sleeping pills dissolved into the minestrone I just ate.

Coffins and Entombed Nuns

Maybe I'm dead.

The thought is not as scary as it probably should be. I'm so calm, so comfortable. The coffin lining is soft beneath me, and it's fairly roomy; I'm touching the side with my right shoulder, but that's okay. I don't feel cramped. Of course, it's pitch-black, but that's strangely comforting. I roll over and realize there's a pillow under my head. *How very nice of them to put a pillow in my coffin. Really thoughtful.*

Memories of vampire and zombie books I've read trickle slowly through my mind, people waking up in coffins, screaming their heads off as they realize they've been buried alive, pounding at the lids, clawing their way out to the surface. *Honestly,* I think, yawning as I cuddle into the pillow.

Silly them. When it's so lovely and cozy in mine. I could sleep in here happily for the rest of my life. . . . No, wait a minute . . . not the rest of my life, that's obviously wrong. . . .

The other thing that's wrong is that when I yawned just now, my throat hurt. Really, really badly. Like if I coughed, it would be so painful I'd think my head was coming off. And clearly, when you're dead, you don't feel any pain.

So maybe I'm not dead after all.

I am obviously very dozy, because that thought is not as comforting as you'd expect.

I swallow. Ow. My throat's as sore as if someone strangled me till I passed out. Now, that would be Gothic. Or serial-killer-ish. *Perhaps*, I reflect, *I read too many novels.* The pain in my throat reminds me vividly of the events of what was probably last night, because it feels as if I've been sleeping for a while.

No one's hovering at my bedside; no one's coming in to bother me. This is lovely. Either it's still the middle of the night, or I've just been left to sleep after my pukefest of yesterday evening. I shudder as I remember it. You can tell yourself as much as you like that you can't help it if you start to vom, that it's just something your body does over which you have no control, that last night you weren't chucking up minestrone because you'd been an idiot and drunk too much, that it wasn't your fault in any way. You can keep saying that, and I do, but in the end it comes down to the fact that everyone else in the Villa Barbiano saw me sobbing on the floor of the downstairs loo with puke everywhere.

At least Elisa wasn't there, I think, clinging to this one little piece of consolation. *At least she didn't see me like that. She'd probably have taken pictures on her phone and shared them with everyone she knows. Sent them to Luca, even.*

I bury my face in the pillow with embarrassment. Why did I ever wake up? I should just go back to sleep, for days and days, and by the time I do eventually emerge from my room, so much time will have passed that everyone will have forgotten all about it. . . .

My stomach's churning as I remember last night. *It can't have been something in the soup that made me puke like that. I was really, really sick, and no one else was.*

Unless they got sick afterward, of course.

And it couldn't have been the biscotti and *vin santo*, because we all had that, too. From the same plate, and the same decanter.

Okay, now I'm definitely not going to get back to sleep. My brain's spinning.

How on earth did I get that sick?

Oh God, and what if Catia called my mum to tell her what happened? She's probably already jumped on a plane to come and get me!

Shoving the pillow behind me, against the wall, I haul myself slowly to a sitting position. It hurts, more than I had expected. It's not just my throat that's sore. My esophagus aches all the way down to my stomach, which is equally painful. It's as if all that violent throwing up, all those cramps, have bruised the entire inside of what my biology teacher would have called my upper digestive tract. I'm thirsty; I want some water, but I have the unpleasant feeling that drinking anything, swallowing anything, is going to hurt a lot.

Still, I'm awake now, and restless. *No wonder I was happier when I thought I was dead.* I pull the sheet off my legs and swing them slowly over the edge of the bed. I heave myself to my feet, and gasp, because standing up sends tremors through my body, and my stomach really is very sore indeed. Patting the wall with my hands, I work my way along it to the window, and the shutters, which I unlatch. Light pours in, white and clear: I squeeze my eyes shut, letting the sunlight filter through my eyelids, getting myself accustomed to daylight.

Well, it's definitely not the middle of the night.

I look down, opening my eyes gradually, and see that I'm wearing a nightie. Someone undressed me, took off my stinky vomitty dress and my underwear, and put a nightie on me while I was unconscious. Somehow, that realization is particularly hard to bear, the thought of my naked body flopping around, all my squishy bits on full display as someone—Catia? Kelly?—pulled off my bra and knickers. The humiliation just never stops. I stand there biting my lip, feeling increasingly thirsty and miserable, holding on to the side of the shutter for support, wondering whether I should just follow my first idea and stay in bed for days until everyone's forgotten all about the events of last night.

The bedroom door opens: Kelly's standing there.

"You're up!" she exclaims. "Wow! Great! How are you feeling?"

"Pretty awful," I say, trying very hard not to cry.

"I bet! Do you need the loo?"

I think about it and eventually shake my head.

"You haven't got much liquid in you, I suppose," she says, considering this. "It's all come out already. Ooh, I should get you a glass of water. The doctor said you should be drinking fluids when you woke up. And when you keep that down, you're supposed to have yogurt with salt in it to balance your tummy out again."

I nod. She goes off to the bathroom and by the time she returns, I've sat back down on my bed again, feeling wobbly at the knees. She hands me the water. I sip it slowly, wincing with every swallow, as she says earnestly:

"Luckily, the doctor came really fast. He lives down in the village and Catia got hold of him right away. He said it was lucky too. You were really sick. He pumped your stomach, to make sure you'd thrown everything up, and then he washed you out with the stomach pump."

I raise my hand to my neck, touching the band of muscle there. No wonder it feels bruised.

"They put a tube down my throat," I say, realizing what must have happened.

"It was *so* awful," Kelly says, shivering. "You were completely out of it, which was the only good thing. I helped. Well, I was holding back your hair and stuff. And Benedetta was brilliant."

I can believe that. Benedetta is the cook. Earlier this week she had us learning how to make pasta dough. She doesn't speak a word of English and rattles away in Italian so fast that sometimes I literally cannot distinguish a single word, but the cooking demonstration was tons of fun.

"It was really important the doc got there in time," Kelly's saying. "You have to do the pumping and washing thing almost straight after people have eaten whatever bad stuff that's poisoned them for it to work. Otherwise, you'd have had to go to the hospital."

"I don't understand what did it," I say, handing her back the empty glass.

"Well"—she frowns deeply, looking very concerned—"that's it, isn't it? That's the problem. Benedetta's in a right state. She was really worried that it was something she made that gave you food poisoning."

I shake my head.

"It can't have been," I say. "We all had the minestrone. We all had bread from the same basket and grated cheese from the same big piece. I didn't have anything here that anyone else didn't eat."

"I *know*." Kelly grimaces. "The doctor went through everything you ate here with Catia and Benedetta. But he thinks you can't have had whatever made you sick long before you started upchucking."

"Lunch was ages before," I say. "It can't have been that."

"No." She turns the glass in her hands. "We all had the biscotti and *vin santo* at the castello. . . ."

She's still looking down at the glass, revolving it slowly between her palms.

"Look," I ask nervously. "Do you happen to know if Catia rang my mum at all?"

A couple of hours later, the doctor has been summoned to check me out, given me the all-clear, and gone again. Catia has flapped around me like a worried hen; she *did* ring my mum to say I had food poisoning, and got the full force of Mum's panicked maternal instincts. I can't help smiling a bit—even though she told Mum I'd been resting after the doctor came to pump me out, and that he'd said to let me sleep it off, Mum's been calling practically every hour. Catia looks very, very tired. She brought me the house phone and practically dialed the number for me, desperate to give Mum the reassurance she needs that I'm alive and well.

I was dreading the call—Mum panicking about me is always really exhausting—but the good part is that I barely had to talk at all. Mum's flapping made Catia's look like amateur hour; she rattled on for half an hour, barely pausing to take a breath. I put the phone on speaker, propped it on a pillow on my chest, and lay back as her voice streamed out, sympathizing, worrying, suggesting ways to rehydrate myself, reminiscing about a trip to Jamaica in her modeling days when she ate dodgy shellfish and was the sickest she'd ever been in her life, and the stylist and the photographer were sick too and they had to postpone the shoot for a couple of days because they were all weak as kittens afterward. Mum had looked positively gaunt in the photos because of all the weight she'd lost throwing up and, you know, the other end too. They hadn't had retouching in those days and they could barely use the photos because she looked like a skeleton—that was before being so thin was all the rage, of course.

She'd been on the verge of flying out to see me—she'd practically booked a ticket to Pisa for the first flight out this morning—but then she'd thought, No, Violet wouldn't want me to make a fuss—I give a particularly enthusiastic murmur of agreement at that bit—but she's been on *tenterhooks,* and *so* relieved the doctor's saying I'm okay, but I must make sure to rest up . . . unless I want her to come and get me and take me home to recover? There's a flight this evening; she could easily make that. She'd just throw some clothes in a bag. . . .

That's the only point where I need to stir myself and reassure her that no, I'm fine, I really am, that whatever I ate is long gone now, that I'll be back to my studies here tomorrow, and please, Mum, *please* don't make too much of a fuss. It takes a long time to keep repeating that so she can hear it and take it in. But after thirty minutes of pleading with her not to come over, let alone take me back home, she runs down like a toy with its batteries slowly going dead. I mumble what feels like endless "I love you's" and even more "I miss you's," say "I'm fine" over and over again, and finally stab the red Off button, shove the pillow under my head, and slump back, exhausted.

I'm *so* not ready to go back to London.

"Hey," Kelly says, pushing open our bedroom door. Her laptop's tucked under her arm, and she's carrying a bowl, which she places on my bedside table. "Here's the yogurt with salt in it. Benedetta says it's just what you need to get your stomach lining back to normal. She went down to the village and got special probiotic stuff for you first thing this morning."

I wrinkle my nose.

"No, really," she says seriously, putting the laptop on her bed. "I tried some. It's not bad at all. She says once you get that down and digested, she's making you some lunch *in bianco.* That means 'white,' and it's what you eat here when you have a bad tummy. It's, like, rice that's boiled with veggies, no fat or anything. Oh bollocks, what did I say?"

Because I've involuntarily retched at the mention of vegetables.

"It's just, when I was throwing up," I say feebly, "there were all these little bits of carrot and celery from the minestrone coming out of my nose. I don't think I can face veggies for a little while. . . ."

"I'll pick them out myself," Kelly offers, sitting down on her bed, facing me. "Before I bring it up."

I'm weak and feeble, and tears of gratitude actually prick at my eyes when she says this. Dutifully, I reach for the yogurt bowl and put a spoonful into my mouth. My body is very disoriented by the violence of my pukefest. I don't know whether I'm hungry or thirsty, or if I need the loo. So I have no idea how it's going to react to the yogurt. Kelly watches me alertly as I swallow the first spoonful; its cold, slippery texture is very gentle on my sore throat, and the taste isn't bad at all—she was right. We both sit there for a few minutes as the yogurt slides down to my stomach, waiting to see if it's going to come right up again. But it doesn't. It feels good, actually.

I manage a grin for her.

"It's nice," I say. "Thank Benedetta for me."

"I tasted it first," Kelly says, watching me carefully. "You know I said I tried some."

I spoon some more yogurt into my mouth and swallow it slowly.

"Thanks," I say, just as carefully.

"I don't mean to sound paranoid," Kelly says. Her red hair's brushed back into a ponytail, and she pulls the ponytail around to one side of her neck, stroking it absentmindedly, like she's concentrating hard on what she's about to say. "But I think you should be careful about what you eat and drink from now on. You were *really* sick. And no one knows what caused it. I've been looking stuff up on the Net. People can eat from the same plate of mussels and clams and some of them get sick and some don't, 'cause you can get a single dodgy one. But what we all had—there's no way you could have got so sick from that."

She twists her head to look at her ponytail now, as if its ends are hypnotically fascinating.

"Unless," she adds, "someone put something in what you ate or drank."

My throat's already feeling much better; though it hurts to swallow, the yogurt is really nice and soothing. So my voice is much clearer when I say:

"Yes."

Kelly lets her ponytail go, and her eyes meet mine. They're clear hazel, framed by pale sandy lashes, and full of sharp intelligence.

"At the castello," she clarifies, making sure we're both on the same page. "Because I heard what the doctor was saying to Catia. I'm really managing to understand a lot of Italian—I've got this whole course on my MP3 player, and I've been listening and listening to it. He was saying it was something you must've just eaten." She grimaces. "'Cause, you know, it came straight back up. I mean, it didn't have time to go through you and out the other side."

I grimace too, setting the spoon back in the bowl as my stomach rumbles a bit.

"Sorry," she continues. "But I had to say it. And Benedetta thinks the same. She says whatever it was, you ate it only an hour or two before you started upchucking."

Kelly gets up and walks over to the bedroom door, which is ajar. She closes it, makes sure it's shut, and comes back and sits down on the bed again.

"Violet," she says very seriously, "I told Benedetta that your lips went blue when you were puking, and she went all funny and freaked out. She thinks there's no way this could have been an accident, and she's sure the doctor thinks so too. She says that happens when people eat yew berries. They're, like, *really* poisonous."

Very Difficult and Very Messy

"Yew berries," I echo slowly.

Kelly nods. She's watching me very closely, checking to see if I'm going to freak out at the suggestion. But actually, I'm glad that someone's put a name to what's going on. And that I'm not alone with it.

"I don't want to go home," I hear myself say. "If my mum knew this wasn't just food poisoning, she'd whip me back to London in about thirty seconds flat. And I *really* don't want to go back yet."

"I wouldn't either," Kelly says. "Not if a boy like Luca were after me."

I blush.

"He isn't really after me," I mumble.

"Violet." Kelly rolls her eyes. "I *saw* you two sitting in the window seat. I know what it looks like when two people have just been snogging, okay? You were all . . ."

I'm dying to know what she's going to say. I want to hear that Luca looked completely dazed and blown away, that he had stars in his eyes and was staring at me as if I were the most beautiful girl in the world.

I am tragic.

". . . disheveled," she concludes.

I can't help grinning, which definitely helps; at least it's a moment of light relief.

"I get that you don't want to go back to London," she says, shifting as she leans forward on the mattress. "But don't you see that the reason this happened to you is probably *because* of this whole Luca thing? Because you've made someone really jealous?" She lowers her voice. "Like Elisa! She's obviously dying to get in there and be a flipping princess! Honestly, if I thought Paige were capable of poisoning you with yew berries, she'd be at the top of my suspect list, the way she was going on yesterday."

"How do you even poison someone with yew berries?" I ask, feeling like Kelly's steps and steps ahead of me. She's obviously been doing nothing else since I got sick but talk to Benedetta and go online to research this theory of hers.

"Boil them and make a decoction," Kelly says promptly. "Just a few drops would be plenty. And there are loads of yew trees around here. I checked. It's really toxic to horses, for some reason. Hang on a sec." She grabs her laptop, flips it open, and reads: "'Symptoms include staggering gait, muscle tremors, convulsions, collapse, difficulty breathing, coldness, and eventually heart failure. Fatal poisoning in humans is very rare, only occurring after eating a lot of yew foliage. The wood is also poisonous. Some bow makers are reputed to have died from the frequent handling of the wood in their craft.'"

She looks up from the screen.

"That's Wikipedia," she says. "But the *New York Times* website had lots of other symptoms, including vomiting and blue lips."

"It feels really creepy to think of someone making this stuff," I say slowly. "You know, they'd have to have boiled up the berries, I suppose. Done it in advance."

"Exactly!" Kelly shuts the computer with a snap and pulls her legs up onto the bed, crossing them. "You couldn't just whip this stuff up in a second—you'd need time, and a place to do it, somewhere you wouldn't be seen. Violet, this is scary. I know you don't want to go home. I mean, I think you probably should, to be honest. But I do get why you don't want to."

She looks at me really seriously.

"I think it must have been in your glass of *vin santo*," she says, her Italian accent already sounding better than it did just a couple of days ago. She's a quick learner. "It would be easier to put it in liquid. Did you leave it alone at all?"

I nod. "On a side table when I was looking at this book of watercolors. Who came back in from the terrace when you were all out there? Anyone?"

Kelly's ahead of me; she's already thought this out. "*I* didn't," she says. "Kendra might've—she wandered away to the side of the terrace, and I didn't see her for a bit. I'm sure Paige was there the whole time—she was sucking up to Luca, doing all that hair-flirting she does."

Jealous as I am of anyone cozying up to Luca, I can't help sniggering at the term "hair-flirting." It's perfect.

"And Elisa?" I ask.

Kelly raises her eyebrows.

"She went back to get her cigarettes," she says. "And I remember thinking she was gone longer than you'd expect, because I thought she'd shoot right back to make sure Paige wasn't all over Luca."

I'm not surprised. Not at all.

"And earlier?" I ask. "When someone shut me in the passage?"

"Okay," Kelly says. "I thought about that, too. I was up ahead with Catia and the principessa, but Paige and Kendra were sort of dawdling behind. They could have sneaked back and done it. But they'd have had to do it together, unless one of them said she was going off to look for the loo, I suppose. I really don't see Paige going off by herself, though, do you? Or letting Kendra go off without her? She'd freak about getting lost."

I nod. That's spot-on about Paige's character: she hates to be alone. Even if she'd needed a loo, and found one, she'd probably have wanted Kendra to stand outside so she could chatter to her through the door. It's not proof of anything, but it sounds right.

"I saw Catia the whole time," Kelly's saying. "But the principessa did go off for a bit. She said she was going to check that Maria was bringing the drinks to the Gold Salon. She must have been gone about ten minutes."

My heart drops. I stare at Kelly, my mouth gaping open. "The principessa? I *totally* assumed it was Elisa," I say.

"All I'm saying is that she wasn't there the whole time on the tour," Kelly says. "And she could possibly have got up and put something in your drink without Catia seeing."

I'm speechless. This idea had never entered my head before.

"All that stuff about you looking like her husband's sister," Kelly's saying. "That was pretty strange. She definitely went on about it a lot." She pulls on her ponytail again. "Basically, if you're going to stay, you need to be really careful around Elisa. Make sure she's nowhere near anything you eat or drink. *And,*" she fixes me with a stern look, "you shouldn't go *near* the Castello di Vesperi, or the principessa, ever again. It's just not safe for you."

But that's why I'm here! I want to protest. In a deeply weird way, the entire scene at the castello yesterday, plus my poisoning, has only confirmed what I thought when I looked at that portrait in the museum in London: that there's a mystery centering on the Castello di Vesperi and the family that's lived there for centuries, a mystery of which I'm very much a part.

I'm not going to tell Kelly about the girl in the portrait. *Let her keep thinking I'm staying here just because of Luca.*

And despite the gravity of the situation, despite the fact that someone—maybe Luca's mother!—has made me very sick, I can't help smiling at the thought of Luca.

Even if the portrait didn't exist, I find myself thinking, *even if that weren't a reason in itself to be there, it'd be worth staying in Italy just for the chance to kiss Luca again.*

231

Luigi, the art teacher, holds up his brush, and we all do the same. I'm not quite sure why we're mirroring his action, but Luigi is very compelling, more than capable of making four excited girls calm down and concentrate on what he's telling us. I think it's partly because he's very serious. Either he doesn't have a sense of humor, or it's extremely well hidden. This, as I'm perfectly aware from years of a girls-only school, is a crucially important quality for male teachers. There aren't that many of them in a girls' school, and unless they look like the back of a bus, they inevitably become huge crush-objects. Little girls follow them around in packs, giggling madly, turning bright red and running away when the teacher turns to look at them; older girls wear the shortest skirts and tightest tops they can get away with, and do a lot of what Kelly calls hair-flirting. Male teachers are usually pretty good at coping with the flirting techniques: the best way to get under their skin, forge a special bond with them, is to share their sense of humor, make them laugh.

The clever girls know this; the pretty ones usually don't, because they tend to rely too much on their looks. Of course, the ones who are both clever and pretty do especially well, but that's true for everything in life.

I look over at Kendra, who's both clever and pretty. I'm surprised to see that she's staring, wide-eyed, at Luigi, absolutely mesmerized by him.

"We put the paint on thee brush, then thee brush on thee paper, and you see. . . ."

Luigi demonstrates, dipping his brush into black tempera paint from a tube he's mixed with water and put on his palette, then flicking the tip of the brush swiftly across the paper. "It dries almost immediately. As you pull the brush across, it is drying already. You see?"

We nod in unison. Luigi has executed a perfect stroke on the paper, like a ribbed black branch stretching from one end to the other.

"That is why watercolor is thee most deefeecult way to paint. You will cry, maybe. You weel be vairy frustrated." He smiles. "Is good for life, to learn sometheeng vairy deefeecult. And one day, perhaps, if you are vairy good and try vairy hard, you will be able to do thees."

He dips the brush into the black paint again and, with a few more strokes, sketches in a few branches and twigs flowing from the main branch; then, with a deft, practiced twist of his wrist, he cleans the brush in a can of water, wipes its bristles off on the edge, loads it with red paint, and taps little flowers as plump and pretty as cherries onto the branches, seemingly at random.

He steps back: we all gasp. The picture he's just made is so simple; it looks as if it would be the easiest thing in the world to do.

"I study in Japan," Luigi says. "That is my style. I weel teach you a number of styles, but we start today weeth the most deefeecult. Today, you will all try to do thees, the tree branch with flowers. You must 'old the brush very steady. You weel make many meestakes and be vairy un'appy. Okay!" He claps his hands, making us all jump. "We begin!"

I'm excited. Only two days ago, at the castello, I was looking at watercolors, and now we're learning how to do them—even if it does include making many mistakes and being very unhappy. I was absolutely determined to make it to our first art class today, so much so that after spending the day in bed yesterday eating more yogurt and plain boiled rice, I hauled myself down to dinner to show Catia that I was okay to restart the normal daily program. Elisa, unfortunately, was there with Ilaria, oversympathizing with me in a way so exaggerated it was almost offensive. I can't believe that Catia doesn't realize what a bitch her daughter is. Every time I picked up my fork, Elisa would lean forward to make a comment:

"It's so good you have your appetite again, Violet!"
and:
"Oh, you finish *all* your pasta! You feel much better, yes! You eat everything!"

While, of course, leaving most of her own pasta on the plate. Catia was smiling approvingly at Elisa, just as if she really believed the face value of all her daughter's nasty snarks. She's oblivious to Elisa's deeply unpleasant personality. *She's probably always let Elisa get away with murder, I reflect, and this is why Elisa's such a spoiled little horror.*

Around me, the other girls have all made tentative starts on their watercolors. We're in a converted barn in the gardens of the villa, big skylights set into the roof, so light pours down, clear and white, onto the equally big trestle table in front of us. Catia runs art courses at Villa Barbiano when she isn't hosting summer schools, and the barn is done up as a full art studio, with canvases propped against walls, easels stacked at the far end, even a plinth for a model to sit on. There's a huge stainless-steel sink for washing up; a long built-in marble shelf running the whole length of one side holds a dizzying array of paint tubes, acrylics and oils, paintbrushes, and wooden palettes, all battered and paint-stained.

I look down at my own palette. It's metal, because, as Luigi explained, wood is absorbent, and the water-based tempera would just soak into it. I have black mixed into one of the dips in the palette, and pale pink in another. Inspired by Luigi's Japanese-style painting, I have the idea of trying to do a cherry-blossom branch.

I pick up my brush and dip it into the black; just as I'm drawing it across the top sheet of paper, Kelly, next to me, rips her first attempt off with a deep groan of disgust, and the sound makes me jerk. Just a little, but more than enough; to my dismay, the straight line I'm trying to paint wobbles and bends the way only the weirdest, most deformed branch would do in real life. Thinking fast, I don't fight it. Instead, I follow the bend, tail it off as best I can, lift the brush, and then add another line, continuing the original branch. I don't think it looks brilliant, but I've sort of saved it, and before I can lose my nerve, I take just a little black paint, the way Luigi did, on the very tip of the brush, and sketch in some twigs coming off the branches.

He's right; the paint dries almost before you've taken the brush off the paper. It's a terrifying pressure to be working under. Around me, I hear tuts of exasperation, sighs of annoyance, more paper ripping off the sketch blocks, but I'm in a kind of zone now and I tune the noises out. At least the speed with which the tempera dries means that I don't have to wait for the black to set before I start painting the blossoms. If I stop, I *will* lose my nerve. I know that instinctively. So, barely breathing, heart pounding, I clean my brush, clouding the water with an inky black swirl, dip it into the pale pink, and dot blossoms on the twigs. I can't picture cherry blossoms in my mind, see exactly what they look like, but when I've done them, they look unfinished somehow. Bare.

Quick. Think fast. What does it need?

There's some green in Kelly's palette, next to me. Kelly isn't painting at the moment; she's at the sink, chucking out the water in her can, having already used several colors and made the water too murky. She took a different approach from mine and mixed up loads of colors before she started; along with the green, which is bright and grassy, there's an equally bright yellow on her palette. I wash my brush one more time and dip a bare three millimeters of the tip into the green, dotting miniature centers onto each blossom. Then I wash it one more time and dot tiny yellow circles overlapping the green ones, and add a light wash of yellow to one of the weird black branches. I think I've added depth, but I'm not really sure.

Stop now, the voice says firmly. *Now. Don't touch it any more.*

I step back, breathing normally again, and look at my sheet of paper.

It really isn't very good. Not when I compare it to Luigi's, which he's propped up at the end of the trestle table.

But for a first attempt, I honestly don't think it's that bad, either.

I look around at the other girls' sketchbooks. Kendra's got a decent-looking branch, but only after numerous tries, while Paige and Kelly have a lot of crumpled-up sheets at their feet and dejected expressions on their faces.

"I *suck* at this," Paige sighs.

"Stick to flower arranging," Kendra suggests, frowning hard as she dabs some bright red flowers onto her branches.

"Oh, hey," Paige says gloomily to Kelly, "you can't be good at everything, right?"

"I'm *rubbish* at everything," Kelly says, grimacing.

"Oh, shut *up!*" Paige waves dismissively at her. "You did an okay bouquet, you're really good at wine tasting, and your Italian's the best of all of us. I hate when girls put themselves down. Kendra's mom's always lecturing us on that—she says women should always be confident. She's really smart. She's a research scientist at a global pharma company, and Kendra's dad is too. Major brainboxes."

"*Paige.*" Kendra's voice has an edge. "Don't."

Paige pulls a comic face. "Kendra doesn't like it when people know what her folks do, 'cause they think that it's, you know, Big Pharma making drugs too expensive for poor people. But your mom's doing all this really cool stuff, Kendra!" She swivels to us. "Really complicated, like herbal remedies, but it costs gazillions in research. It's not all animal experiments."

"*Paige!*" Kendra snaps.

"Sorry!" Paige mimes zipping her lips, and then promptly continues:

"My mom doesn't do anything. And my dad basically plays a lot of tennis at the club. Kendra's parents are regular grown-ups, so when her mom tells me what to do and what not to do I kind of like it."

"You wouldn't if you had it all day long," Kendra says sourly. "My mom expects daily emails telling her what we've learned and what I'm going to put on my college applications. She never lets up. It's all right for you, Paige. You just want to go to Miami and party. I'm destined for Ivy or death."

Paige nods. "Yep, I wanna go to college in Miami," she explains to me and Kelly. "Big party school; great weather."

"I can't even *imagine* what my mom would do if I went to college anywhere but New England," Kendra says, shuddering. Just then, Luigi interrupts:

"Okay, *basta chiaccherare!* You have tried to paint, and I let you talk because I know it ees deefeecult. But now, we look at what you have done."

We fall silent immediately, recalled to order. It doesn't hurt that Luigi is very good-looking in a grown-up way. Unlike the tall, slim, almost lanky boys we've met so far, Luigi is short and stocky, with a hairy chest (you can't fail to notice the tight dark curls of hair poking out from the neck of his denim shirt); equally hairy, muscly forearms; and a strong, bullish neck.

And though he's a bit too manly-looking for my tastes, he's obviously exactly what Kendra likes. As soon as he spoke, her head whipped around and her huge slanted dark eyes went dewy; she's staring at him with her head tilted to one side. I doubt she's listening to a word he's saying. She's just watching his full lips move as he talks.

"Who does not like to paint the watercolors?" he asks.

Paige and Kelly's hands shoot up.

"*Bene,*" he says, shrugging in a way that would be really

238

rude in Britain, but somehow in Italy isn't dismissive. "You may try the oil paints. They are easier. But you, and you?" He looks at me and Kendra. "I begin looking at what you have done."

He walks around to stand behind Kendra.

"*Allora,*" he says, looking at her branch and blossoms. "A good start." He nods. "There is confidence here. *Bene.* We work on the technique."

Kendra preens as he walks around the table toward me.

"*Eccecente,*" Luigi says, his bushy brows rising to mingle with his dark ringlets. "You have done thees before?"

"No," I say, my heart shooting up into my mouth, because that question can only be positive.

"*Molto, molto bene,*" he says, nodding in short, sharp jerks of appreciation. "*Complimenti.*" He reaches out to touch the blossoms, pointing to the green and yellow centers. "Why did you do thees? Eet ees your memory of the flowers, how you have seen them?"

I shake my head.

"They just needed something," I say. "It didn't look finished without them."

"*Benissimo,*" he says, nodding sharply. "*Complimenti.* The green and the yellow, thees is vairy nice. I like. You have correct instincts."

I'm bright red with sheer happiness. I know I am, but I don't care. Kendra's scowling, and I don't care about that either.

You can have Luigi, I say to her. *Honestly. He's not my type and too old! All I want is to learn how to paint, okay?*

I'm loving everything about being in Italy, I think with a rush

239

of sheer happiness. *The countryside, the beauty, the yummy food, and most of all, learning to paint. Oh, but then—Luca. Luca Luca Luca . . .*

But I realize to my surprise that while I was painting, I didn't think about Luca at all, not once. I was completely absorbed; I could do it all day long. I absolutely love it.

I so don't want to go home.

After all, Kelly and I have no proof I was poisoned, I tell myself firmly. *It could have been just a fluke. A reaction to something, a bout of nasty food poisoning. I'll be careful what I eat and drink from now on.*

But Kelly's probably right, I think, wincing. *From now on, maybe I should stay away from the Castello di Vesperi. . . .*

Something Out of a Fairy Tale

"Par-*tee*! Par-*tee*!"

Paige clatters downstairs, whooping happily, all hair and tan and teeth, looking as if she's come straight out of a Southern California reality show. Her cork-soled wedges make her legs seem endless, as do her white short shorts. I always thought you had to be really thin to wear shorts like that, but Paige isn't, and she totally makes them work. Mind you, the glorious American tan helps too. I've been sunbathing, but it'll take me some time to get as lovely and golden as Paige is.

"*Madonna santa,*" Leonardo says devoutly, goggling at Paige.

"*Bellissima,*" Andrea agrees. He looks around at the rest

of us girls, all clustered in the hall waiting for Paige to take out her hot rollers and get herself downstairs, and smiles at us.

"*Bellissime tutte,*" he continues. "You are all beautiful."

Even Kendra, who's so cool and poised, can't help looking smug at this flattery; Kelly and I positively coo with pleasure. I don't think I've ever been called beautiful by a boy in my life. It's definitely not an English-guy thing; in London, we pride ourselves on our irony and sarcasm. You're lucky if you even get a backhanded compliment from a boy. "Your hair doesn't look terrible today"—that kind of thing.

If boys only realized how much girls love attention and compliments, I think, *they'd do it more. I mean, we absolutely melt when one of them kisses our hand, or tells us we're pretty—even beautiful. To be brutally honest, they don't even have to mean it a hundred percent. They just have to say it.*

I glance at Paige and Kendra: yep, I'm willing to bet that American boys don't throw around words like "beautiful" either. They're both glowing like hundred-watt bulbs. Kendra has sort of poofed up her hair into a big smooth chignon at the top of her head, and in her white halter dress she looks sophisticated enough to challenge Elisa for Chicest Girl at the Party.

"*Andiamo!*" Leonardo says, throwing back his dark hair from his face and holding out his hand to Paige like a medieval courtier; she giggles madly as she places hers in his and totters out of the house and down to the car, wobbling in her wedges.

"If she has a drink," Kelly mutters to me, "she's going to fall on her face in those heels. Fashion victim or what!"

"There'll be plenty of boys ready to catch her," I point out as we follow.

Andrea is escorting Kendra, catching the pale pink cardigan that's sliding off her shoulders—she's wearing it in a very Michelle O way, like a cape—and handing it back to her with a gentlemanly flourish. The pairing-off is going on already, I notice. I really hope that at least some boys at the party are interested in talking to me and Kelly. I don't know if Luca's coming—I was much too proud to ask Leonardo and Andrea if he was—and actually, I don't mind being a wallflower if, as Luca predicted, Italian boys don't generally find my looks that appealing. If Luca isn't there, I'm still going to dance and hang out and make friends.

But Kelly won't be happy to be a wallflower, I know. She's dressed up within an inch of her life, eye makeup layered on, wearing a black top and skirt that make her look slimmer, her white skin gleaming against the black. It's almost translucent, her skin; you can see a tracery of blue veins beneath its lightly freckled surface. She's geared up for this party, having missed the last one. I'm really glad she's coming along.

We pile into the jeep, which Leonardo has special permission to drive, and bounce down the driveway and through a winding maze of asphalt and dirt roads, blue signs with white lettering flashing a series of little villages called Vagliagli, Tregole, Capriolo. The white dust of the roads, kicked up by the tires of passing cars, is thick in the hedgerows, making them seem ghostly in the headlights; there are no streetlights, none at all, and around us it's completely dark, apart from the bright stars and a yellow moon that

243

hangs low in the sky, behind the branches of the oak trees on the ridges of the hills. The radio's playing loud dance music, and by the time we turn a curve and see a line of cars parked on each side of the road, angled up on the sloping tree roots, my heart's surging with anticipation. I *love* parties.

Leonardo drives the jeep right up onto the bank, at the end of the line of parked cars, going so high that the jeep tilts and we all scream, scared and thrilled by what feels like the imminent danger of tipping over. He cranks up the handbrake, turns off the engine, and we literally tumble out the road side of the jeep, because the higher side is blocked by a tangle of brush.

"Wow," I breathe as we walk along the road past the parked cars, and come to an arched gate set in a low wall, a drive slanting steeply downhill through the archway. A few Vespa scooters are leaning against the wall, by the gate-posts, and at the bottom of the drive is a small house, all its windows blazing with light, music pouring out into the dark velvety night air. It's like something out of a fairy tale. A modern fairy tale, where Hansel and Gretel don't get put into a witch's oven, but dance all night under the stars.

And maybe there'll be a prince to make the fairy tale complete, I can't help thinking, before I firmly forbid myself from specu-lating about whether Luca will be here. I'm determined not to make my happiness dependent on whether Luca's at a party or not; I've never done that before with the boys I've dated. I've managed to keep myself from being one of those pathetic girls who can't get out an entire sentence without wedging the name of their latest crush into it. But I have the horrible feeling that Luca is going to test my ability to stay strong and independent like never before.

Basta, as they say over here. Enough. I push him to the back of my mind as we pass through the gate and start picking our way down the steep gravel drive to the fairy-tale party house. Horses neigh, and we do a double take, realizing that the fences on the right of the drive enclose paddocks: one horse ambles up to the rail as we pass by, its silhouette looming huge and dark against the sky. Kelly squeaks in shock.

"It's so, big," she says nervously, shying away to put me between her and the horse. "It can't jump the fence, can it?"

"Of course not!" I say as confidently as I can, though actually I have no idea.

"I've never been that close to a horse before," she confides. "We're not big on the countryside in my family. We go to the sea. You know? Fish and chips on the pier, and the arcades. My gran likes bingo."

The horse nickers amiably and wanders away. A cat slips across the path in front of us, its eyes gleaming orange in the dark; an owl hoots in the distance, a white shadow flitting through the sky. Kelly jumps again. *Everyone's out for the night,* I think, smiling. *Looking for their own particular party.*

We're at the base of the drive now, in front of the house, which looks very small from this angle. A wooden door is slightly ajar, golden light spilling out from inside, but Leonardo and Andrea ignore it, taking a stepping-stone path down the side of the hill that curves around the house, revealing it to be built into the slope. A stone terrace, lined with lemon trees in terra-cotta pots, stretches out over the edge of the hill, with what must be, in daytime, a wonderful view of the valley below.

But no one's looking at the view tonight. Huge yellow candles are burning in shallow stone dishes, and an insistent bass is pounding at the walls of the house, forcing its way free and out into the evening air. The terrace spreads out into a rough oval, the dance floor. As at the club in Florence, there aren't that many people actually dancing. I remember Luca saying that Italians prefer to stand around and show off their outfits.

Agh! I catch myself. *Stop it with this Luca stuff! You're getting as bad as the pathetic girls you just said you despised!*

So instead, I think: *Great—more room on the dance floor for me!* and follow the boys, Paige, and Kendra as they head along the terrace and through the wide french doors, thrown open to let people flow in and out of the house. The first thing I see inside is gobsmacking.

"Is that *wine?*" Kelly exclaims.

It's a huge glass bottle of wine. No, not a bottle. A vat. A huge glass vat of wine shaped like a bottle, standing on a solid wooden table, with a plastic tube coming out of the top and finishing in a plastic spigot. The tube is hanging over the edge of the table, over a big plastic tub that's presumably there to catch the drips. Leonardo picks up the spigot and presses a lever, holding a series of plastic cups underneath it, filling them one by one, gesturing to us to come over and take a cup each.

"*Omigod!*" Paige yodels, and everyone who hadn't noticed our group before looks over and keeps looking. "It's like a *keg party!* Only with *wine!*"

I see Leonardo wincing at the loudness of her voice, and realize that it's because she's called attention to the fact that an Amazonian blonde and a stunning black girl have arrived. It's a feeding frenzy. Boys swoop in from all directions to surround Paige and Kendra, trying to cut the girl of their choice off from the rest of the group, peacocking in front of them, showing off their clothes, their command of English, their handsome smiles. Kelly and I edge back by the side of the table and stand watching the attempts of Leonardo and Andrea to wedge their way back to Paige and Kendra.

Kelly sips some wine and makes a face. "It's a bit rough."

"It isn't even in bottles," I point out. "What do you expect?" Thank goodness my stomach's back to normal; I sip some myself. "Oh, come on, it's not *that* bad. Just 'cause you've got the good palate, you're showing off now."

Kelly grins. "I am not," she says.

"Really?" I tease her.

"Okay. Maybe just a little bit," she says. But then she looks over at the group around Paige and Kendra, and her face falls. I think that it's basic envy of the sheer level of attention they're getting—envy I totally share—until I realize that her stare is fixed on one particular person; her head's turning to follow his movements.

It's Andrea. Kelly likes Andrea. Who's forged a path to Kendra's side and is doing his best to shoulder away all the other guys as he monopolizes her with quick-fire conversation.

Oh dear, I think. *Kelly doesn't stand a chance with Andrea.* My heart sinks. I want her to be happy, have a great time—

And then a stocky dark boy wheels up in front of us. He doesn't even look at me; his gaze is entirely fixed on Kelly as he says to her, smiling appreciatively:

"*O bella rossa! Come ti chiami?*"

"*Mi chiamo Kelly,*" Kelly says carefully in Italian, and I realize that he called her a "beautiful redhead." Wow. What a way to start talking to a girl. No wonder Italian boys are famous for being incredibly charming.

"*Io sono Gianbattista,*" he says, and he takes her hand, the one that isn't holding the wine cup. "*Andiamo a vedere le stelle.*"

He starts to pull her away, and she throws me a look over her shoulder, wide-eyed, brimming with incredulity, her cheeks flushed, her freckles standing out on her nose.

"I'm going outside with Gianbattista. To look at the stars," she says, trying to sound matter-of-fact. I notice that she glances over hopefully to see if Andrea's noticing that she's made a conquest.

"They don't mess around here, do they?" I say, because Gianbattista has already got her halfway to the french doors. "Have fun!"

"*Che bonona,*" another boy says, staring after Kelly as she disappears onto the terrace with her star-viewing guide. I make a mental note to remember that word and ask what it means as I take another sip of wine and look around the room, which is a big open-plan living room, a kitchen visible through an archway at the far end. I can barely see the furniture because the room is full of Italians, lounging on the sofas and flicking through coffee-table books of photographs, standing in groups waving their hands around as they talk in the loud, emphatic way that I'm coming to realize doesn't mean they're arguing or even disagreeing with each other: it's just their way of having a conversation. They're wearing white linen and blue denim. Their hair is shiny; they're well groomed; the boys are smooth-shaven or sporting designer stubble, the kind you do very carefully with an electric razor to get the effect just right; and the air smells of perfume and aftershave.

I know it's early in the party—the huge wine bottle's still almost full, and the night is young—but I'm impressed at how good everyone looks. And sober. No one's pink-faced and stumbling, no one's slurring their words. The groups of people are all mixed. It's not like the London parties I've been to, with boys at one end of the room getting drunk enough to build up the courage to talk to the girls, who are at the other end giggling and pretending to ignore them.

This is impressively grown up.

And Luca was bang-on in his assessment of me. I'm standing here alone, no one coming to talk to me. I think I look pretty nice: I did myself up in my best makeup, dark smoky eyes and red lipstick. I wish I could wear white, like Kendra, who looks amazing in it, but I'm a little too body-conscious for that. Kendra has an athlete's body, and I don't. I'm okay with not being really thin, but I'd feel like a great white whale if I wore a white outfit.

Is it a whale? I wonder. *Or a shark?* I shrug. These are the kind of questions you find yourself pondering when you're at a fantastic party, all your girlfriends have been snapped up on sight, and you're busy propping up the drinks table with your bum because no one wants to talk to you. There aren't any girls to talk to just to look busy.

Get a grip, Violet. No self-pity. And no more than one glass of wine.

I walk out onto the terrace, watching the flames burn liquid in the big shallow terra-cotta dishes. The wax inside is yellow, the color of the lemons in the little trees. *Citronella candles, I think. To keep off mosquitoes.* My grandmother burns them in Norway, by the lake, but I've never seen ones this big; the scent is sharp, a chemical citrus. I prop my elbows on the stone balcony and watch the party in full swing around me; it seems like everyone knows everyone else, but then it always does at parties when you don't know anyone at all—apart from your three girlfriends, who you can't even see because they have boys packed around them three-deep.

Something else that's different about Italian boys, I realize. If they see a girl they fancy, they go up to her and start talking. If an English boy likes you, he'll mostly avoid you not to seem too keen. Which is barking mad, of course.

Generally, things on the dating side do seem to run much better here. *Except if you look like their sister.*

Luca's voice is in my head again. Naturally, I've been scanning the terrace, but I haven't seen him.

Right, that's it. I'm not going to stand here any longer, looking like a lemon, mooning over Luca and not talking to anyone; what would he think if he came onto the terrace and I am all by myself? He'd laugh, tell me he'd been right, that he's the only one who's interested in me. I try not to lie to myself, and although I'm head over heels about Luca, I have to admit that he is not the nicest boy I've ever met in my life. The sexiest, definitely, but not the nicest. He can be sarcastic, abrasive, cynical, even mean and bitter.

And I'm not giving him the opportunity to tease me.

If there's one thing I can always do at parties, it's dance. I march across the terrace, dropping my cup in a bin as I pass, and merge into the small group of people on the dance floor. The music isn't my usual kind of thing: it's really retro, songs that were cult hits years and years ago, like sixties remixes done in a clever, knowing kind of way. But although I'm more used to modern stuff, I know exactly how to dance to this kind of music. Milly, Lily-Rose, and I love it, though it's usually just one song, dropped into the end of the evening. We look cool, because we've practiced in front of full-length mirrors for hours. Singing into hairbrushes, giggling madly.

Obviously, I don't mime singing into a hairbrush now. I'm not a complete idiot. But, like at Central Park, I may not be the girl that all the boys fancy, but I can show these Italian trendies how to dance properly.

And after a few songs, we're jumping all over the uneven stone floor, laughing, pushing our hair back, wiggling our bums, doing comic hand movements, really getting into it as the candlelight flickers over our faces. One song stops and we catch our breath, smile at each other, and wait for the next beat to start. It's so dark I can't see the faces of the other dancers in detail, just smiles, shining eyes, and tanned skin gleaming as we synchronize together.

I'm going with the music, following where it takes me. I'm getting a bit sweaty, and I don't care. Paige would say I'm working it out, and that's what it feels like: working everything out, letting everything go, all the tension and all the stress. A wacky song comes on with a chorus that goes "You can't touch this"; it has lots of stops and starts, and we find ourselves choreographing an improvised routine to it, involving freezing wherever we are when it stops, like a game of musical statues, which probably looks like the stupidest thing ever from a distance, but is hilarious when you're in the middle of it.

By the time the song finishes, I'm knackered, laughing, my feet are a bit sore, I think I need the loo, and I'm totally relaxed and happy.

"Oh, American! Nice to dance with you!" says a boy in a bad American accent, and holds up a hand to high-five me.

"English," I say, and duly high-five him.

"Ah, English!" he says, and starts to add something, when I feel myself butted in the back, a shove that sends me off balance. I tip forward a couple of steps to avoid falling over, and the boy reaches out to steady me.

One of the girls, I think. *A bit tipsy and overfriendly.* I look around rather crossly, because it was a big shove, and then I scream my head off.

Because standing right behind me, baring a terrifying set of big yellowish teeth, its face almost level with mine, is a very large gray donkey.

Drop It and Pop It

I've never been this close to a donkey before, and I don't like it one bit. Its teeth are really very large indeed, and it's staring right at me as if I'm a head of lettuce it's about to bite into. I shriek and back away, which is probably the wrong thing to do.

Now I've shown fear. The donkey will sense that, and attack me with its enormous teeth. You should never show fear. It's like with sharks—you're supposed to swim away from them slowly, not flap around frantically, because then you look weak. Like prey.

But what are you supposed to do when you're faced with a grimacing donkey that just butted you in the back?

And then the boy who steadied me laughs and reaches past me, stroking the donkey's nose.

"*Ecco Golia!*" he says, rubbing her head. "*Sei venuta per tuo vino?*"

He turns to me.

"She like wine," he says.

"You what?" I stare at him blankly, thinking I must have misheard. But he's already turned away, and I jump again, squeaking in shock, as the donkey pushes past me to follow the boy, its big gray hairy shoulder shoving me out of the way. Thank God, it—or she—has lost interest in me; I watch her lumber through the crowd. Her back has a dark cross on it: a thick black line across the shoulders, a longer one following the bony line of her spine.

The boy goes inside the french doors, and the donkey's still following, its front hooves stepping over the threshold. I watch, amazed, as someone else gently pushes her back with a hand between her eyes. Then the boy reemerges with a bowl, which he's carrying carefully because it's half full of red wine. He sets it on the flagstones by the wall of the house, and then jumps out of the way—the donkey's big head is already ducking to the bowl, her hooves shuffling dangerously close to the boy's feet.

"You see?" he says, coming back to where I'm standing on the edge of the dance area, goggling at the sight of the donkey lapping up red wine. "She like wine! Only for the party. Then she will dance with us."

He looks at my wide eyes and open mouth, and bursts out laughing.

"You not see this in England," he says, grinning at me. "*Un asina* who like Chianti."

"No!" I finally manage. "No, I've never seen that in England."

"You like Chianti?" He tilts his head to one side. "Come, we drink some too. Like Golia."

"That's her name?" I ask, following him back to the house. We pass the donkey, who's completely absorbed in licking up the wine.

"*Si, Golia.*" He pats her as he goes past: greatly daring, I do too. Her thick coat feels just like a hassock, rough and coarse.

"I am Sebastiano, and your name?" he asks.

"Violet," I say as we step over the threshold.

"Violetta!" he says, throwing his arms wide. "English girl, Italian name!"

And across the room, I see a dark head turn in our direction. That much taller than the rest of the boys, he stands out, his straight black silky hair falling over his face, his blue eyes as bright and cold as the water of the fjord next to my grandmother's summer rental cottage. I was looking for him before and couldn't see him anywhere; now that I've been distracted by dancing and a Chianti-drinking donkey, he's spotted me. His gaze flicks like a knife between me and the boy, who's at the gigantic wine bottle now, filling cups and handing me one.

"*Salute!*" Sebastiano says, touching his cup to mine, and I glance up at Luca, seeing that he's taking this in, too.

A rush of confusion fills me as I toast. I'm glad that

Luca's seen me with someone else, that I haven't been a wallflower at this party, that I've proved him wrong, even a little bit, because there's a boy here who seems to like me, who's talking to me, anyway, getting me a drink. In films, in books, flirting with a boy is a surefire way to get the one you actually like interested in you, draw him over to your side. They're supposed to like competition, the challenge of going after a girl who's popular.

But maybe real life doesn't quite work that way. Because Luca arches one black eyebrow, his mouth quirks up on one side in a sneer, and he turns pointedly away, sliding a cigarette into his mouth and lighting it with a flip of his Zippo.

Disgusting habit, I think as firmly as I can. *I'm glad he's not coming over, smoking a nasty stinking cancer stick.*

It's awful when you lie to yourself. I *do* think smoking is foul, but I'm also more than aware that if Luca strolled over to talk to me, with that cigarette dangling from the corner of his mouth, I wouldn't walk away, complaining about the smoke; I'd stand there staring up at him, trying not to grin as widely as a five-year-old meeting Cinderella at Disneyland.

Well, Luca doesn't seem remotely interested in coming over. He's clearly one of those boys who like to mess girls around. I've seen them before. Their favorite thing is to have as many girls running after them as possible, like those circus performers who can keep loads of plates spinning on different sticks at once. This kind of boy rarely has a steady girlfriend. He doesn't like to commit, because if he's linked to one girl, it's harder to keep all the other plates spinning.

I glance over at Luca. He's turned away, resolutely not looking at me. I realize where the expression "give someone the cold shoulder" comes from. And then I see a hand reaching up to push his hair back playfully, a girl's hand with a heavy gold bracelet on it, big chunky coins dangling from the chain.

I recognize that bracelet at once: *Elisa*. My whole body stiffens. *He's over there letting Elisa touch his hair, rather than coming over to me.*

I put my cup down on the table and smile so brightly at Sebastiano, he's visibly surprised at my sudden enthusiasm.

"Let's go back and dance!" I say loudly.

"Benissimo!"

He follows me outside into the soft night air, and I can't help gasping at the sight of the donkey, Golia, who's now in the middle of the dance floor, swaying happily from side to side. People are dancing around her, stroking her head as they pass, avoiding the ropelike, flapping tail.

"I tell you she like to dance," Sebastiano says cheerfully.

"Will she be okay?" I ask, charmed by the sight of the dancing donkey, but obviously feeling that animal-rights activists might have strong feelings about dosing a donkey with wine.

"Oh yes," he says. "We give her wine because at the party she drinks from the glasses, in the hands, and people were . . ."

Not knowing the word, he mimes fright, opening his eyes wide, throwing his hands up in fear. I giggle as I say, "Afraid."

I bet they were afraid, I think. *I'd have a heart attack if a donkey came up to me and shoved its nose in my cup of wine.*

"*Si!* They were afraid! So is better to give her in the

257

ciotola." He points to the bowl. "Then she is happy, she no drink from the glass. And she drinks the water too. She no have bad head."

He scrunches his face up, miming a headache, or a hangover; I giggle again.

"She is my donkey," he says, "so I know she is happy. I live here."

"Oh! It's lovely," I say sincerely, looking around me. "You're really lucky."

"I know!" He beams. "Come now, we dance, Violetta."

He takes my hand and pulls me toward the dance floor, just as Kelly's admirer pulled her outside. I can't imagine an English boy doing that—they'd be worried about getting slapped. But somehow it's charming with the Italians, even if it's not the Italian boy you really want to be taking you somewhere, and I let Sebastiano do it. As he grabs my hand, over my shoulder I see Luca emerge onto the terrace, with Elisa.

I speed up almost to a run. I'm running away from Luca, from the pain that seeing him with Elisa causes me, from the confusion and conflicting feelings he makes me feel, the tremendous attraction and the fear of thinking I'm special to him when really I'm just another of his many spinning plates. Another of the foreign girls he messes around with every summer.

Sebastiano and I arrive, breathless and laughing, on the stone oval of the dance floor. I'm delighted to see that Kelly's there too, dancing with the dark stocky guy, Gianbattista; she shoots over to my side, yelling:

"Did you see the *donkey*?"

"No," I say, deadpan, "what donkey?"

She takes a moment, then howls with laughter. I think she's a bit tipsy by now.

"You're *soo* funny!" she yells. "You're *hilarious! Soo* funny!"

She whirls away, dancing like a dervish, and I give Gianbattista a narrow glance, the one that means *My friend is a bit drunk, but if you try to take advantage of her, I will remove my heels and hit you over the head with them.* He looks taken aback, and I think the message has got over loud and clear. The music's great—lots of songs we're all dancing to in London, and no slow ones that mean boys are going to grab you and shuffle back and forth while pressing bits of themselves into you that you really don't want to be aware of. I dance and dance. I don't look anywhere beyond the bobbing heads, the waving arms, the smiling faces. I don't look beyond the flames of the huge citronella candles, the fairy lights suspended in the branches over the dance floor.

I don't look onto the rest of the terrace. I don't want to see Luca and Elisa, wrapped in each other's arms. To see him kissing her as he kissed me, his arms around her, his dark head bent over hers, his silky hair falling in her face. The only time I do look out from the confines of the dance area is when Paige appears, tumbling hilariously on the rough stone terrace, Leonardo's arm a firm bar under her arm holding her up.

"Dance!" she calls happily. "Dance time! Drop it and pop it!"

She collapses suddenly; it looks as if her knees have given way, but a second later I realize that she's actually doing a would-be sexy dance move, sticking out her bum, throwing her knees wide, her hands on her thighs, like a dancer in a hip-hop video. The trouble is, once she gets down, she can't get up again. Leonardo bends down and tries to haul her up, but she's laughing too hard to help him and almost pulls him over with her; Andrea dashes over, grabs her other arm, and gets her back to her feet again.

I'd be mortified at getting stuck down in a sexy squat. Absolutely mortified. I give Paige huge points for coming up laughing even louder, and exclaiming to Kendra, who's come over too:

"Ken! Didja see? I dropped it but I couldn't pop it! Ha! I couldn't pop it!"

She's howling with laughter, her head thrown back, her blond curls tumbling everywhere.

"I dropped it!" she yells. "But I couldn't pop it!"

"*Ma cosa dice?*" Sebastiano says to me. "What does she say?"

I look at him helplessly. "I can't explain," I say finally. So I throw my hands wide in apology for not being able to translate, and start dancing again, only to stop a moment later as Paige yells:

"*Oh! Em! Gee!* I am *sooo* out of it!" She's pointing at Golia, the donkey. "I'm, like, *seeing* things! I thought you were supposed to see pink elephants—I'm, like, seeing a *horse*! No, it's a pony! My Little Pony! Cool! Is anyone else seeing a—"

"I think it's time we took her home," Kendra says dryly to Leonardo.

"Oh." Leonardo's face falls. "*Ma no,* she is okay. We sit her down a little bit, she is fine. . . ."

Paige staggers, and Andrea has to shove his arm more securely under her shoulder to hold her up.

"I really think she needs to go home," Kendra says firmly. "I'll go too."

Leonardo clearly doesn't want to leave the party, or be responsible for a tipsy Paige; he doesn't say a word. It's Andrea, wanting to be in Kendra's good books, who says swiftly:

"I take you, Kaiindra. *Leo, dammi le tue chiavi.*"

Leonardo fumbles in his trouser pockets and hands Andrea his car keys.

"*Ecco,*" Andrea says to Kendra, smiling triumphantly. "I take you and Paige home, okay?"

"Thank you," she says, with a rare grateful smile that makes him flush with pleasure.

Kelly nudges me. Her cheeks are pink, her face shiny, her hair's come down with dancing and is sticking to her forehead, and when she speaks she's doing her best not to slur.

"I think I sh'd go home too," she says. "We sh'd all go."

A realization hits me in the rib cage, as if she'd punched me rather than nudged me lightly. She's right; we've been here for hours, we've had a good time—some of us, frankly, look like they've had too good a time. Andrea's going back to the villa now with Paige and Kendra, and we should definitely go with him. Leonardo doesn't seem to consider himself responsible for getting us back, and the last thing I want to do is throw myself on Elisa's mercy, or trust a stranger who might be drunk, or not have the best of intentions, or isn't even quite sure where to find Villa Barbiano, to give us a lift home. In London there are always late buses, or minicabs, at a pinch; here in the countryside, things are very different. You're at the mercy of someone with a car.

But the punch in the rib cage isn't because I've realized that we're dependent on a sober driver. It's because I have to admit to myself that I want to stay: I'm still hoping that Luca will turn away from Elisa and come and find me. Take me for a walk somewhere dark and romantic, kiss me again, make me melt.

I'm pathetic. I am not going to be this person.

"You're totally right," I say to Kelly firmly.

And I shove Leonardo aside with little ceremony, taking his place supporting Paige. He grumbles at being manhandled, but I couldn't care less. He's handsome and charming, but he's fallen in my estimation; a boy who hangs around while a girl drinks a bit too much, happy to have a good time with her but not to help get her back home, doesn't rate very high on my points scale.

"Come on," I say, grunting as Paige goes limp against me, heaving her up, determinedly refusing to glance back along the terrace to see if Luca's blue eyes are looking in our direction. Regretting that I'm leaving before he made his move.

You're an idiot, Violet. Stop it right now.

"Time for all of us to get going," I say loudly. And I really try to mean it.

A Stupid, Silly, Impossible Fantasy

Hauling Paige up the long sloping drive to the wrought-iron gates, and then along the rutted dirt road to Leonardo's jeep, is not the most fun I've ever had in my life. I'm really glad I didn't wear high heels; balancing myself, as well as Paige, would have been a much more difficult task. Luckily, I've danced off any effect the wine I drank might have had, and Andrea, too, seems sensible and sober. As, I realize, did most people at the party. They were happy and laughing and fun, but that was about it; Italians nurse a couple of glasses of wine all evening. They don't seem to drink to get plastered, not like English people do.

When we reach the jeep, Andrea props Paige on me like a gigantic doll while he gets in, turns on the engine, and bumps the jeep down to the road so it's level. No way would we have managed to heave Paige into the jeep when it was parked at such a steep tilt up the slope.

Andrea's unlocked the back door, and Kendra and I push and shove Paige in. She flops down inside with a long sigh of relief, collapsing on the backseat.

"It wasn't a pretty pony," she says, desolate now. "It was all gray. My Little Pony should be pink and shiny."

"O-kay," Kendra says. "Can you shift up, Paige? 'Cause we all need to get in."

"You sit here, Kaiindra," Andrea says eagerly, leaning over the front passenger seat and patting the upholstery with his hand.

"Subtle," Kelly mutters to me.

"Italians don't seem to be subtle," I mutter back.

"No," she says wistfully. "When they like you, they let you know."

And even in the moonlight I can see that she's looking at Andrea sadly. He doesn't even notice her or look our way: his attention's all on Kendra, who, in turn, is totally focused on Paige. Who isn't budging.

"Need to lie down," she mumbles. "Not feeling too good. Need to lie down."

"You have to sit up!" Kendra says crossly, her hands on her hips. "We all need to get in!"

"Need . . . to lie *down*," Paige insists, her speech getting slower and slower.

"If you make her sit up, she might puke," Kelly says with blistering frankness. "And no one wants that."

Off in the paddock, one of the horses neighs as if in

agreement. It's such a beautiful dark night, clouds scudding across the yellow moon, a faint breeze barely lifting the leaves on the trees that line the road, stars bright pricks of light in the black sky. *Really black, I realize. In London, because of the streetlights, it's a mauvey pink; here, it's so dark you can see every single star.*

Kelly's over at the jeep now, gingerly picking up Paige's feet with her high studded wedges dangling off them. It's as if Kelly's playing with a gigantic Barbie.

"I can squash in and sit down if I put her feet on my lap," she announces. "That's okay, I don't mind."

"But what about Violet?" Kendra points out. "You can't both sit like that, there isn't room."

We look dubiously at the very back of the jeep, which Catia uses for loading all sorts of stuff; not just suitcases, but rubbish. It's fenced off from the rest of the car and lined with some nasty, filthy old scraps of blanket. I'm *not* going to volunteer to climb in there and ride back in the dirt, clinging to the wire screen like a prisoner. And, to be fair, no one even suggests that I do.

"You could maybe squash into the front seat with me," Kendra says doubtfully.

"Is not safe," Andrea says, shaking his head.

"We could see if we could get the seat belt over both of us—"

"*C'è qualche problema?*" comes a soft voice from behind us, and we all jump, startled.

He has a way of sneaking up on you like a cat, I think savagely, annoyed at being taken so off guard. Everyone turns but me, because of course I know who it is straightaway. It's as if I have a special radar setting for him: I would recognize his voice anywhere.

"Luca!" Andrea says, sounding relieved, and rattles off a long stream of Italian.

I don't want to swivel to look at Luca directly. So I step back a couple of paces, closer to the wall that borders the paddocks, widening my range, and see him leaning against one of the gateposts, looking very amused. His eyes are gleaming, his hands shoved in his pockets, as he speaks equally rapid-fire Italian at Andrea.

I just glance at him swiftly, and then away again. He's been ignoring me all evening, and I'm not going to give him the satisfaction of staring adoringly at him now. Something on the wall catches my attention; it's a cat, maybe the one that crossed our path before, padding along the top on velvety paws, big and confident, pausing in front of me, staring at me with flat glassy eyes that gleam orange in the dark night. I reach out tentatively to stroke it, and when it doesn't hiss and scratch, I tickle under its chin. A purr starts up immediately, rattling deep in its chest, and it closes its eyes and shoves its head heavily into my hand, showing me exactly where it wants to be scratched next. I pull lightly on its soft silky ears, smooth down its thick fur, and distract myself so thoroughly that it's only after quite a while that I sense eyes on me and look around to see that everyone has fallen silent and is staring at me.

"*Allora?*" Luca says, a mocking edge to his voice. "*Vieni con me, Violetta?*"

That can't mean what I think it means. My heart catches in my throat. The cat, realizing that I've been distracted, jumps down from the wall, landing with an audible thud, and pads off through the gate to chase food for its dinner. *Poor field mice,* I think ruefully. *Between the owl and the cat, they'll have a miserable night of it.*

Then I look at Luca, and have the horrible suspicion that I'm a mouse and he's the cat, playing with me, letting me run away and then reeling me back in. His eyebrows are raised, his mouth quirked in an amused smile of inquiry.

"Sorry," I say, not to him but to Kelly and Kendra. "I missed all of that."

"Luca's going to take you back to the villa," Kendra says briskly. "'Cause we can't all get in the jeep."

I panic. Stone-cold panic, bringing out sweat on my palms. *I can't be alone with him. This isn't fair.*

"Kelly's coming with us too, right?" I say overloudly. "It'll be nicer than sitting under Paige's feet."

Luca nods his head sideways, and for a moment I don't get why. Then I do, and I can't breathe. He's indicating the line of Vespas parked by the gatepost. *He didn't come in his car. He came on a Vespa. I'm going to ride back home on his scooter.*

This is not happening.

"Okay!" Kendra says brightly, climbing into the jeep. "See you two back at the villa!"

"Have fun," Kelly adds, squishing in under the recumbent Paige's feet and leaning over to shut the door.

I grimace at her helplessly, but they're gone. Clearly, from the tone of her voice, Kelly thought that I'd be pleased at being marooned here with Luca. She caught us in the hallway of the castello; she knows that I like him.

But I'm not pleased. I'm furious, actually. Not with them, not with Kelly and Kendra. I can see how they'd think this was an ideal solution to the problem of Paige being passed out in the back of the jeep.

No, I'm furious with Luca. I feel trapped, played with. He's spent all his time at the party not with me, but with Elisa. And now he thinks he can stroll up here, exploit a problem we're having, and pick me out of the group to ride off with, without even *asking* me. As if I should be *grateful* that he's spending some time alone with me.

I'm bristling like a hedgehog.

"*Andiamo?*" Luca says, pulling his hand out of his pocket, dangling a key with a black fob. Without looking to see if I'm coming, he walks over to his Vespa. It's a faded, scraped pale blue, big and clunky, with old-fashioned dials on the front panel.

Luca is bending over, retrieving two helmets from under the seat. He puts one on, leaving the buckle loose, holding the other one out to me.

I haven't moved. I'm still standing by the wall. I stare at the helmet, my heart pounding, words rising to my lips. I want to yell at him, to complain that he's taking me for granted. But then I bite my lip, choking down the words, because I'd make a fool of myself if I said them. I've got no rights over Luca. I'm not his girlfriend, or even close to it. I'm just a girl who's kissed him a couple of times, and from what Elisa's said, Luca's kissed a ton of girls. For all I know, the days I haven't seen him, he was in Florence, or at other parties, kissing other girls, other foreigners visiting that he can play with, avoiding long-term consequences because he knows they'll be going back to their own countries at the end of their holidays.

No, the best thing to do is to act as if you just don't care. As if you've been kissing other boys, too, every night he hasn't seen you. As if you can barely remember his name.

Sometimes I think I'm too proud, too self-protective, but then I see other girls making idiots of themselves over boys and I change my mind. I'd rather be too proud than make a laughingstock of myself. I think of how my mum acted when my dad left her for the awful Sif: no matter how upset Mum was, she never threw scenes, never begged him to stay. Maybe she lavished too much attention on me after he went, kept me a little too close, but I really admired how she behaved through the separation and divorce. Dad admired her too, I know. I've never been prouder of her. And I want to be like her. I won't chase after a man; I won't seem desperate or needy. I'll be as cool as my mum.

So I smile as best I can, saunter over to the Vespa, take the helmet, and say casually as I put it on:

"*Grazie!* I've never been on one of these before."

Luca promptly paralyzes me by leaning down, pulling the helmet strap tight, and fastening the buckle under my chin. His aftershave smells like seawater, cool aquamarine, fresh and light; his breath on my face is warm and touched lightly with wine.

"*Ecco,*" he says softly. His fingertips touch my skin. "It must be tight."

He wheels away from me and swings one long leg over

the seat, putting the key in the ignition. Over his shoulder he says:

"You must hold on to my waist. And when I lean, you must lean with me. Okay?"

He's waiting for me to get on. I mustn't hesitate, or I'll look as if I'm scared; I hike my skirt up and climb onto the back. The little scooter's revving up, rattling noisily and cheerfully, like the cat purring on the wall; Luca looks back and says, *"Aspetta."*

Quickly, he shrugs off his jacket and hands it to me. It's leather, butter-soft, like fabric in my hands.

"Put it on. It is not cold, but there is wind when we drive," he says.

I slip it on, my head spinning. The collar smells of him, as if he's wrapped around me. And then, in turn, I wrap my arms around his narrow waist, I feel his warm skin beneath the light cotton of his shirt. He's just lean muscle over bone, almost skinny, but as the scooter kicks into motion, I can instantly tell how strong he is, because he controls it with small, seemingly effortless flexes of his muscles. His shoulders bunch lightly, taking the strain of bouncing an old Vespa with two people on it over a road that suddenly feels much more rutted and potholed when you're not traveling in a jeep with good suspension.

Dust kicks up from the Vespa wheels, white dust that scatters up to the banks of trees on either side, adding to the pale traces that are already there. It's like a ghost road, a sliver of moon gleaming through the dark branches, everything black and white but for the yellow headlight of the Vespa swiveling back and forth as we bump down the road, a cone of light showing our way. If I had any idea about not holding on too tightly to Luca, that vanished the instant the scooter shot off; from the first jolt, I clung on for dear life. It's like we're the same body, leaning in unison against the curves, my head tilted into his shoulder so our helmets don't bump, his chest rising and falling with his even breathing, his shoulders flexing with the strain of holding the Vespa steady, keeping us safe.

Being so close to Luca, pressed so tightly against him, synchronized with him, is so heady and intoxicating that it would be enough, on its own, to make me dizzy; but the extra factor of having to hold on to him so tightly as we bounce over ruts and swerve to avoid potholes makes me feel as if we're in a bubble together, isolated from the rest of the world.

We pull onto the asphalt road, and the ride becomes instantly smoother, faster, the scooter puttering along, cars occasionally whipping past; to me they seem terrifyingly close, but Luca doesn't tense up, doesn't flinch in any way, which is hugely reassuring. The yellow cone of light from the headlight is tiny on the black road, and I can barely see anything until we rattle through a village with some streetlights. All the shops are shuttered up, the bar is closed, not a soul about, barely any lights on in the houses. It's very late, I realize, and a wave of tiredness hits me, a reaction to the excitement of the party, the adrenaline rush of dancing, and the thrill of being on a Vespa with Luca. My body sags, and I find myself relaxing against him, my head nudging more comfortably into the curve of his shoulder.

As if we knew each other really well, as if he were my long-term

271

boyfriend taking me home from a party, our bodies familiar and cozy with each other, I think. It's a dream. A silly, impossible fantasy. But I'm tired, and it's late at night, and I let myself indulge in it for the rest of the ride. I rest my head against his helmet and I close my eyes, the scent of him and his aftershave and the petrol fumes from the exhaust all mingling in an oddly intoxicating haze.

The Vespa turns and starts to bump up a gravel drive. I know this means we're back at Villa Barbiano, but I'm in denial. I keep my eyes shut, my head down, even when the scooter crunches to a halt beside the jeep, and Luca's leg shoots out to kick down the stand.

I draw in a long breath, and then it catches in my throat as his hand closes over mine, still wrapped around his waist.

"*Siamo arrivati,*" he says gently.

I have to get off first, I realize. And I'm embarrassed that it takes me a while to unwind my arms. Luca starts to turn and I realize with horror that my skirt is practically up around my waist: this galvanizes me and I jump off so fast I nearly fall over, dragging down my skirt so he can't see my thighs. I'm wobbling, shaken up by the ride, and I hear him huff a little laugh of amusement as he swings his leg over to sit on the seat facing me, unbuckling his helmet.

"You like to ride on a Vespa?" he asks.

I take my helmet off and hand it back to him.

"Well, it's bumpy," I say.

I can't really see his face, it's so dark out here. There are a couple of lights on the villa walls, one over the main door, but that's higher up; the parking lot is around the side, barely illuminated.

He stands up, towering over me, and puts the helmets down on the seat.

"And loud," he says. "You know what *'vespa'* means?"

I shake my head, my mouth suddenly dry, because he's taken a step toward me, and his legs are so long that one step means he's already standing in front of me, close enough to touch.

"It means 'wasp,'" he says softly. "Because it makes a sound like a wasp. How do you say that?"

"Buzzing," I manage. "It buzzes."

"Buzzes," Luca says, and his accent makes the word sound so funny that I can't help laughing.

"You laugh at me?" he asks, and though he's put on a serious voice, as if he's annoyed, somehow I know he isn't. "Girls never laugh at me. You are the only one."

"Well, maybe they should," I say without thinking.

"No," he says firmly. "Only you can laugh at me."

I don't know what to say to this. I stand there, tongue-tied, which is very unlike me. It feels simultaneously as if we're very close, and also miles away. I yearn for him to touch me, but I'm scared I'll slap him if he does. I won't let him take me for granted. Not after he's spent the entire evening, as far as I know, with Elisa and not with me.

I think he's read my mind, because after a brief pause, he asks, "You have a nice time at the party?"

There's only one answer to this.

"Lovely," I say, and I actually toss my head as if I were a heroine in an old film, being coquettish with an admirer.

"I danced and danced," I add airily. "With lots of people. I didn't see you at all."

"I see you," he says, "with Sebastiano. You dance a lot with him."

I answer lightly, "Oh yes! He's very nice. I really liked him."

Luca's feet shift on the gravel.

"He has lots of friends," he says rather snappily. "Lots of girls."

"Like you," I snap back. "Elisa says you have lots of girl friends too. Foreign girls."

Luca sighs heavily, and reaches up to run a hand through his hair.

"Elisa—" he starts, and then halts, as if he's choosing his words very carefully. He sighs again. "Elisa," he finally continues, "can sometimes be not very nice. Even to her mother, she is not very nice. It is maybe better not to listen to what she tells you."

"This just in," I mutter. "Breaking news revelation."

"*Come?*" Luca stares down at me, fine streaks of black hair now tumbling over his forehead. "*Non capisco.*"

"*Elisa,*" I say in Italian as careful as his English, "*è una stronza.*"

He bursts out laughing.

"*Brava,*" he says. "*Complimenti.*"

And he's very clever, because he uses the laughter to carry him toward me somehow, on a quick step forward, and the next thing I know he's taken my hands and is holding them in his.

I don't know what to do. I look at our clasped hands. It feels as if he's cleared the ground, swept away Sebastiano and Elisa; has tried to tell me that he saw me dancing with Sebastiano and was too jealous to come over, and that he doesn't like Elisa that way.

Of course, he might just be telling me what I want to hear.

"Violetta—" he starts, and I look up at him, which is a huge mistake.

Because he promptly kisses me, and I'm not ready.

I'm still not sure that Luca hasn't had a lovely evening flirting with Elisa, then decided, on a whim, to pursue me instead. For all I know, he's going to go back to Elisa and tell her I'm not very nice. I don't have enough to be able to trust him. I remember Elisa winding her arm through his, taking him out onto the terrace at the castello, and him walking with her without even glancing back in my direction.

My brain says I shouldn't be kissing him. *Hold him off at least once!* it advises. *Don't kiss him every time you see him! This is not cool behavior!* But it hasn't sent the message through to my body, which is tilting up toward him, closing my eyes as his lips come down on mine. Our hands are still clasped together, and that's weakening my awareness that I should stop the kiss, because the handclasp feels magically romantic, a knot held tightly against our hearts. Luca is the opposite of boys I've kissed before. He doesn't push, he doesn't grab, he doesn't do anything until I'm desperate for him to do it. It's incredibly seductive, because it makes me want more and more, more than just our lips parting, our tongues meeting, our mouths drowning in each other. I want everything, I want him so badly. My fingers wind through his tightly, pressing into our chests, and the surge of feeling that rises in my body frightens me with its sheer force.

I'd do anything. I'd do anything with him.

It's too much. I wrench myself away. If I'm feeling like this, when all we're doing is kissing, not even with our arms around each other, just holding hands, for goodness' sake—how on earth would I feel if we were in a room together, with the door closed and no one to interrupt us? What would I do? How far would I go?

I know the answer. And that's why I panic and pull myself away, untwisting my fingers from his, and blurt out, in a crude attempt to push him away verbally as well as physically:

"Luca—did you know I got sick after I was at your house? The castello? Catia had to call the doctor. I was really sick."

"*Cosa?*" Luca looks completely shocked. "I did not know."

"Stomach pain," I say, patting my tummy. "I was really sick."

"*Ma cosa dici? Violetta*—" He catches himself and goes into English with a visible effort. "With you—"

He paces away, striding in a wide circle, running his hands through his hair.

"With you, it is difficult!" he says finally, halting in front of me. "I do not know what you will say next. Or do next. I find you in my home locked into the *passaggio segreto*, and you say someone has locked you in, and now you say you are sick after you make the visit, and my mother—*la mia mamma!*—says you are very, *very* like my *zia* Monica, like her *gemella*—twin—and that is strange—*everything* with you is strange. I don't know why it is so. And difficult!"

He buries his hands deep in his hair, the picture of frustration.

"What do you mean, you were sick?" he demands, staring down at me.

"I sort of fainted," I say frankly. And even though it sounds gross, I add, "I threw up. Lots. The doctor pumped my stomach."

"*Dio mio! Violetta!*" Luca's genuinely horrified. "You are all right now?"

He reaches out and brushes hair back from my forehead, curls that got stuck there under the helmet. It's such a tender gesture that a lump forms in my throat, and I swallow hard. I nod, and his hand stays in my hair, stroking it gently.

"Oh!" I say, remembering something I wanted to tell him. "I downloaded some albums of that singer you mentioned before. Jovanotti. He's really good."

"You like him?" Luca smiles. "He is very good."

"Yes, I'm teaching myself Italian by translating the lyrics."

He smiles again. I just want to wrap myself around him and hold on tight. Keep him smiling forever.

Above us, a door bangs in the villa, someone hisses a "Shh!" and we hear footsteps coming along the stone path above us. Whispered conversation, muffled giggles.

"Guys!" comes Kendra's voice, pitched low and discreet. "Are you down there? We heard the scooter come up the drive."

Nice and tactful, I think gratefully. *If Luca and I were having a major snog, that'd give us enough time to disentangle ourselves and get decent.*

"We're here!" I whisper back. "Did you get Paige to bed okay?"

"Yes and no," Kendra says quietly, coming down the steps to the parking lot. Andrea's following on her heels like an obedient dog. "We got her upstairs, but she was all messed up and crying about the pony not being pink, and she woke up Catia."

"*Bollocks*," I say, with feeling.

"What is 'bollocks'?" Luca asks, sounding very interested.

"Never mind," I say firmly to him. "Is Catia really pissed off with us?"

"We have to have a meeting tomorrow morning after breakfast," Kendra says gloomily. "To set new house rules."

"Oh *no*," I sigh.

"Yup. We should go to bed now. I don't think Catia really cares that much." Kendra adds cynically, "She's just going through the motions. But, you know, we shouldn't look like we're—"

"Taking the piss," I finish.

"*Taking the piss?*" Luca echoes, his accent so funny that I stifle a giggle. Not quite well enough; he hears it and aims a playful smack to the back of my head, which I dodge with another giggle. That's the thing about Luca. One moment we're teasing each other, then we're kissing, then we're fighting, or being serious. And it can change so fast, it's dizzying.

No wonder I don't feel in control of anything when I'm with him. And honestly, cool as he seems, I don't know if he's any more in control of what's between us than I am. One moment I'm doubting him, watching him let Elisa stroke his

278

hair; the next I'm feeling a connection between us stronger than anything I've experienced before.

"O-*kay*," Kendra says, with an intonation that perfectly conveys what she wants to say. She jerks her head toward the steps.

"We should go," I say. I look at Luca hopelessly. "Get home safe," I manage, shrugging out of his jacket, which I've only just realized I'm still wearing, and handing it to him.

He takes it and flourishes me an elaborate bow, the jacket dangling from his outstretched hand, which should look stupid, but actually feels as romantic as when he held my hands while kissing me. I know I've gone bright red.

"Kaiindra—" Andrea begins, but Kendra's already walking swiftly up the steps.

"Text me," she says over her shoulder.

I follow her up. At the top I turn and look briefly at the parking lot. The two boys are standing there, looking up at us. Luca's staring straight at me, and I have to look away to avoid breaking into a silly smile. *Honestly, they're so gorgeous. The kind of boys you dream of meeting if you come to Italy. Who'd have thought it? How lucky are we?*

"Andrea's really good-looking," I say to Kendra in a low voice when I hear the Vespa and the jeep start up.

"Whatever." She shrugs. "The weird thing? I love to, you know, hook a boy on the line, but when I do? I don't care about 'em anymore. I'm funny that way."

I digest this. "So you're not really keen on Andrea?"

She shrugs again.

"Not now. He's gotten all needy."

"Wow," I say respectfully. "You're very tough."

"I can't help it," she says simply. "I've always been like that. I get bored really fast."

"Wow," I say again. "You're like a nasty guy. So look—don't get upset—but if you don't like Andrea, do you think you could leave him alone? I think Kelly really likes him, and if you don't care one way or the other—"

"Sure," she says casually as she pushes open the front door of the villa. "No prob. Plenty more fish in the sea."

I shut the door behind me. And maybe because I'm tired, and it's dark, and she's been so nice about leaving Andrea alone, I ask:

"Are you okay about forgetting that nasty comment Elisa made? You know, about you being exotic?"

"Because I'm black?" Kendra wheels around to look at me directly, stopping in her tracks. "Yeah, I was really mad about that. But then I thought, what am I going to do, not date anyone or have fun the whole time I'm here? Elisa would *totally* win if I did that!" She smiles, her teeth beautiful and white, but there isn't an ounce of humor behind it. "I had a really good time tonight. Tons of boys hanging off me. And I could see it was really messing with her head—she kept giving me these dirty looks. So I'm going to get as many boys as I can running after me this summer. Just to make Elisa really . . ."

She pauses.

"What would Kelly say? *Narked.*" Now her smile's real. "I want to make Elisa *narked.*"

I smile back: the English word sounds really cool in her American accent.

"Is there anyone you do like?" I ask as we tiptoe upstairs to bed. "Obviously not Andrea . . ."

"Maybe," Kendra says as we reach the top of the staircase. "But I don't actually like boys."

I'm so taken aback by this I stop, trying to read her expression, and she laughs softly, turning away to the room she shares with Paige. "Just messing with you a little there," she says, flashing me a smile over her shoulder that, even in the moonlight, I can see is genuine. "When I said I don't like boys—I meant, I like men."

And she whisks herself into the bedroom, closing the door behind her on the perfect exit line.

It's Much Better This Way

Luca, I am all too aware, has still not asked for my phone
number. A few days after the party, floods of texts are still
swamping both Kendra and Paige's phones, and Gianbattista's already rung Kelly several times, asking her out.
The only girl at Villa Barbiano who doesn't have a boy getting in touch with her is me. Sebastiano wasn't interested in
me that way, I know. He was just a dancing mate.

It's incredibly annoying.

The thing is, when I'm with Luca, it's so overwhelming
that I feel swept away, as if I'm struggling all the time to
keep my balance. It never occurs to me when we're together
that he isn't asking for my phone number. But it means that
afterward, I can't expect a text or a call from him. There's no

way for him to get in touch and make plans for us to meet again. It's really unbalanced. He knows where I am most of the time—at Villa Barbiano, doing lessons, hanging out. And if we do go out in the evening, to a party or to the bar in the village, all he has to do is get Leonardo to let him know, and then he can drop in and see me if he wants.

Or not, if he doesn't want.

I sigh. It feels incredibly unfair. I've lived in London all my life, in the center of a big city with Tubes and buses and bike lanes. Parties, going out, hanging out with friends are all so easy that I've taken it completely for granted. I never gave a moment's thought to people who live in the country-side or who aren't old enough to drive, or can't afford a car, and are completely dependent on friends for their social life. How do they manage? If you lived somewhere like the place we went last night, gorgeous as it was, how do you get around and see people? Maybe they have Vespas. But how old do you have to be to have one of those? At least sixteen, I'd think. Maybe even older. And they can't be cheap.

Luca has a Vespa, of course. And a car. Maybe he shares the car with his mum, like Leonardo does with Catia, but I can't imagine the principessa goes out much. He can nip around as much as he likes, while I'm stuck pretty much in one place.

Okay, that's enough self-pity, I tell myself. *Concentrate on memorizing imperfect conjugations. Kelly and Kendra probably know theirs backwards already.* It's the afternoon, a glorious sunny day, and we're by the pool, Italian grammar books in our hands. Well, everyone has them but Paige, who's given up even pretending to study and is flicking through magazines. *If you're stuck somewhere, there can't be a better place in the world for it. Don't be spoiled.* It's gorgeous weather, and although I'm being careful to use sunblock, I'm getting a lovely tan. Golden and healthy.

Like an Italian girl. Not one with a Scandinavian mother and a Scottish father.

I bite my lip. Coming to Italy, wanting to find out the reason that the girl in the portrait in Sir John Soane's Museum looks like me, has tangled me up much more painfully than I thought it ever could. I thought there could be secrets buried in my family that I might not want to know about. I never thought about the secrets in the di Vesperi family, how my resemblance might affect them. I never expected that they might see the likeness in me. That definitely never crossed my mind.

How could I possibly have expected that generations down the line I'd meet and feel this way about the son of the family? And what's more, that he would be attracted to me . . .

Thank goodness, I'm leaving all that well alone. What do I care if I saw my own face looking back at me from an eighteenth-century portrait? I have a mother and father who love me, and a really good life. I tell myself that I should be glad Luca doesn't have my phone number. Because if he did, then I'd be on tenterhooks all the time, checking constantly to see if he'd texted, or if I'd missed a call from him. It's better this way. I can actually get on with things here that I care about without being perpetually distracted by the possibility of him getting in touch.

Yes. It's much better this way.

I huff a sarcastic laugh. I am appallingly bad at lying to myself. I look around the pool area: Kelly, wrapped in a towel—she's still very uncomfortable at being seen in a swimsuit—is immersed in one of the textbooks we all had to bring with us for the course, the same one that's lying on my lap. Its cover is shiny and cheerful, stripes of white, green, and red, but its subject, *Basic Rules of Italian Grammar*, is dry as a bone. Still, Kelly's reading it as intently as if it were a torrid vampire romance, her lips moving as she recites irregular verb conjugations to herself, and Kendra, not to be outdone, is scribbling notes in her own copy.

"How do you say 'love and kisses' in Italian?" Paige asks, absorbed in her texting.

"*Amore e baci*," Kelly and Kendra promptly reply, and cast jealous glances across the loungers at the speed of each other's response.

"Who are you writing that to?" I ask curiously.

"Everyone!" Paige says. "'Hi boy, love and kisses!' I'm writing that back to all of 'em. I can't even remember which one's which. *Ciao ragazzo, amore e baci.*" She types it in, sends it, and clicks on another message. "Ooh, what does this mean? '*Sei una favola, bambola mia*'?"

"'You're a fairy tale—'" Kelly starts, looking smug.

"'My doll,'" Kendra finishes for her. "'*Bambola*' is doll."

"Huh. 'You're a fairy tale, my doll'? That's *weird*," Paige says. "Maybe just kisses for him. No love. And what's '*bonona*'? Is that like another doll?"

I prick up my ears, remembering the word from the party: a boy said it watching Kelly walk across the room.

Kelly blushes. "It means a girl with curves. It's a good word. Like a compliment."

"You're kidding!" Paige sits up straight, looking over her sunglasses at Kelly.

"No, honestly," Kelly assures her. "It's a mash-up of the words for 'big' and 'good.' But in a really good way."

"Like big is beautiful?" Paige starts to giggle. "I could be eating *more* pasta, then! And to think I was looking at all those Italian girls at the party and envying how thin they are! When the boys really want a nice curvy girl! *'Bonona,'*" she reads out from her phone. "I don't get all of this message, though. He keeps putting sixes in for some reason."

"Oh, that's 'cause they use the number six in texting to mean *'sei,'* 'you are,'" Kelly explains. "'Cause six is *'sei'* in Italian. It's like us using the number two to mean—"

"Got it," Paige says with satisfaction, scrolling through the message. "Hey, now this actually sort of makes sense! You're super-smart, Kelly."

"It's pretty obvious, really," Kendra snaps. "I worked it out ages ago."

Kelly turns a page in her textbook. "You didn't mention it, though, did you? And you didn't say it just now."

"That's because you're always jumping in first," Kendra says with an audible sneer. "You've just got to be teacher's pet, even when there isn't a teacher around."

I catch my breath, worried that this very obvious attack will devastate Kelly. But I've underestimated her.

"I have to be teacher's pet," she says calmly, not even giving Kendra the satisfaction of raising her eyes from her book. "My family's not rich like yours. I have to use my brain and suck up to the teachers to get scholarships so I can make something of myself."

Wow, I think at this body blow to Kendra. *Well played, Kelly*. I realize that she must have had to deal with this kind of accusation before, from other girls jealous of her cleverness, and learned exactly how to deflect it.

I should say something to cut the tension, but Paige gets in there first.

"Jeez, I completely forgot!" she exclaims. "There were three guys called Riccardo at the party! I called 'em Riccardo One, Two, and Three. Look!" She waves her phone around. "That's how I put their numbers down. Hilarious!" She looks thoughtful. "I sort of remember Riccardo Three having a hissy fit, but hey, it wasn't *my* fault I met him third, was it? But maybe it was Riccardo Two." She pulls a comical face. "I've got a few memory blanks about the party."

Catia was surprisingly blasé about Paige's coming home staggering drunk and sobbing about My Little Pony not being pretty enough; in the next morning's house meeting, she was going through the motions rather than laying down the law. Considering that neither her own daughter or son had yet to return from the party, and that Leo, who'd taken us, hadn't bothered to bring us back, even with Paige in that state, Catia wasn't starting from a highly elevated moral perspective. But I honestly don't think she'd have cared much anyway. Catia limited herself to telling us firmly again that Italians don't drink to excess—something I'd noticed myself—and she wants us to behave like the locals while we're here.

She added something a bit pompous about hoping that

our experience here will encourage us to go back home and show people there that you don't need to get horribly drunk to have a good time. (I'd have been crosser about that if I hadn't had to admit that she might have a point.)

Catia concluded by saying that she knows we're all young, and young people like to go to parties and have fun. We'll have to learn how to moderate our drinking and be sensible, and she's pleased to see that three of us already managed that with no problem at all. Paige and Kendra were goggle-eyed: they were definitely expecting to be read the riot act. Things are clearly a lot laxer in Italy than America.

I realize my gaze has drifted sideways, beyond the rosemary bushes, to the cypresses that line the parking lot, hidden down below the stone wall that borders it. I'm remembering two nights ago, standing there with Luca, still wearing his jacket, kissing him, our hands twined together, and my heart turns over in my chest. I jump off the lounger and walk over to the edge of the pool. It does me no good to turn pictures of Luca over and over in my mind. Especially as I don't know when I'm going to see him again.

Kelly and Kendra have subsided into silence, their heads buried in their books. I shudder to think what kind of atmosphere we're going to have in tomorrow's Italian class; they'll be fighting to show off how much they've learned. *Oh well, at least it'll take the pressure off me and Paige.* Because, to be honest, I'm finding it really hard to do homework with my thoughts so full of Luca.

I'm overheated from the sun; my brain is cooking. I need to cool down, and then maybe I can learn at least the past imperfect. I stand on tiptoes, about to dive into the pool.

"*Oh, Violetta!*" calls a voice from the terrace above, the one outside the dining room. Not Catia; she's out doing errands. I teeter, catch my balance, and manage not to belly flop into the blue water.

For which I'm extremely grateful when Elisa emerges into view, leans her slender arms on the stone balcony, and calls again:

"Violetta? You must come with me. I just get a message from Mamma. She say she is at the Castello di Vesperi, with the principessa, and they want to see you." She sighs theatrically. "You cannot drive, so I must take you. It is very, *very* boring for me."

❧

Don't go, Kelly had said immediately. *I really don't think you should. We agreed you should stay away from the castello.*

How could I not go? My curiosity is much too strong. It brought me here all the way from England; it can't conceive, now, of being so close to the castello and refusing a summons to visit, on my own. Singled out. It would be like doing a marathon and stopping after the twenty-fifth mile.

Besides, as I pointed out to a worried Kelly while I quickly showered and pulled on a dress and sandals, it's not like Elisa's kidnapping me. Both her mum and the principessa are going to be there—we heard Elisa say that, all four of us. They are witnesses. And then, at the castello, the principessa and Catia will be together; it's too far-fetched, even for our lurid imaginings, to picture them ganging up in some bizarre plot against a girl. My resemblance to the principessa's sister-in-law may be freaky, but it's much more likely that they want to discuss it with me in private.

You got really sick there once before, Kelly said, her voice rising anxiously, so I agreed that I wouldn't eat or drink anything I didn't keep my eye on the whole time and that other people weren't having too. But I still find it really hard to think that I might have been deliberately poisoned; it's like something out of a novel, too unreal to take seriously. The more time passes, the more that the memory of being sick fades, the more I look back and think that I must have caught a tummy bug, or had a bout of food poisoning, and that Kelly and I, overexcited by being in a foreign country, where you're always more likely to imagine mystery and intrigue, got carried away and saw lurid conspiracies where there was nothing at all.

And of course, the castello means Luca. The closer I get to it, the more chance of seeing him. I'm honest enough with myself to admit that the Luca factor alone has me putting on some makeup, climbing into Elisa's little Fiat, and sitting there as she bumps it down the drive and along the road that leads through the village and up to the castello on its high hill.

I sort of expect Elisa to launch into a screed of unpleasantness, and have braced myself accordingly. But actually, she doesn't say a word until we turn between the high stone gateposts and into the long, winding private dirt road that leads up to the castello. It's dark, shaded by the cypresses that grow close together on either side, one of those drives that you can see from far away across the olive groves and vineyards, even from the village, a double line of tall, narrow trees like tapering black candles signaling a road that rises to an important house. I imagine all the bats folded up inside the cypresses, hanging inside the densely packed branches, protected from the sun by the thick foliage, waiting for night to come so they can unfurl their wings and fly out to hunt for dinner.

"You are learning Italian?" Elisa finally says.

I consider this, debating my response, and reply:

"Yes, a little. We're all studying hard."

"From my mother," she says, sneeringly. "She is a good teacher of Italian?"

"I don't know," I say simply. "I haven't got anyone else to compare her with."

I'm wondering if Elisa is trying to lure me into saying something that she can repeat to Catia and get me into trouble. I'm not going to fall for that trick. Having been to an all-girls' school has made me very familiar with it. I know, from talking to people who go to mixed schools, that it's different there. But the single-sex aspect of St. Tabby's means that you develop very close friendships, cliques, and rivalries, and it's not just among the girls; the teachers get sucked into it too, or even, in some cases, drive it. There's a handful of teachers at St. Tabby's who definitely have their pets and their hates, as we call them, and the girls who are the pets play it for all it's worth, sucking up to the teachers and even bad-mouthing other girls to win more approval.

"Do you think she has a good accent?" Elisa says snarkily, jerking the car around a tight ascending curve, its engine whining at the high gear it's in.

I honestly don't know how to answer this. I turn to look

at her, not understanding what she wants from me. And I realize that instead of keeping her eyes on the road, she's staring straight at me; I let out an awful little embarrassing whinny of horror and jerk my gaze back to the windscreen again, hoping desperately that she'll follow suit before she drives into one of the drainage ditches on either side of the road, or into one of the cypresses.

"You don't know very much about my mother," Elisa says with great pleasure, her voice full of malice. "She likes to pretend. She is so *fasulla*. False. Everything about her is false."

I'm dying to ask what she means but I bite my tongue, because I sense that the more silent I am, the less I seem to care, the more she will talk.

"My mother, she is not Italian," Elisa says, dragging the wheel around to take another curve. "You don't know that, *non è vero?* My mother is American."

"*What?* Are you joking?" I blurt out.

Okay, she's got that much satisfaction from me. I couldn't help the exclamation of surprise. Out of the corner of my eye, I see Elisa's lipsticked mouth narrow in pleasure.

"*Si,*" she says, delightedly stepping on the accelerator. The Fiat bounds over a bump in the road, and I shove out my foot, bracing my leg against the interior wall of the car, not wanting to let her see me grip the seat to steady myself.

"American," Elisa continues. "But she never says that. Her name is Catherine, but she change it to Catia because that is Italian. It is so sad, tragic. She want to be something she is not. And because she is not a real Italian, she does not know how to keep her Italian husband. That is why my father leaves to live in Florence."

I'm genuinely taken aback by Elisa's revelation. Never in a million years would I have guessed Catia wasn't Italian.

"She meet my father in Florence, she is studying art and the language, like all of you foreign girls," Elisa says, with a nasty twist to the last few words. "She leave everything in America behind, she marry him and immediately she decide she is Italian. No more America. She hate it when I say she is American, or I tell her she say a word wrong in Italian. She did not want to teach us English. English would be useful to me and Leonardo. Just to know. But no, she teaches Italian to *stranieri*—foreigners. It's stupid, *no?* She never go back to America, she never take me or Leonardo to meet her family there, she forget them all. She care only for herself."

I stare at Elisa as she continues contemptuously:

"She is stupid and ridiculous. No one else care that she is American but her. Even my father, he think she is ridiculous. He have an Italian girlfriend now. A real Italian, not a false one like my mother."

We've reached the top of the drive now. Elisa doesn't turn into the parking area, however; with a squeal of brakes and a groan from the gearbox, she snaps the Fiat into a ninety-degree turn and sends it between the walls, through the gateway, in a tight scary loop till she comes to a halt sideways, on the cobbled courtyard where the family leaves their cars.

"*Ecco*," she says. "Here you are. And now you know."

I simply don't know how to respond to her stream of angry revelations. I'm reeling from this new information.

It makes Catia seem what Elisa's called her, fake. She's deceived us, effectively, and that makes me feel really weird, insecure. It makes me feel sad for Catia too. Why should she pretend so hard to be something she isn't, and alienate her own children in the process? I'm overwhelmed with confusion. I wish Kelly were here so I'd have someone to share the surprise with. Paige and Kendra, as Americans, will be even more freaked out, I imagine.

Elisa makes no move to turn off the engine or get out. I realize with great relief that I can get away from her: she doesn't intend to come inside, to hear whatever the principessa and Catia have to say to me. I scramble out before she can change her mind. Closing the car door, I smell burning rubber from whatever bit of her car's engine—the clutch?— she's overstrained from driving so fast up the hill to get rid of me as quickly as possible.

But Elisa has to have the last word. She swings the car around farther in its circle, pointing it at the gateway, and rolls down her window, propping her heavily bangled arm on the frame as she says:

"Luca is not here," with a fake smile. "You can see, his car is away. You are disappointed, I think."

She gestures at the parking area, where there's only the small, dented old white Panda.

"You said that last time," I snap, "and he showed up anyway. Some Italian guys prefer foreign girls," I add. "Like your dad did when he married your mum. Luca obviously does too."

It's my turn to stun her into silence. I turn on my heel and walk swiftly up the raised path toward the castello's main entrance. Behind me, I hear Elisa's car shoot out of the gateway so fast I almost expect to hear a crunching noise as she grinds her chassis against the stone of the wall. I've pressed the button for the bell and am listening to the awful pulse of the electric scream slowly die away when something occurs to me.

As Elisa just pointed out, the only car parked in the courtyard is the Panda, which I honestly don't think can possibly belong to the principessa; it's far too ancient and sagging. And where's Catia's jeep? True, she might have left it in the parking lot, but it's so big I think I would have seen it as we passed, even at the high speed Elisa was driving.

Did Elisa lie to me? Did her mother not ring her after all? But why on earth would she lure me here and leave me when no one's here but—

The little door inside the bigger door swings open. And standing there, in her black dress and awful shoes, is Maria. The housekeeper.

The Most Important Things in the World

I have a moment of sheer, absolute panic as I look at Maria's small dark figure. Memories of films I've seen, books I've read—*Rebecca* in the forefront, with awful Mrs. Danvers the housekeeper, in her black dress and pulled-back hair, whispering over Mrs. de Winter's shoulder as she stands at the edge of the window frame, egging her on to jump. Horrible, scary old bat. And here I am, with neither Catia's nor the principessa's car visible, and just Maria in the castello—Elisa's long gone already, not that I'd accept a lift back from her. . . .

I can walk back down, I think quickly. At least to the village, it's all downhill and mostly in the shade. I don't have to stay here. Maria can't make me.

And then I see that she isn't standing back to let me in, but is still firmly planted in the center of the doorway, her wrinkled brown face creased into a tracery of fine lines, looking taken aback. Surprised. Not at all as if she's expecting me, as if she's lured me here to do something awful to me.

Which is pleasantly reassuring.

"*Signorina?*" she says, frowning in puzzlement. "*Ma cosa fa qui? La signora non c'è.*"

She's asking what I'm doing here. I summon up the fragments of Italian I've managed to grasp so far, and say:

"*Elisa mi porta qui. Dice Signora Catia e la principessa qui. Per vedere me.*"

God, that was terrible. Really bad Italian. But I've managed to explain, because she's frowning deeper, in an I'm-thinking-about-this way, not a what-on-earth-did-you-just-say way, and she says in her croaky voice:

"*Ma loro non ci sono.*" They're not here. "*Non capisco.*" I don't understand.

She raises her shoulders and lets them fall in the big, theatrical way Italians shrug, as if they're pantomiming it. She doesn't move from the doorway. I shift my feet on the hot cobblestones, which are beginning to warm up the thin soles of my sandals. A bead of sweat runs down from my hairline, melting unpleasantly against the plastic of my sunglasses, which are clammy on my lightly sweating skin. I didn't put on sunblock, and I can feel my forehead, the bridge of my nose, starting to get pink.

"*Posso venire?*" I ask, which I think just means "Can I come?" but I can't remember how you say "inside." "*Caldo,*" I add, which I know means "hot."

I gesture up at the sky, a clear bowl of swimming-pool-tile bright blue upended over us, not a wisp of cloud to shelter me from the scorching afternoon sun. *What am I going to do if she doesn't let me in?* I brought my phone; Kelly and I agreed I'd text her urgently if anything bad started happening, though I don't think either of us had a clue what she could do to help. *I'll find some shade, sit out here, and text Kelly,* I decide. *Then I'll start walking down to the village.* I don't have any money on me, I can't even buy a coffee at the bar. I suppose I'll have to walk all the way back to Villa Barbiano.

Doubtfully, I look down at my sandals, which are decorated with lots of silver studs, definitely designed for prettiness rather than long walks on dirt roads. I have the nasty feeling that forty minutes of walking—because that's how long it will take me, minimum—is going to give me some awful blisters.

Maria sighs, and I look back at her. She's shuffling away, down the corridor, which seems pitch-black from the bright courtyard.

"*Vieni,*" she calls over her shoulder. "*Puoi aspettare in cucina.*"

"Come," I decode. And something about kitchen—"*cucina*" is "kitchen," and "*aspettare*" means "wait." *You can wait in the kitchen.*

Well, she's not exactly rolling out the red carpet, but again, that's reassuring; I certainly don't get the feeling she's planned this in advance. I walk inside, and the cool of the stone walls and floor is an instant relief after the hot sun, like entering an air-conditioned shop. I sigh in pleasure, pushing my sunglasses once more to the crown of my head.

Then I turn, knowing that I'm expected to shut the door. And that's the hard part. My hands don't want to move. For a long moment, I simply stand there, arms by my sides, looking at the bright rectangle of the open doorframe.

In or out? It's not too late to change your mind, Violet. Instinctively, I know that nothing bad will happen to me outside, nothing worse than sunburn and sore feet, and perhaps the social embarrassment of having lugged myself home in the blazing sun rather than wait, like any sensible person, for my hostess and her friend, who are doubtless just stuck in traffic or had a flat tire or something equally explainable.

But I also know, just as instinctively, that here is where the answers lie. Here, inside the castello. And the only way I'm going to get them is by being brave. Not by running away.

I take a deep breath, reach out, and close the door behind me. It squeaks shut with such an ominous, *Young Frankenstein,* horror-film groan of rusty hinges that I can't help smiling, despite my nerves being on edge. The castello is not some awful, lurking trap. Maria is not Mrs. Danvers from *Rebecca.* And more than likely, no one gave me yew poison either—that was Kelly and Benedetta working themselves into a big, silly flap.

I wonder quickly if I should text Kelly to let her know what's happening. But Maria's disappeared from sight, shuffling off on her clog-shoes somewhere deep in the bowels of the castello, and I turn and run after her, hoping the kitchen isn't too hard to find. I know all too well what can happen if you take a wrong turn in this place. . . .

✍

I'm a bit taken aback, frankly, at the state of the castello kitchen. I remember Catia telling Maria she ought to get the creaky door hinges oiled. She didn't tell Maria she should dust, but it was everywhere, on the brass fittings of the pictures, collecting in the frames, on the inlaid table in the hall. Maria can't possibly be responsible for having to clean this entire place herself; even someone young and enthusiastic, without slow clumpy shoes, wouldn't be able to manage it. I suppose there was no reason to expect the kitchen to be any cleaner than the rest of the castello. My shock is more that it's like walking back in time, stepping through a portal and going back fifty years.

It's huge, with a cavernous ceiling, and a gigantic, ancient range, its enameled sides peeling away, the roof above it black with soot. The fridge is equally enormous and old, humming so noisily it's like having a third person in the room. Next to it is a butcher's block, sagging in the middle with age; it's been used so much over the years that it's no longer flat. I don't know how anyone can even cut bread on it. The wood is greasy and dark and, to be honest, pretty revolting.

I look away swiftly to the walls, which are lined with shelves and random credenzas, display cabinets stuffed with china and glass, like a bric-a-brac collection in an old-fashioned antique shop. Jelly molds hang high up on one wall, beautiful, elaborate copper shapes now green at the edges with tarnish and festooned with cobwebs. I stare around me with my head tilted back, mouth open in amazement, taking this all in.

Maria's at the range, putting a huge old kettle on one of the hobs, a dirty old rag wrapped around its handle so she doesn't burn herself. I stand awkwardly near the door, not knowing what to do with myself. Part of me thinks that they should clear out all this old stuff, put in a nice new kitchen, and start afresh; the other part is fascinated by all the random stuff in the cabinets—whose glass, I notice, is also smudged and sooty. I peer more closely at one. Teapots. Lots of teapots, delicate and exquisitely painted, but most with brown stains—age or neglect, I don't know. Some have matching cups and saucers, very small by comparison with the ones people use now, the saucers with scalloped edges, decorated in pale greens and blues and pinks.

I think of the tea parties little girls have with their dolls and their friends. Or the Mad Hatter's tea party in *Alice in Wonderland*. If I'd grown up here I would have pestered the adults nonstop to let me take all this china out and play with it. I picture myself sitting outside on the grass, a cloth spread out, my dolls sitting in a circle, Milly and Lily-Rose with their dolls too, all of us with utterly serious faces as we choose our favorite pieces and assign them to the perfect recipient.

"*Siediti,*" Maria says, and I spin around to see her lugging the kettle onto a trivet in the center of the kitchen table. I dash over to help her but she shoots me such a withering look that I retreat, and sink into the chair she's pointing out. The table is made out of a slab of wood as thick as my forearm, battered and covered with so many dark burns that in places they merge together.

The kettle clatters down onto the trivet, iron clashing against iron. Maria turns away again, retrieving a teapot and two cups. The teapot's enameled and chipped; no nice china for me, I notice with some amusement. She grabs a bunch of herbs from the butcher's block and leans across the table, pretty much rubbing them in my face. I rear back in shock, the sharp fresh odor of peppermint rising to my nostrils, the edges of the big mint leaves rough and tickly against my skin.

She nods with satisfaction, her cheeks creasing in a half smile, takes off the lid of the teapot, and shoves the entire bunch of mint inside, cramming it down. Then she heaves up the kettle, shooting me another warning glance not to help, and pours a stream of boiling water over the herbs to steep them.

"*Infusione alla menta,*" she says, sinking down into a creaky old armchair opposite me. "*Fa bene allo stomaco.*"

She pats her tummy, hidden under the black folds of her dress. I nod. My mum drinks a lot of mint tea. She's really into herbal stuff and health foods.

"*Menta.*" I repeat the word for "mint." I've seen it in ads here, for chewing gum.

"*Si.*" Maria nods approvingly.

The mint smells delicious as it heats up, fresh and green. I remind myself I need to wait until Maria drinks it too, just in case.

"*La principessa è come mia figlia,*" Maria says, her black

302

eyes intent on me, wanting me to understand what she says. "*Capisci? Come mia figlia.*"

"*Figlia,*" I think, means "daughter." I take my time, piecing the words I've heard together: the princess, she's saying, is her daughter? No, "*come.*" Which means "like." *The princess is like her daughter.* I've got it.

"*Principessa come figlia,*" I say, forgetting the word for "your" but pointing at her to hopefully convey it instead. The downside of learning a language is that you feel like an idiot stumbling over the words, bodging a sentence together as badly as a three-year-old. The upside is the pride in actually being able to communicate, no matter how basic your words are: I feel a huge rush of achievement as Maria nods vigorously in approval.

"*Sì! Sì! Lei è come la mia figlia! E Luca, è come il mio figlio anche,*" she says, her eyes still fixed on mine, the dark pupils boring into me like twin electric drills.

I think I'm blushing at the mention of Luca. It's so awful when you have a crush on someone, the way that you long to hear his name spoken, going out of your way to drop it into conversation, or leading the subject around to him in the hopes that someone else will mention him first and give you the excuse to talk about him. And hearing his name just once isn't enough. It's like a drug, you want it again and again. I look at her expectantly, wanting her to keep talking about him.

"*È un bravo ragazzo,*" Maria says, nodding again, agreeing with her own words.

I know that: it means he's a good boy. And to my surprise, part of me immediately thinks: *I'm not so sure.* I remember his words to me, the last time I was here: *Sometimes I am not very nice.*

No. I'm honestly not sure whether Luca is a good boy.

But I look around me again and think, *This is where Luca lives, in this eerie Gothic castle with all its treasures decaying.* It must be like living in a museum that no one visits. Pictures dusty, rugs fading, collections of stained crockery in the kitchen, which is sort of filthy itself. Just the principessa and Maria for company, and honestly, they're a very odd pair. *No wonder he's the way he is,* I think. I know he's the same age as Andrea and Leonardo, nineteen, but he seems older. More grown up, less carefree. Cynical, even bitter sometimes. I think of the way Luca talked about his father, how much he hates the situation between his parents. What must his childhood have been like, growing up here?

Maria's reached out to the teapot, swirling it in practiced circles, making sure the water infuses completely through the mint leaves. Then she picks it up and pours it into first her own mug, then my own. Steam rises from the mugs, deliciously scented, and the pale green transparent liquid is so pretty I almost hesitate when Maria opens a jar of honey, spoons out a dollop, stirs it into her mug, then pushes the jar across the table to me; it seems a shame to ruin the lovely color of the infusion.

"*Miele di lavanda,*" she says. "*Lo faccio io.*"

She can tell by the blank expression on my face that I don't understand a word. Tutting, she gets up, goes to the far end of the kitchen, and returns with a handful of something she clumps around the table and holds out to me: dry herbs. Her hand is ancient, deeply lined, more like a claw;

cautiously, I sniff what she's shoving under my nose and then nod in recognition.

"Lavender!" I say.

"Sì, sì!" She taps the jar of honey with the other claw. "Miele. Di lavanda."

"Miele di lavanda," I say as she nods vigorously. Lavender honey. Now I have to take some. I stir it in, watching the sticky, sugary honey dissolve. My brain's checking everything: the tea, made by Maria in front of me, poured from the same pot; the honey that she's had too, serving herself from the same jar. Nothing that could remotely hurt me. I pick up my mug.

Maria's shuffled around the table and sat back down, facing me.

"La principessa è la cosa piu importante per me nella vita," she says. The princess is the most important thing for her. "Lei e Luca. Le uniche cose per me nella vita."

The principessa and Luca, the most important things for her. I nod seriously, showing that I understand. And part of me, a silly, fantasizing, dreaming part, thinks that maybe she's aware of the connection between me and Luca, that she's trying to welcome me, with the lovely fresh mint tea, her own homemade honey. That she's telling me how important the family is to her because she wants me to respect that, to treat Luca well.

Has he mentioned me to Maria? Confided in her? The mere idea of Luca talking about me to someone makes me flush with excitement.

The tea's cooled enough to drink now. I pick up the mug and raise it to my lips.

. And then I jump almost out of my skin. The heavy oak kitchen door at the far end of the long room swings open with such force that it slams against the wall. Sunshine floods in, and I realize how dark it was in here, how little natural light this kitchen has. A figure's silhouetted against the brightness outside, tall and lean, and in the next moment it tears toward us threateningly, footsteps ringing loudly on the stone flags.

It's Luca. Heading straight for me, towering over me, his expression grimmer and more angry than I've ever seen, his blue eyes narrowed with fury, his mouth a long straight line. It's all I can do not to shrink back. I'm afraid of him, afraid of what he might do; that realization straightens my backbone and I sit up with posture so perfect that my mother would thoroughly approve, and I stare back at him in defiant challenge.

I've done nothing wrong! I was asked to come here, brought by Elisa—I haven't foisted myself on his home like some kind of pathetic stalker. He has no right to be angry, to glare at me like this—

And then his hand rises, and despite myself I flinch. I should have stood up to confront him, but he was so fast, his long legs crossing the room in a split second. In a small, rational part of my brain, I absolutely know that Luca isn't going to hit me, but that's exactly what it looks like, and I stare up at him in utter shock and disbelief at seeing his hand come down with lightning speed toward me. What he does is completely unexpected: he grabs the mug in my hand, rips it from my grasp, and sends it flying toward the wall in one swooping swing of his arm.

The mug flies into the display cabinet like a cricket ball

being thrown. It smashes everything it hits, and it shatters into pieces itself. The sound of glass and china splintering is deafening. I scream, and the next thing I know Luca has his arms around me, spinning me away, suffocating me against his chest so my scream is muted, my open mouth squashed into his shirt.

I'm stronger than I look. I wrestle free a moment later, feeling my eyes stretched as wide as they can go with shock and sheer fury.

"What do you think you're *doing?*" I yell at him. "Have you gone *mad?*"

I didn't think I could get even angrier, but when he doesn't answer, just turns and goes running around the table away from me, I do. If I still had the mug in my hand, I think I would have hurled it at his head.

"How *dare* you?" I shout, but he isn't looking at me; his focus is entirely on Maria. He grabs her, pulling her up from her chair, and shakes her like a rag doll.

"*Cos' hai fatto?*" he's yelling into her face. "*Ma cos' hai fatto?*"

She's yelling back at him, so fast I can't understand a word she's saying. I can only stare in horror as, eventually, Luca lets her go, and she sinks back down into the chair again, sobbing, her hands over her face. Luca turns back to me, and his face looks terrible, paper-white, skin stretched tight over his cheekbones, his eyes dark with utter sorrow and misery.

"I am so sorry, Violetta," he says, his voice rough and hoarse. "I am so very sorry that this happens in my home. She has just tried to—"

He clears his throat, and I see with complete shock and disbelief that he's crying. I don't think he even realizes it; he doesn't raise a hand to wipe the tears away. They're falling slowly down his pale cheeks as he says slowly, painfully:

"Maria has just tried to poison you."

He's Like Snow White

It's two hours later. I feel as if I've been through a tornado, caught up in the tight spiral of a cyclone and deposited somewhere else, in a totally different landscape, aching right through to the bone. So though I'm sitting out on the terrace beyond the Gold Salon, looking out on the cypress trees from which we watched the bats pour out on our last visit, it's as if I'm seeing everything with new eyes. I don't know what to think, how to react.

Which, I suppose, makes me normal. I mean, who *would* know how to react if they were told that someone had tried to poison them?

"It was in the *tazza*," Luca's telling me. He's sitting next to me on the stone bench, being very careful not to touch me. I reacted so badly when he grabbed me and pressed my face into his chest so I wouldn't get cut by a flying shard of glass or china, he's probably nervous about how I might respond if he tried to hold my hand or put his arm around me.

"The what?" I say dully.

"The cup," he says. "She put it in the cup before she put it out in front of you. And also the wineglass for your *vin santo*, before. Just a few drops. Not enough to . . ." He swallows, hard. Out of the comer of my eye I see how tense his jaw is, how tightly clenched.

"Not enough to kill me?" I finish.

"No!" He swivels to face me, his eyes intense. "Violetta, she swears, not that. She never meant . . . that. Just to hurt you, to make you afraid, so you would not come back here, never again. Maybe to make you leave Italy."

I prop my elbows on my knees, burying my face in my hands.

"But *why*? I've been thinking and thinking about this, and I still can't see why. . . ."

I've had some time to go over this in my head. Not during the awful scene Luca had with Maria, where she cried and pleaded with him, where he threatened to call the police, where he strode over to the liquid that had been in my cup, now dripping down the wall and pooling in some of the cups and saucers that had survived, pointing at it furiously, telling her he would have it analyzed by the police if she didn't tell him everything. When he rang his mother, who came home ashen-faced, and on sight of whom Maria broke down completely, wailing and sobbing like a banshee.

The principessa told Luca to ring Catia, to come and

take me away, but I wasn't ready to go. I think I must still have been in shock. I could barely walk, let alone envisage getting into a car, going back to Villa Barbiano, and having to tell everyone there what had happened, when I barely understood it myself.

That was the other factor, apart from the shock: how could I leave without a full explanation? Without understanding what had gone on here, why on earth Maria would want to drug the *vin santo* and mint tea of a girl she'd seen only once—not only that, but to lock me in the passage too? Because she confessed that to Luca as well. She'd sneaked up, seen me lagging behind in the gallery, and opened the door to the passage, hoping I'd take the bait and assume that was the way everyone else had gone. Once I'd gone down the stairs, she locked me in and slipped back to the kitchen in another attempt to scare me away from the castello.

"I know it's because of the way I look," I say, summoning up the bravery to sit up straight and take my hands away from my face. *The face,* I think bitterly, *that has caused all these problems.* "From the way your mother and Maria reacted when they first saw me. I mean, it was really odd and weird."

I don't feel I can tell him about the portrait in London. Not yet, maybe not ever. I can't deal with the possibility that he might somehow blame me, think I'm at fault for having deliberately come to the castello knowing that I was a dead ringer for a girl who lived here centuries ago.

He's nodding.

"Yes," he says slowly. "It is your face. And your body. Everything."

He gestures at me, and I feel really self-conscious,

because he's encompassing everything about me. He's really looking at me up and down.

"My mother says," he continues, "that you look like my aunt Monica when she was your age. My father's sister at seventeen. Moh." He pulls a face. "I do not know Monica when she is young. When I know her, she is older, she tints her hair blond, she is very thin, too thin. I do not see that you look like her. Not at *all*."

The emphasis is very reassuring; I bristled when he said that I didn't look like Monica, who was thin, but the "too thin" immediately afterward was a huge relief.

"But what my mother think, what Maria think, is not good." He draws a deep breath. "My father," he says, "is a very bad husband. He always has girlfriends, always. My mother always know but she will not leave. You know, I tell you this. I hate it."

The stone bench is very cold beneath my thighs, but I register that without doing anything about it. I don't move. It's as if I'm carved from stone myself, like one of the statues in the castello gardens.

"They think because of this that you may be the daughter of my father," he says, all in a rush. "Because you cannot be the daughter of Monica, it is not possible. She has two children, they are your age and my age. Not possible that she has another. But you are so like the di Vesperi family. Even I see that. I look at the pictures, the *ritratti di famiglia*, and I see it. I do not want to see it. But I do."

From the moment I discovered that Luca was of the di Vesperi family, somewhere deep down, I've been afraid that we might be related. But this is a horrible, profound communication of my worst fear.

"Is that why Maria tried to poison me?" I say, barely able to move my lips now; I feel overwhelmed with misery.

"*Sì*. Seeing you, it upsets my mother very much. She know my father have girlfriends, she accept that. But a child, that she does not know about, makes her very sad."

"We don't know that it's true!" I exclaim.

Luca jumps to his feet and, shoving his hands into his jeans pockets, starts to pace up and down the terrace.

"No," he says bleakly, ducking his head forward so his hair falls over his face. "We do not know."

I pull my knees up to my chest and wrap my arms around them.

"I always realized I looked different from my mum and dad," I say in a small voice. "My mum's Scandinavian, tall and blond. And my dad's Scottish, he has red hair and freckles."

Luca mutters something under his breath that sounds like a curse.

"How did you know?" I ask him, a question that's been on my mind ever since he stormed into the kitchen. "How did you guess what was going on?"

He heaves a deep sigh and leans against the stone balustrade that wraps around three sides of the terrace. Fishing in his pocket, he pulls out a pack of cigarettes and taps one out.

"Maria comes with my mother when my mother marries my father," he explains. "Maria is from the village where my mother's family has their villa. She is always very *fedele*." He thinks for a moment. "Faith-ful," he translates, his accent making it hard for him to pronounce the *th* sound. "She has always made remedies, with the herbs. Once, many years ago, she became angry with my father because he behaved badly. She make him sick. He never knows, he think he have eaten the bad fish. My mother knows. Maria is good at pretending, she pretend she like him and he does not suspect anything."

"She *is* good at pretending," I agree, thinking of her pinching my cheeks on my last visit to the castello, telling me I was pretty; of the way she feigned surprise when she opened the door to me this afternoon. I would never have guessed that she knew I was coming, that she had planned to give me tea, to push a cup toward me that already had some drops of yew decoction in it.

Luca nods.

"But the person she cannot pretend with is my mother. Mamma know and she tell Maria never, never again. *Mai.* Never must she do this thing to give him herbs to make him sick."

He lights his cigarette with a metallic click of the Zippo.

"And I remember. I am young but I remember. I try to look after Mamma, keep her happy when my father is not here. I hear when my mother tells Maria never again. So when you tell me you are sick . . ." He takes a long pull on the cigarette, staring straight ahead, avoiding my eyes, his expression still bleak. "I guess what happens. *Maybe,* I think, *it is Maria.* But I do not know, not to be sure, and I am wondering about what to do. But also"—he looks directly at me now, his blue eyes blazing with intensity—"I think you are

314

safe, because you do not come here again. I think I have time because you are safe with the other girls.

"And then I stop into the Casa del Popolo this afternoon, for a coffee, and I see Elisa. She tells me you are here, because Mamma ring on the phone and say she is with Signora Barbiano and they want to see you. At once I think, but why? This is very strange. It does not make sense. So I ask Elisa, but did you speak to my mother, how did she sound? And she say no, she speak to Maria, it is Maria who give the message from my mother. So then—" His eyes narrow. "Then I am very scared for you and I get in my car and drive very very fast to come here to make you safe."

"Thank you," I say. It seems inadequate for what he's done for me. My arms are still wrapped around my calves; it's like they're a barrier, giving me security, protecting me. I feel incredibly vulnerable and alone.

"*Di niente*," Luca says bitterly, which I know means "Not at all." He looks at me and lets his cigarette butt fall to the terrace, stubbing it out with a turn of his boot heel, and walks over to the bench. To my amazement, he drops fluidly to his knees in front of me; he's so tall that his face is still almost level with mine. I stare at him, feeling really awkward with my knees bunched up like this.

"You look so sad," he says. "I am so sorry. *Mi dispiace cosi tanto*. It is for you to say what should happen to Maria," he continues seriously. "My mother says this too. If you want, we will call the *carabinieri*. The police."

Instinctively, I shake my head. No police. No publicity. No one but us must know about this awful family secret. I slide my legs to the side, along the bench, pulling my skirt over my knees, and the next thing I know Luca has reached out and taken my hands. I shiver, and his long fingers wrap more tightly around mine, giving me reassurance.

"She cannot stay here," he says firmly. "It is not possible. She must leave. She is not good for my mother, I tell Mamma that very often. Maria want to *padronare*"—he thinks—"to rule. To rule the castello. She no want help to clean, to cook. My mother offer often to get more women to clean, to help, but Maria say no. She want to rule my mother. Now I tell Mamma, Maria must leave."

"If you call the police, there'll be a big scandal," I say slowly, trying to work out how I feel, what's the best thing to do. "I don't want that."

Luca is agreeing, but he isn't pushing me; I feel nothing coming from him but concern for me.

"What else could happen, though?" I say hopelessly. "If your mother"—I would normally say "mum," but it feels completely disrespectful to call a princess "mum"—"sent her to an old people's home, she might start—I don't know, putting stuff in the tea of other people she didn't like. Or the nurses. It wouldn't be safe."

Luca's listening intently, and I'm talking slowly. He nods sharply as I talk, confirming that he's taking in what I'm saying.

"I know this too," he says. "She is not safe. When she do this to my father . . ." His eyes go cold, his face taut. I'm realizing that he always looks like this when he talks about the principe. "He is sick in the stomach, but who cares? He is very bad with my mother, he make her cry, he tell her lies. So maybe, he is sick one time . . ." He shrugs eloquently, still holding my hands. "But with you . . ." His eyes flash in anger. "You are innocent. You have done nothing. It is very wrong and bad to make you sick."

He lifts one of my hands and raises it to his cheek, a gesture so tender and unexpected that my breath catches in my throat. I feel the blood rising to my cheeks, and I look down at my lap. I can't meet his eyes.

"Is there somewhere Maria could go?" I ask in a very small voice. "Maybe"—I have a flash of inspiration—"maybe a nunnery?"

Luca's face goes blank. I have to explain "nunnery" to him, and that involves hand-waving as I describe the black clothes and white headdress, so I have to retrieve my hands, for which, on balance, I'm very grateful. When he finally gets it, he laughs, throwing back his head; he stands up and props his bottom against the edge of the bench, looking down at me with a great amusement in his eyes; Luca never stands when he can lean.

"*Povere suore,*" he says, smiling. "Poor nuns. Maria would try to rule them too. No, if you agree not to call the police, my mother thinks she send her back to her village. To her old house. They know her there. Her mother too, she make the drinks with herbs. Good drinks," he adds seriously. "I promise. It is not all bad, she makes many good remedies. But they know Maria, they live all on the land of my mother's family. If my mother send her back, they will all be warned."

Relief sweeps over me. I take a deep breath. *Never to have to see Maria again, not to have her in the castello. No scandal, nothing.*

"It's perfect," I say. "*Perfetto.*"

317

"Good. I think so too. *Perfetto*. She must leave tomorrow." He shakes his head. "I would say she must leave today, but it is late now, too late for the train to the Veneto. But tomorrow, she go, and someone my mother knows will take her so we know she gets there." He pulls a face. "The only thing that make me cross is that it will make my father happy. He does not like Maria."

He reaches out his hand to me.

"It is late now," he says quietly. "Soon I take you back to Villa Barbiano."

I take his hand and stand up, facing him. And I realize that I have a sudden craving to be away from here. I need to process everything that's happened this afternoon: my head's swimming, dazed with too much information, too much drama.

I have a powerful, almost overwhelming wave of nostalgia for my own bedroom back in London, a room I don't share with anyone, my safe, lovely, cozy, pink nest. My mum, fussing around me, making me my favorite comfort food. *I wanted adventure*, I think wryly, *and I got it. In spades. And now all I want to do is run back home to my mum*. But then I wonder, *Is she my birth mom?* and even more quickly, *Does it matter?*

It is eerie and uncanny how Luca has the ability to read my mind.

"Will you go back now to London, Violetta?" he asks, his black brows lifting, his expression concerned. "*Italia* has not been good to you. Maybe you think you should go home, where these bad things do not happen."

"Do you want me to go?" I ask, feeling very insecure. *I*

couldn't blame him, I realize with huge sadness. *We're in a real mess. Perhaps the best thing would be for me to go away and never come back.*

Luca's lips tighten into a hard line. Slowly, he shakes his head. "It's hard to know what's best," he says. "But I do not want you to go."

"I don't want to go either," I say in a whisper.

He takes in a deep breath and lets it out again. We stand there silent, because we don't know what more to say. I realize that shadows are stretching across the terrace. The air is milder, an evening breeze blowing softly. There's a rustling sound from the cypress trees in the garden below, and we look over to see the first few bats emerging from the branches, circling slowly in the darkening sky. I think we're both grateful to have something else to concentrate on. We walk across the terrace and lean on the stone balustrade, elbows almost but not quite touching. And we watch the black shapes rise and fall, the red streaks of sunset fading from the sky, and a clear white curve of moon rising slowly behind the dark silhouettes of the trees.

I know, in that moment, that I'll stay on. I can't just run away—not now, not when I feel as I do about Luca. All we have is speculation: nothing's definite. We can't possibly be *sure* that I'm Luca's half sister! Everything's up in the air—how can I leave and never know the truth?

Because in my heart, what I want, more than anything else, is for Luca and me to be together.

There's so much uncertainty, so much confusion. I want to reach out and touch him so badly, but I know I can't. The space between us is tiny, but right now it feels as wide as the ocean.

And as darkness falls, I make a resolution. That whatever the truth is about who I am, whether Luca and I really are related, I'll stay in Italy until I've found it out.

I learned another Italian word recently, painstakingly working on the translation of Jovanotti's lyrics: *storia*. It means "history," but it can also mean a relationship. If you say *nostra storia*, "our story," that's like saying "our relationship," or "our love affair."

I cast a fleeting glance sideways at Luca and realize he's looking at me, his eyes the dark blue of the night sky.

Our story isn't over. It's not possible. Not so soon, when it's barely even begun . . .

Follow Violet and Luca's story in the upcoming
kissing IN ITALIAN

Acknowledgments

Many thanks to Beverly Horowitz, my brilliant editor, who shepherded this book along with great care and attention; to Kenny Holcomb, who continues to give me covers that make everyone ooh and aah in amazement and wonder at their gorgeousness; and to Krista and Rebecca, whose efficiency and help is hugely appreciated.

Equally huge thanks, as always, to my wonderful agent, Deborah Schneider; to Cathy and Victoria, who do the best job of looking after me I could possibly imagine; and to Random Burns, the number one fan, plotter, and title suggestor for my YA books.

And to all the fans who've followed me to this new series: I hope you enjoy it just as much as you did the Scarlett Wakefield books. I miss Scarlett, but it's been so much fun starting a new series. I hope you love my new characters as much as I do!

About the Author

Lauren Henderson is the author of the Scarlett Wakefield mystery series: *Kiss Me Kill Me, Kisses and Lies, Kiss in the Dark,* and *Kiss of Death.* She is also the author of several acclaimed "tart noir" mystery novels for adults, as well as the witty romance handbook *Jane Austen's Guide to Dating,* which has been optioned for film development. She was born and raised in London, where she lives with her husband. Visit her online at laurenhenderson.net or on Facebook as Lauren Milne Henderson.